Cage of Nightingales

Elizabeth Hopkinson

Winnipeg, Canada

Editors: Craig Gibb & Francisco Feliciano

Published December 2023 by Deep Hearts YA, an imprint of Deep Desires Press and Story Perfect Inc.

Deep Hearts YA
PO Box 51053 Tyndall Park
Winnipeg, Manitoba R2X 3B0
Canada

Visit deepheartsya.com for more great reads.

Cage of Nightingales

I am young, Italian and castrated
and seek my glory only through singing.
~ Filippo Balatri, 1676-1756

The magic flute will protect you,
Support you in the greatest misfortune.
With it you can you behave all-powerfully,
To transform people's passions,
The sad will be joyful.
~ *The Magic Flute*, Wolfgang Amadeus Mozart & Emmanuel Schikaneder, 1791

Part I

1. A Crow Amongst Nightingales

"Fight! Fight! Fight!"

Tammo bit his lip. There was blood on it and he hadn't even thrown a punch yet. Across the circle of boys, Paolo was waiting, mouth curled in a sneer, black eyes flashing.

"Come on, then."

"Yes, come on, Crow. What are you waiting for?"

Tammo snapped his head round but he couldn't catch who had spoken. Called him Crow. The early September sun was low in the sky and shone in his eyes. Any one of the pinched, pale faces waiting for the kill like gamblers at a cock-fight could have spoken the word. Dark blue cassocks lifted and settled in the breeze as the traitors leaned in. Blood pulsed in Tammo's head like a crazed ostinato.

"Give us a song, then."

That was one of the tenors for certain. Atto or Salvatore or one of those. Clumped behind Paolo as if he was going to protect them. Fat chance. There was no way this term was going to end like the last. No way they'd get the better of him this time.

"I don't think he's got the balls, lads. You're not a eunuch, are you? Firebrand."

Tammo's punch struck Paolo on the ear, making it bloom red. The other boy's face was a gargoyle's, ugly with rage. Tammo couldn't even feel the kicks and struggles. He was a lion, a bear, an avenging angel. He would break Paolo's teeth so he would never sing again. Calling him Crow was one thing. He hated the name with a passion, but he could have shrugged it off on a good day. Even *eunuch* he could cope with, since anyone who had heard him sing knew in an instant that he wasn't one. But no-one—no-one from the red-nosed girl in the laundry to the Duke of Angelio himself—called him Firebrand and got away with it. He was riding Paolo like a donkey now, drumming down blows to the back of his head.

"Go on, Crow!"

"Go on, Paolo!"

"Teach the freak a lesson!"

The sudden dying of the battle-taunts registered with Tammo before he became aware of the thumb and finger on his collar. The mad ostinato was still playing in his head, his arms and legs still flailing wildly; only now he was two inches above the courtyard, buckled shoes kicking to reveal yellow stockings. Paolo was cradling his ear, eyes wet and smouldering. The rest of the boys were like so many statues, held in a variety of guilty life-studies.

The hand let go and Tammo fell to the cobbles, grazing the palms of his hands. No one dared to laugh.

"Is this the behaviour of gentlemen of the Conservatorio Archangeli? Is this the behaviour of the servants of St. Michael?" Tammo would recognise that voice anywhere. He risked a glance over his shoulder to see Maestro Aquila—the flute master—glaring down his long nose. "Is it, gentlemen?"

"No, maestro." A woolly and unconvincing bleat.

"I beg your pardon?"

"No, maestro." Now halfway to a shout.

"I never wish to see such displays of mindless aggression in this courtyard again. You are students of the art musical, not savage beasts. And if I find my words have gone unheeded, recreation time will be abandoned forthwith and replaced with extra counterpoint practice. Do I make myself clear?"

"Yes, maestro."

"Now repair to your dormitories immediately. And be ashamed. Paolo Agresto."

Paolo lurched to his feet, still holding his throbbing ear.

"You are a nasty piece of work, young man. Go and wait in the rector's lobby. I'll deal with you later. Tammo Capell. I am thoroughly ashamed of you. On your feet, boy."

Tammo stood up with a groan. The blows he hadn't felt in the heat of the fight were beginning to throb, and he'd started to shiver. But that was nothing to the sick stomach he'd felt at the sound of that voice. Of all the maestri, why did it have to be Maestro Aquila who'd caught him fighting? Tammo would have to have been on his death-bed to admit to liking a tutor, but with his dying breath he might have named Maestro Aquila. He was the one maestro who had been known to smile at Tammo occasionally, and that was a rare favour from anyone. In his bad graces, Tammo had the feeling the next term would become the gateway to Hades.

"So, would you care to explain what that was all about?"

Tammo shrugged and looked down at his shoes. The toe of one was now scuffed. They would make him polish that later.

"Don't know." The croak of Tammo's voice sounded loud in the courtyard, now the two were alone. The dormitories and the plastered facades of the maestri's houses seemed to close in on him. A trickle of cold sweat ran down his back.

It was an hour after midday. The sun, where it shone, still had the strength to burn, although there was a chill to the back of it and a clarity to the blue of the sky that spoke of reddened leaves and a harvest of pears to come. The bell in the campanile sang out its one contralto note, followed shortly by a sonorous tenor from the dome of Sancti Michaelis Archangeli, the one you could hear all over Angelio. From an upper window came the sound of a solo voice singing passaggio excercises, a sound of such crystal transparency that visitors to the conservatorio might be forgiven for thinking they heard angel song. Tammo knew better. There were no angels here.

Maestro Aquila gently turned Tammo by the shoulders to face him and lifted his chin with a finger. It hurt. The intensity of the eyes made his cheeks burn. The maestro let out a breath through his long nose.

"Tammo. Boys do not hit out at other boys without knowing the reason why. Why were you fighting with Paolo?"

"He called me Crow."

Tammo wriggled out of the maestro's gaze and looked down again. There were several cuts across his knuckles and one of them was swelling. On the right hand, a thin snake of blood ran right across the tight skin where his scar began, twisting and pulling everything out of shape all the way to the elbow, then stopping before it began again on his neck. Firebrand. Even to Maestro Aquila, he wouldn't admit that Paolo had called him that. It was too shameful, too close to things he didn't care to remember.

"Crow. I take it this amiable nickname is in reference to your voice?"

"I suppose."

He could feel his whole face flaming now. Worse yet, there was something wet on his eyelashes. He blinked hard and set his jaw to stop the shivers. This was doubtless the part where Maestro Aquila would tell him a gentleman of the conservatorio should not rise to the bait of name-calling. That the maestri's reserve of second chances had now run out. He would give the news that Tammo dreaded to hear, the news that would part him from the only consolation he'd found in this prison of torture.

"Sweet Michael," he prayed. "Don't let them take my flute lessons from me. Please. I'll do anything." Life without flute lessons would be worse than hell. Every student in the intermediate grade knew him to have a crow's voice, and treated him accordingly. It wasn't just Paolo he wanted to beat into mincemeat. Most days, he wished he could pulp the lot of them.

Maestro Aquila gave a deep sigh.

"What am I to do with you, Tammo? Come with me."

It took a moment before Tammo glanced up and realised that the sound of heels on the cobbles was that of his maestro turning and walking across the courtyard. With the baffled air of a man at the gallows on whom the rope has just snapped, Tammo gritted his teeth against injuries and followed.

Maestro Aquila's long strides took him to the far side of the courtyard, to a house with wreaths and lyres in bas-relief over the doorway. A manservant hovered uncertainly in the passage as the door swung open. The maestro waved him away with a hand and strode on into the main parlour. Tammo followed him into a room filled with books, sheaves of manuscript paper, huge folios that would reach to your waist when stood upright, and yet more books and sheaves.

Tammo's eye was drawn to one wall, where a flute hung in a specially-constructed rack. Looking down its perfectly straight length, Tammo could almost feel the warmth of the dark wood against his fingers, the touch of his lips against the mouth-hole. He could hear how it would soar and flutter, a second breath to his own breath, a songbird soul to lead where his own couldn't follow. With approval, he noted the detail worked into the exterior: a curling vine the length of the flute's body, hiding figures of linnets, finches, orioles. He drew in his breath and squared his shoulders, determined to look anywhere but at that magical instrument.

Maestro Aquila found a place to stand between a crewel-worked stool acting as a book-rest and a green leather folio lying propped against the window sill. He tucked his hands beneath the tails of his coat and gazed out of the window for several moments, before looking back over his shoulder.

"Which class do you sing with at present, Tammo?"

"Bass."

Tammo shuddered. This was now the second time he had been assigned to the bass class. In the past two terms, he had moved from contralto to bass to tenor and back to bass again; and the best that could be said of his suitability was that his lips moved in time to the music.

"And how are you finding it?"

The maestro massaged his chin, swept the books from the stool with one stroke and sat down to face Tammo, his hands steepling towards his lips.

"I am aware, Tammo, that this is not the easiest of schools for you. I know that you were taken in as a charity boy under circumstances… Well, the less said, the soonest mended perhaps."

Tammo nodded stiffly and scowled.

"And I am aware that these circumstances have left you with certain…disadvantages when it comes to the practice of the art that we all serve here. You must be aware that this is not easy for the other boys either. Most of them had to petition for entry on the strength of their vocal abilities alone. It may appear to some that boys such as yourself are stealing the bread of the more talented."

"But, maestro!"

Without realising it, Tammo had stepped forward and clenched his fist. His upper body trembled with outrage. Surely, the maestro wasn't siding with Paolo.

"Take that look off your face, Tammo. I do not excuse the actions of the likes of Paolo Agresto. That intermediate tenor class is a disgrace. I've said it to the rector more than once, and I'm not alone in saying so. But you must understand the way things are in this world. We do not go around striking out at every perceived injustice to ourselves when others may perceive an injustice just as great. We trust in St. Michael to weigh it in the balance. I hope you have learned that here, at least."

"Maestro." A sullen mutter.

This was it, then. The punishment not cancelled but merely deferred. The rope re-tied and the noose re-tightened for a second swing. What was it to be this time?

"However—as you would be aware, did you not persist in your belief that St. Michael's scales are permanently tipped against you—there are other talents we choose to recognise here besides singing. And when you put your mind to it—when, I say, you put your mind to it—you show a vast amount of promise, Tammo. A promise I do not want to see going to waste.

"What age are you now?" The maestro's abrupt question made Tammo flinch. "Have you passed your fourteenth birthday?"

"Yes, maestro."

Maestro Aquila scratched his chin. Tammo heard the sound of tiny bristles.

"I thought as much. You're not a child any more, Tammo. You have taken the first steps toward manhood. You may even think—as many boys do—that you have already reached that goal. But trust me when I say that to be treated as a man you must first act as a man. Not as an immature infant who shirks his duties and cannot control his temper. You must learn to shoulder responsibility. Until they see that you can do that—*until I see* that you can do that—the maestri of this conservatorio will continue to treat you as a child."

Tammo sucked the bead of dried blood on his lip and looked away.

"Look at me, Tammo. Are you ready to begin being a man?

Tammo drew in a deep breath through his nose, squared his shoulders like one of the Duke's Guard, and looked up. "Yes, maestro."

"Good. Very good. I'm proud to hear that. In that case, I will put it to the rector that you be excused from rehearsing to Maestro Allegri and come instead to me for further lessons in the flute. When you do, you may play that flute there."

"Maestro!"

For a moment, Tammo forgot to keep up his guard in the rush of emotion that came to him. The maestro was pointing to the dark flute, instrument of the gods! He would show Maestro Aquila that he was worthy of it. He would show them all.

"Of course, you understand that this is entirely dependent on your behaviour during the rest of the week. One more instance of fighting or truancy and you will be back to singing with the other boys, regardless of whatever names they choose to bestow on you. Do you understand me?"

"Yes, maestro."

He was getting the dark flute. He could stick a hundred

of Paolo Agresto and his crew. He'd like to hear them play it as he had.

"This is a serious matter, Tammo. My reputation as a maestro is at stake. Disobey me in this and the punishment will be severe. Extremely severe."

"Yes, maestro. Thank you, maestro."

Maestro Aquila sighed and shook his head.

"Very well, then. You are dismissed. Go and wait out the rest of recreation in the courtyard until the bell sounds. And stay out of trouble."

Tammo made the bow he knew the maestro was expecting, turned on his heels, and ran.

It was difficult to know where to put himself, Tammo realised, after his third circuit of the piece of courtyard between the first three maestri's houses and the students' dormitories. All Tammo's grade had been sent to their dormitories in disgrace and, much as he wished to be left alone, he didn't want to be quite as alone as this.

He began to climb the lime tree that grew by the side of the dormitory building. From its branches, a song thrush was calling over and over again. Could he reach it? Like him, wild birds didn't trust anyone. But if you got on their side—if you didn't look at them too much or move too fast and tried to speak their tongue—they might tolerate you around them. Tammo had tried it before. You had to lie very still. You held your hand out and whistled a bit of its song, looking at it only for a moment, then away somewhere else, then back again. If you were very lucky, then it might start hopping along the branch.

Tammo fixed his eyes on the bird's speckled body. For one minute, he was sure its bright eye caught his own with a knowing look. Then, with a sudden flash of feathers, it alighted on a twig high above the dormitory window, letting out a peal of trills that sounded too much like laughter.

Tammo swore in his head. He had almost had it; he knew he had. It wasn't going to get away from him now. Just a bit higher. Just a few branches more and he would coax the mocking creature for sure.

Something yanked him from behind. Tammo's throat went suddenly tight and sweat burst from his forehead. Momentarily, he hung suspended by his middle, before clutching wildly at twigs and handfuls of foliage to steady his balance. He looked over his shoulder, heart thumping. His cassock had come unfastened from his belt and was tangled in the branches. Gripping tight with his left hand, Tammo tugged at the rough-woven cloth. There was a slight rip; the branch bounced sickeningly. He was still tangled. Tammo tugged again. The whole branch was bending now. He had to get out of the tree before he lost his balance. He didn't care about the thrush any more.

Tammo gripped firmly on a hunk of cloth near his buttocks, clenched his teeth and pulled. The nauseating plunge of the branch told him he had succeeded. Panting through pursed lips, he scrabbled to the end of the bough, now swaying up and down in rebound. The plastered windowsill was just above him. This was going to hurt a lot, Tammo thought. With a leap that reminded him sickeningly of the day he got his scars, he threw himself so that the stone sill caught him full across the stomach. Tammo gave an audible croak as wind came out of him and tumbled into the room within.

It was a misfortune that he landed directly between two beds. Tammo's back came down hard on the floorboards in what was practically a somersault, his head hitting the wall a moment later. Tammo sat up slowly, clutching the back of his neck, and peered between the iron bed pallets and grey blankets.

On the far side of the room, a boy was standing with his back to Tammo, singing at his own reflection in a mirror. It was a good mirror and a good reflection. The singer was well-grown and remarkably healthy for a conservatorio boy. He had a face like a cherub in a grand painting: rounded cheeks, full lips, eyes any girl in Angelio would have been proud to call her own. He was standing in a heroic pose: one foot a pace in front of the other, one arm behind his back, the other extended before him in declamatory fashion. He was watching his own expression in the mirror, as his voice rose and fell in a endless series of trills and mordents, all in the high upper register. What made the performance slightly ridiculous was that the mirror—which was large and had a fine pear wood frame engraved with leaves—was balanced upon the singer's bed, and the singer himself was declaiming his wordless passions over the top of a washstand. Added to the fact that he was wearing precisely the same indigo cassock and cropped hairstyle as Tammo, his heroic persona took some imagining.

The boy finished off his song with a long, drawn-out note, far higher than Tammo could have hoped to reach, which waxed loud and then soft by degrees, before coming to rest with a graceful appoggiatura. He made a little bow to himself in the mirror, then spun round on his heels to fix his attention on Tammo. The beginning of a smile plucked at the corners of his lips as he looked the intruder up and down. His eyes sparkled.

"So kind of you to drop in."

He spoke as though he was making conversation in a salon. He crossed the room and held out a hand to pull Tammo to his feet.

"You do know this is the eunuchs' dorm?"

Tammo scowled. He would have guessed if he had been thinking straight. Everyone knew the eunuch class had their own private dormitory at the top of the house. He ignored the proffered hand and staggered painfully to his feet.

"I fell out of the tree."

"Oh. Are you hurt?" said the boy, in a much more natural voice. He spoke clearly, lightly, in something like the unbroken register of the little boys, but with a touch more resonance. It was a voice of beauty, Tammo thought reluctantly. It made his own harsh caw sound more corvid than ever.

"I'm fine. I just needed to rest. I'll be out of your way in a minute."

The boy furrowed his eyebrows.

"Have you got a cold?" he asked, not unkindly.

Tammo snarled. Within one step, his eyes were level

with the boy's throat. His battered knuckles were ready for action. He was about to counter with, "Have you lost something?"—the standard insult for eunuchs—but the look of genuine terror in the lad's eyes silenced him. He had never seen a boy flinch so quickly from a blow that hadn't even been struck. His wide eyes were, for a moment, as stark as those of a cornered doe. Then he seemed to calm himself with deep breaths. The refined, salon face he had worn at first settled over him like a mask. He gave a nervous smile.

"I do apologise. My mistake." He made a curious little bow. "Carlo Bianci, at your service."

"*The* Carlo Bianci?"

Tammo's curiosity elbowed its way past his natural defences. Every boy at the Conservatorio had heard the name. It was held up to them as an example by maestri weary of mediocrity and whispered in the dormitories with a mixture of awe and crippling jealousy. In fact, Tammo now recalled that he had seen this overgrown cherub sitting at the eunuch's table in the refectory and singing solo in the chapel with that same angel's voice. Carlo Bianci. Castrato.

The other boy smiled, amused. "*The* Carlo Bianci? Let me see."

Carlo looked over his shoulder, as though searching for further intruders. He then checked his face in the mirror, gave a sly wink and turned back to Tammo.

"It would appear so. Yes."

Tammo fought off the urge to smile back. The eunuch had made a joke. Tammo couldn't decide yet if that meant he was mocking him or not.

"Is it true what they say about you?"

Carlo put one hand to his throat, and raised his eyebrows in an overly dramatic gesture.

"How should I know that? What is it they say?"

"Well, that…you know…that you're Maestro Sarastro's pet."

"His pet?" Carlo sat down on the edge of the nearest bed and tucked his hands under his thighs. He leaned forward with an expression of infantile curiosity. "What sort of pet, I wonder? A monkey? A parrot? A sweet little spaniel?" He batted his long eyelashes.

He looked so funny that Tammo wanted to laugh, but he was still too wary to let laughter come out. He turned it into a cough instead.

"I mean, they say you're a prodigy."

A shadow passed over Carlo's face. If Tammo had had to guess, he would have said his question made the other boy feel weary. He bit his lip.

"Don't they call you the Nightingale?" Tammo asked.

"Don't they call us all nightingales?" Carlo's tone was a little too airy. "Isn't that the name they have for this place out there on the streets: The Cage of Nightingales? The place where they cage up all the little songbirds and teach us to sing until we soar to the heights? Or something like that."

"They don't call me Nightingale." A sullen croak.

Carlo's voice softened. "What do they call you?"

Crow. Firebrand. Charity boy. Freak. Tammo swallowed hard and stuck out his chin.

"Tammo. Tammo Capell."

"Pleased to meet you, Tammo Capell."

He actually meant it. Tammo let himself look into the other boy's eyes. Behind the girly eyelashes there was honest openness. And sadness too, Tammo thought. He tried to hide it, but it was there. This boy had suffered too. Tammo wouldn't have let torture drag the word from him, but had he admitted to the name of Firebrand, he believed Carlo might have understood.

"So, what were you doing up the tree?" said Carlo, at the exact moment Tammo began to say, "So what were you doing, singing at that mirror?"

"I was trying to catch a song thrush." Tammo decided to get his explanation in first, laying on an air of finality so the half-truth would stick. It was mostly true, anyway. "That's how I came to fall through the window. I would have got it if my cassock hadn't got tangled round a branch. I can catch any bird I like. It's easy."

Carlo eyed Tammo's torn cassock and moss-stained appearance with a look of guarded disbelief. Tammo shrugged.

"Well, mostly it's easy. I'm still working on it. I'm better at it than anyone else."

"I'm sure you're the most graceful tumbler in Angelio," Carlo said smoothly. And then before Tammo could decide whether to take offence: "But how close did you truly come to catching the song thrush? I was listening to him, you know. Echoing him. Or trying to." Carlo gave a modest smile. "It's what Maestro Sarastro teaches me to do: to listen to birdsong and try to copy it. He calls it nightingalising." A cringe of embarrassment from Carlo as he spoke the word nightingale yet again. "Only the rector says the conservatorio can't afford to buy caged birds from the market, and our class isn't allowed off the premises, so we never get to hear them in the woods. That's why I try to practice near this tree."

"You're not allowed out of the conservatorio? Not ever?" Tammo's freedom-loving spirit latched onto the part of Carlo's speech that most offended it.

"Not unless we're going to sing somewhere, and then we're always chaperoned. We can't go to Carnival or the opera, or even dine with our parents." A black look Tammo would not have imagined possible for such a cherub flickered across Carlo's face. "Not that I want to." He gave a dainty shrug.

"I don't either," Tammo lied. He had much rather keep the conversation away from parents. He went back to the topic of the mirror.

"So you need that mirror to copy birdsong?"

Carlo's laughter was like a peal of fairy bells.

"Of course not, silly. Don't you use them in your class? To ensure you keep a noble expression when singing? Like this?"

He instantly struck a pose of such exaggerated grandeur that Tammo burst out laughing through his nose, and forgot to retort that he'd never stayed in any class long enough to find out what they did. Carlo was fun, he thought. Eunuchs were supposed to be stuck-up and spoiled, throwing tantrums every two minutes. Carlo wasn't like that at all. In fact, he was much friendlier than the boys Tammo was forced to rub shoulders with, day in and out.

"So, what kind of birds…?" he began. But at that moment, the campanile sang out two chimes.

"Hell!" Tammo swore. "Afternoon class!"

He glanced about the dormitory. He could go for the tree again, if he jumped at the right angle, but what if someone was watching?

"It's all right," Carlo said. "You can take the stairs. If you go by the left-hand staircase, you ought to miss the maestri. They never come in that way." He winked at Tammo. "Never mind how I know."

"Right." Tammo hurried across the room and put his hand on the doorknob. What was it after recreation? Theory of music. Then counterpoint. That was right below the dorms anyway. He should get away with it.

"Wait."

Carlo had crouched down and heaved a travelling case out from under his bed. He rummaged around for a moment or two and produced a clothes brush.

"You can't go looking like that."

With the practised action of a high-class manservant, Carlo swept the bits of leaf and twig from Tammo's hair and cassock, brushing out the moss dust and tucking the rips out of sight as far as they would go. A pity he couldn't do anything for the marks of the fight, Tammo thought. He doubted he would get through a whole afternoon without comment on those, but that was the pattern of his life.

Carlo finished off his ministrations by playfully tickling Tammo on the nose with the brush.

"There. Perfect." He smiled. "Good luck, Tammo Capell. I'll watch out for you in chapel."

"Thanks, Carlo," said Tammo.
And he meant it.

2. A Nightingale Amongst Crows

A bell rang. Carlo threw off the itchy blanket and touched the floorboards with his bare feet. His lips formed the words of the familiar song before he even knew he was awake.

"*Laudate pueri Dominum.*" Children, praise the Lord…

He'd been singing this song for the last four years, ever since Signor Bernardi had first brought him to Angelio at the age of ten, awkward in new shoes and sleeves too long for him, gazing up and up at the great buildings, fearing they would fall on his head. He had wept at the porter's lodge when he had to say goodbye to his old village choirmaster, although Signor Bernardi had done little more than pat Carlo's curly head before heading off to the tavern, a fresh purse of silver at his belt.

"*Auxilium meum a Domino.*" My help comes from the Lord…

Carlo shivered as he turned to make his bed. It was early and the sun hadn't yet risen. The two meagre candles on the prie-dieu were the only illumination the boys had to get them through their morning ritual. Carlo had braved the cold water with his usual feeling of sick dread, glad of the warm towel that wiped it away so quickly. In just two more months they would begin lighting fires at the extremes of day, praise to the seraphim! Above all things, Carlo hated to be cold. The chill to the blood. The ice… No, he would not think of it. He could never forget, but he would not think.

"*Benefac, Domine.*" Bless, oh Lord…

The boys lined up down the centre of the room, prefects at the head, followed by the other eunuchs in ascending order of age. At the prie-dieu, little Luca looked back, eyes wide, still uncertain he was doing the right thing. Carlo nodded toward the kneeling-cushion with an encouraging smile. He liked Luca. The cropped curls the colour of chocolate and the large eyes lost in eagerness to please reminded him of his own reflection not so long ago. He would tell him a story tonight, Carlo decided. The little boy had not yet left off crying at night and calling out for his mother. Secretly, Carlo wondered how recent Luca's surgery had been. He seemed very small. A story would calm him and Antonio both, and stop them from being corrupted by the older boys' talk. They were too young for that yet. Let them stay innocent as long as possible.

The boy at the head of the queue rose from his knees and walked out the door. Carlo knelt at the prie-dieu, hands clasped over the open Psalter. The flickering candles lit up a triptych of the Virgin and Child, flanked on the right by the Archangel Michael delivering her from the dragon, and on the left by the first Duke of Angelio kneeling in homage to the city's patron. Like a true Angelian, Carlo kissed the Archangel's hand. The grateful figure of the Virgin Mother caught his eye as he sat back on his knees again. After four years, Carlo had begun to forget what his own mother looked like, yet her words came back to him whenever he saw that picture.

"Carlo, my beautiful boy. My sweet little angel."

He tried not to wonder where she was now. Whether she was safe. It was best not to think of such things. He dipped his finger in the receptacle of holy water.

"Mighty St. Michael, guard us and grant us justice. *In nomine Patris, et Filii, et Spiritus Sancti.* Amen."

He had only just left the dormitory when a hand touched his shoulder.

"Hey, Nightingale. The rector wants to see you after chapel this morning. His study. Don't keep him waiting."

"This is great honour for the Conservatorio Archangeli. And a serious responsibility for you, Carlo. I trust you understand that."

The rector spread his fingers across his amply-filled waistcoat. The white, curly wig of his office was touched with a halo by the first morning rays.

"This is the first time I have permitted someone so young to sing at the Sancti Michaelis. But Maestro Sarastro tells me you are ready."

Behind the rector's chair, the Duke's own Master of the Art Musical watched Carlo from beneath forbidding eyebrows. Maestro Sarastro had taught the great Morestelli himself, along with half the virtuosi in the Apostolic Empire. It was his operas that filled the Duke's theatre every carnival season; his chorales that inspired thoughts of heaven in the hearts of worshippers beneath the silver dome on feast days. Carlo hadn't expected an engagement like this for at least another year. But if Maestro Sarastro said he was ready, then no one would dare suggest otherwise.

The rector took a sip of his early morning chocolate and replaced the cup carefully in its porcelain saucer. A boy with a silver chocolate-pot in his hand stepped forward to refill it.

"You do understand what this means, Carlo? To sing at the Seraphim Mass? The sacred duty you are to perform. Permission to speak, boy."

"Yes, rector. I understand. It is an honour beyond words."

There would be few in Angelio who didn't understand. Seraphim Mass was not one of the cardinal feasts of the Archangel. Only the very greatest of the virtuosi ever sang at those. But as the feast honouring the army of St Michael's host—and consequently the Duke's army as well—it was an important occasion in civic life. Everyone would be there. The Duke, the ruling families of the city, the leading clerics of the Sancti Michaelis: all the people whose favour Carlo would need if he was to make it as a virtuoso. All would be expecting to hear music that would echo that of the seraphim themselves and open channels of blessing from the Archangel to the city's defences for another year. There would be no room for error, no excuse for nerves. The occasion demanded perfection.

"You will have to work very hard at this, Carlo." Maestro Sarastro's rich voice betrayed nothing of pride in his pupil, only stern admonition. "Further rehearsals beginning today, in addition to your vocal exercises."

"I understand, maestro. I won't let you down."

The rector turned awkwardly in the chair. He looked like a brocade-covered seal manoeuvring on the sand.

"Is that really necessary, maestro? Carlo has been forced to miss a number of non-musical classes as it is."

Maestro Sarastro gave a dismissive snort.

"An hour or two off religious studies or prayers is hardly going to hurt."

The chocolate cup went down with a clatter.

"Maestro Sarastro. May I remind you that the Conservatorio Archangeli has a religious foundation going back to the days of the second Duke? We teach the art musical as being sacred to Michael himself. It cannot be divorced from the boys' devotional lives."

"And may I remind you, rector, that your boys' musical offerings to St. Michael are what bring in the funds for your precious school? Without them, you would find your chocolate-pot sadly empty."

Carlo felt a familiar twinge in his stomach. The rector and Maestro Sarastro were notorious for arguing over the training of talented students. The trouble was, neither of them could bear not being in charge. It made interviews such as this close to unbearable sometimes. When they started, Carlo wanted to wrap his arms over his head and hide under the table, just as he had done back in the village. It took everything he had learned about heroic poise to keep a straight back and his head facing forward. He was a gentleman of the conservatorio now. He wouldn't cower like a peasant.

The rector picked up a linen napkin and dabbed at the corners of his mouth.

"I don't intend to create a scene in front of the boy. I suggest we discuss this in private. Like gentlemen."

Maestro Sarastro's cheeks quivered.

"As you say, rector. We wouldn't want the boy tainted by low behaviour."

The rector snapped his fingers impatiently at the chocolate-pot boy. The boy bowed and hurried from the room.

"The maestro and I will discuss this further, Carlo. You are free to go to breakfast for now. Is there anything you wish to ask? You will, of course, receive your usual share of the fee. The bursar will credit it to your account."

That was another thing to distance him from the other boys. The more singing engagements a student secured, the greater the amount in his personal account. Was his whole life to be envy and segregation from now on? No. Carlo's heart gave a little flutter as he remembered. Tammo Capell, the boy with the crow's voice who had tumbled into his room. They were destined to be friends. Brothers. Two lonely outsiders drawn together by a tilt of the Archangel's scales. And Carlo had a plan to make sure it happened.

"Thank you, rector. Everything is perfectly clear." Carlo made a bow, making sure it took in the Duke's maestro as well as the head of the conservatorio. "God save you both."

There was very little time for what Carlo had in mind, but

then there was very little time for anything. The trick was to catch the stolen moment.

The eunuch class was still chewing on tooth-sticks and putting on their outdoor hats when the first hint of opportunity arrived. Or, rather, *someone* arrived. Wheezing and heavy footsteps in the passageway sounded the alarm. The little boys stood to attention. Giuseppe—a florid boy of fifteen—hastily pushed a snuff box under his pillow and scrubbed away the evidence with a handkerchief. His companion—alabaster by comparison and sporting an illicit ringlet—gave an effeminate giggle.

A short-winded voice called out. "Master Bianci? Are you in here?"

"Yes. Come in, Rubin."

Giuseppe and the others deflated with relief. Carlo gave a pale smile as the rector's manservant stumped in, leaning heavily on the door. In spite of his swollen nose and pot belly, Carlo liked Rubin. He'd been Carlo's chaperone since his first concert and, when Carlo was small, had let him play a while in the piazzas on the way home. Carlo could guess why he'd come calling at this time of day.

"It's about my rehearsal with Maestro Sarastro, isn't it?"

"That's right, lad. No walk for you this morning, I'm afraid. Straight to the rehearsal room." He gave a phlegmy cough.

"Sure you can make it that far, Rubin?" Marco, one of the prefects spoke, a smirk on his lips.

"Sure you can, Marco?" the alabaster boy shot back.

At nineteen, Marco had already begun to carry the

extra weight that was the curse of so many castrati. Feminine softness could so easily turn to flab.

Marco scowled at the alabaster boy. "Is that rouge on your lips, Giovanni?"

Giovanni touched his mouth self-consciously. His eyes flickered towards Rubin. "Natural beauty." He made a flirtatious pout. "Why don't you come here and kiss me, Marco?" Marco reddened. "Why don't you kiss my—"

"Come now, gentlemen, that's enough," said Rubin.

"He should respect me as a prefect." Marco looked down his wide-set nose.

"He respects you as a very Hercules." Carlo broke in with a grand theatrical gesture, catching hold of the bedsheet and draping it over Marco's shoulder as a toga. "A Titan of the dormitory. A demi-god of prefecture. As indeed we respect Giovanni as our Paris of Troy." He gave Giovanni an exaggerated kiss on the cheek. "And Master Rubin as our very own Mercury, messenger of the gods!"

He went down on one knee and trilled out a few bars of a bravura aria, ending in a note high enough to break windows on the far side of the courtyard. Most of the boys laughed. Nicolo and Luca applauded.

"Always the little peacemaker, aren't you, lad?" Rubin ruffled Carlo's cropped curls as the other boys trooped out for their walk.

"That's why I pass all understanding." Carlo got to his feet and dusted down his cassock.

The truth was, Carlo hated arguments. Maestri or students, it was all the same. Arguments led to bad things.

They made pains come in his stomach and spoiled his voice. That was why it was so important to cultivate friendship.

Carlo turned to Rubin.

"Grant me two minutes. Then I'll be with you."

The quill was scratchy, and the inkwell almost dried out in the sun, but there wasn't time to be too particular about handwriting. Carlo frowned. That wasn't as he would have wished it. He hated to produce ugly work. It couldn't be helped, though. The sentiment, at least, would be as pretty as he could make it.

My dear and newly-discovered twin...

Carlo stroked his bottom lip with the feathered end of the quill. Perhaps not. He might be certain he had met his soulmate in Tammo, but the other boy was as wary and unpredictable as a wild bird. He might think Carlo was poking fun at him.

He scored two lines through the first sentence and began again.

My dear and newly-discovered companion:

I hope you felt, as I did, what a joy it was to meet a friend, especially one who loves songbirds. If you can find in your heart even a part of the affection I already feel for you, then come to the roost of the song thrush tomorrow after vespers. I promise you will always have a listening ear and never an unkind word from your

Affectionate and loyal friend,

C.

It was as good as an aria, Carlo decided. No one could

fail to be moved by that. With a deft movement, he sanded the ink and blew on it, then quickly folded the letter into quarters. He hoped it didn't blot too much. For a moment, he tickled his bottom lip again, wondering what to write for the direction. Of course, what else? The quill scratched the folded paper, spraying tiny bursts of ink.

To the graceful tumbler.

Carlo pocketed the letter, snatched up his school things and galloped out of the door. He was ready for his rehearsal now. And for whatever else the maestri chose to surprise him with. The strength to keep going was right here in his pocket.

He had to wait until after grammar before the chance came to dispatch his heavenly message. Maestro Sarastro had worked him hard in rehearsal. The piece Carlo was to sing at the climax of Seraphim Mass contained enormous vocal leaps and a slow, gradual descent from the soaring upper register. And, of course, the maestro had wanted to begin with the most difficult parts straight away, even at such an early hour of the morning.

"No, no, Carlo," he had exclaimed, arms everywhere. "Your voice must rest, as it were, on the clouds. Fill your chest with the divine air. Fill it, boy!"

And he had. Over and over and over again. At one point, he had felt certain he was going to swoon. The ceiling of the rehearsal room swam like the pool of the Morningstar Fountain and blood pulsed in his ears. But he breathed and stayed conscious. By the end of the session, it had become quite exhilarating. No one composed sacred music like Maestro Sarastro. Carlo felt sure he must have come someway close to echoing the seraphim. It wasn't a bad way to begin your lessons.

By the time second period was over, Carlo could feel the letter weighing in his pocket like a stolen peach. He had to get rid of it before he accidentally sang out his secret and spoiled his new friendship before it had even begun.

The stairwell of the main school building was crowded with boys—coming up, going down, leaning over the ornate banister railings to call to one another—before the rap of prefects' rods returned the noise to a murmur. Two floors beneath him, Carlo could make out a group of boys much of a height with himself, standing by a colonnade. They were pushing and jostling a smaller, slighter boy with cuts on his face. Voices that had broken with a vengeance drifted up the stairwell.

"Where do you think you're sloping off to, Crow?"

Crow. So that was what they called his twin. Carlo frowned.

"Speak up, Crow. Don't cheek your elders." A poetry textbook clipped Tammo's ear in a deliberate accident.

"What is it to you?" Even from two floors up, Carlo could sense Tammo's anger. And his fear.

"That's *signor* to you, freak." The textbook made a return journey, forcing Tammo's head down. "A little bird saw you coming out of Maestro Aquila's yesterday, smiling. Smiling! Must have cracked the cobblestones. So, what do you have to smile about? Paolo wasn't smiling when he came out of the rector's, I can tell you."

"He just wanted to see me. Now shove off, Riccardo, or I'll finish you too."

"Like hell you will! Want to know what I heard? That Maestro Aquila's giving you classes on your own because you're scared Paolo will punch your ugly head."

"Your ugly head, you mean!"

"Poor old Crow! Can't even think of his own insults. Why don't you run along and toot your flute for Maestro Aquila? You know he only has you playing the thing because he can't stand the sound of your voice."

Carlo saw Tammo hunch his shoulders about his ears and lower his head. The twinge in his stomach came back. Why did people have to be so unkind? The flute part was interesting, though. Tammo had never mentioned that yesterday.

"Off to class over there! And keep the noise down."

One of the senior prefects was elbowing his way through the swarm of boys. The crowd parted. Tammo shrugged Riccardo away and turned toward the main front door. He was directly below Carlo now. This was the moment. Leaning over the balustrade, Carlo trilled out the call of the song thrush, his melodious voice rising above the hum of noise.

Tammo looked up. So did several other boys. Carlo grinned and made a mock bow, but in the same movement snatched the letter from his pocket. As he had hoped, Tammo held his gaze longer than the rest. Carlo held up the letter by his cheek, raised a playful eyebrow and dropped the letter down the stairwell.

Tammo's heel came down on it in an instant. As Carlo

watched, his potential twin glanced around, knelt with the pretence of tightening a shoe buckle, and slipped the letter inside his own cassock. He didn't risk another glance above, and the next breath swept him outside on the back of the throng. But the message had been delivered. At least one good deed for the day had been done. Now he could only wait and see what came of it.

There was another good deed he'd promised himself he'd do. Carlo was struggling to keep his eyes open by the time all the eunuch class returned to their dormitory at ten, but he couldn't allow himself to forget little Luca. By the time everyone had disrobed and combed their hair, the younger boy was yawning so hard there were tears running down his face. But still he shivered in his chemise and tucked his knees defiantly under his chin when Carlo suggested he go to sleep.

"I want my mamma."

"How about a story instead?" Carlo walked over to Luca's bed and tucked the grey blanket around the little boy's legs.

At the other side of the dormitory, the older eunuchs were playing cards and passing round the box from under Giuseppe's pillow. There were a couple of stifled sneezes. Giovanni giggled.

Bare feet came pattering across the floorboards. "Can I hear a story too?"

Antonio, the second-youngest boy, was only fractionally bigger than Luca and pretended to be brave at night, but he'd woken the boys with nightmares more than once. Carlo let him climb up onto Luca's bed, and stretched the blanket to cover his legs too.

"You shall both have a story."

Carlo fought off the yawn that was desperate to come. He felt like he'd done at least three days' rehearsal in one. A roar came from across the room, as Giuseppe won a hand at cards. Carlo ignored it, and fixed his gaze on his waiting audience.

"Do you know the tale of the Archangel Michael and the first Duke of Angelio?"

"Is it a scary story?" Antonio's eyes widened.

"Of course not." Carlo drew up his own knees and wrapped his arms around them. "It is noble and heroic. Just as you will be when you tread the boards of the Teatro di Palazzo as famous sopranists."

Antonio's fear changed to a broad smile. Luca attempted a more cautious version before grasping hold of the sheets again.

"I want to be primo castrato," Antonio announced.

"So do I." Luca nodded solemnly.

"We can't both be primo."

"Yes, we can."

Both looked at Carlo for confirmation.

"You shall both be primo in turn. And have dozens of admirers." Inwardly, Carlo sighed. Did even the smallest singers have to be rivals? He summoned up a look of theatrical animation. "Of course, you know the Duke is patron of the Teatro. And the Archangel Michael is patron of the whole of Angelio, even the Duke. Well, this is why."

Both little boys were rapt and silent now. From his own bed, Nicolo lay on his stomach, listening too. Francesco and Marco glanced over their shoulders at the scene and shook their heads in amusement.

"Many, many years ago, when Angelio was nothing more than a little village in the woods, the very first Duke was given all the land around here by the Apostolic Father himself, as a reward for his piety. But when he arrived to take up his lands, he found that a wicked Count, who cared nothing for virtue, had taken the village and all the land for himself; and gathered to himself a host of fearsome knights that no one could defeat in battle. Three times the Duke and his knights rode out against them, and three times they were driven back. In his desperation, the Duke retired to a chapel in the woods and prayed for help, and all his knights prayed with him. And, just as day was dawning, what do you think they heard?"

"A cockerel," said Luca, seriously.

There was a guffaw from the other side of the room. Carlo sucked in his cheeks to keep a straight face.

"They heard the sound of heavenly song. And, when they looked up, they saw the whole army of the seraphim coming out of the clouds, shining as bright as the sun. Leading them out was their prince, the Archangel Michael. His eyes were burning gold and his sword was aflame. The angels swept down over the fortress of the evil Count, singing their crystal-clear song. And as they did, the walls of the fortress crumbled. The wicked knights fell to their faces in fear, or ran away into the woods and the haunts of the wild animals. As for the Count, no one ever saw what became of him.'

"He was eaten by the cockerel," someone said.

Carlo scowled and crossed himself against evil It wasn't wise to mock holy stories.

"What happened then?" Antonio wanted to know.

"Well, the Duke was overcome by what he had seen, and knelt to give thanks for the victory. But as he did so, Michael himself swooped down by his side and said, 'Arise, noble sir, for I have great things to show you.' The Duke stood to his feet, and the Archangel led him to a spring of clear water. 'This is the water of purity,' he said. 'If you and your descendants remain pure and pious, then this place will know the protection of the seraphim host forever. All this land you see will become a great city, the most beautiful in the empire. And the sons of your house will always rule over it.'

"It happened just as the Archangel said. When the Duke built his city, he had a church raised in the exact spot where he had met with St. Michael. That was our own Sancti Michaelis Archangeli, whose great bell you hear every day."

"And where you're going to sing, Nightingale."

"Yes." Carlo smiled shyly. "And the spring became the Morningstar Fountain, named for the song the seraphim sang at the time of creation, when the morning stars shouted together for joy. Now St. Michael stands on top of the cathedral, watching over everyone in Angelio to keep them safe. Especially those with no one else to watch out for them. That's why you need never be afraid, Luca. And they do say…" Carlo leaned forward. "They do say that sometimes people in Angelio see him for themselves. He comes near and comforts them when they're sad or in trouble. He may be nearby even now."

"Is that true, Nightingale?" Luca frowned.

"Yes, it is."

The older boys who had been looking round nodded in agreement. To doubt the Archangel was to doubt you were an Angelian. Only fools and foreigners disbelieved.

"Have you ever seen him?" said Antonio.

"No." Carlo pulled the blanket up to the little boys' chins. "But I hope to one day." If he sang beautifully enough. If he made his voice as pure could be. The Archangel might recognise Carlo as one of his own and honour him with a vision of heavenly splendour.

"Bedtime for you as well, Nightingale."

Plump Marco folded his hand of cards and stood up with an elaborately genteel yawn. This time, Carlo couldn't help following suit.

"Come along, gentlemen. Prayers and candles out."

Carlo knelt on the sanded floor. He knew the familiar words about Almighty God granting them a restful night and a peaceful death. He was sure he meant them too. But tonight he had a new prayer. One he meant with all his heart.

"Beloved Archangel, watch over Tammo. And let him come to the tree tomorrow."

3. A Bird in the Hand

The smell of fish was the smell of freedom, Tammo thought. But freedom at the price of humiliation. Along with the salt-tanged scent of air unconstrained by any conservatorio walls or schedule of lessons came the undisguised looks of pity or even disgust.

"Oh, the poor little orphan boys from the Cage! I'm sure I could spare a copper or two. There you go, signor."

"That one's not so little, is he though, Bella? Looks as though he's been fighting to me."

"So he does. Here, you're not trying to trick us, are you, signor? I'm not giving my charity money to ruffians."

"An unfortunate accident, citizeness." Vice-rector Aprile waved away Tammo's bruises with an apologetic gesture. "The boy is truly deserving of charity, I assure you. Orphaned only three years ago in a terrible fire. The conservatorio is his only family."

"Ooh, he's right as well, Modestia. Would you look at those scars?" The woman poked Tammo as though he was a rare beast in a menagerie. "Turns my stomach, that does. He's not the one from that metalworking shop, is he? That was a dreadful carry-on. Do you remember, Modestia?"

Modestia didn't remember—much to Tammo's relief—although Bella remained convinced for another five minutes that she should, and set Tammo's stomach in knots by repeatedly saying:

"It was down by... Just round the corner from here. There was a whole family of them. What was the name now?"

"I really couldn't say, citizeness." Vice-rector Aprile finally brought Tammo's misery to an end. "But all our boys are very deserving, and much dependent on the goodwill of Angelio's citizens. If you could spare anything, for St. Michael's love..."

Modestia eventually relented.

"There you go, young man. You try and stay out of trouble."

Tammo grimaced a smile.

"God bless you, citizeness." Preferably with a brick.

The good side was that every week, for one glorious hour, Tammo got to experience the exhilaration of the marketplace. There was much more to it than just fish. For every basket of crabs and slab of eels, there was a stilt walker, a puppeteer, a man with a musical box that played when he turned the handle. Today, there was a man in a long coat decorated with feathers of all kinds who had taken up residence under the poplar tree down by the riverbank, just upriver from where the fish barges moored. A number of wooden birdcages hung from the tree's branches and stood by his feet. Fluttering behind the bars, Tammo could make out a magpie, a woodlark, several starlings, and linnets.

"Gather round! Gather round, good folk!" the man called. "Such sights as you have never seen! Such wonders as you have never encountered! With a magic learned in great secrecy from the bird-tamers of Mingguo, I will command my birds with only the sound of my flute!"

When the feathered man was certain he had enough of an audience, he drew a flute from his pocket with a flourish. He had tied ribbons of red and pink to the end of it; they fluttered in the morning breeze.

"I beg of you, good folk, do not be afraid by what you see here. This is the most benign of magics, dreamed up by his court magicians for the Emperor of the Jade Throne himself, to ease his troubled spirits. Merely marvel as my birds respond to the irresistible sound of music, as I play for them the song of liberation."

Sure enough, as the showman played, the magpie in the cage to the left of his head started to rattle the cage with its beak. The spectators began to nudge each other and point. The magpie took a firm hold of the bolt that locked the cage door. The showman tapped his foot and dipped the flute, so the ribbons danced. The cage door swung open and the magpie flew free.

There was a smattering of *oohs* and *aahs* from the crowd, but most knew the show had only just begun. The showman changed to another folk song and dipped his flute again. The magpie alighted on the cage of starlings and began to tug at their door too. Several flourishes later, the starlings were also flying free, making a circle about the showman's head.

The cycle was repeated for the woodlark, and then for the linnets. Each time, at a change of tune and a dip of the flute, the magpie would free another set of his feathered companions. By the time the song came to an end, a whole flock of birds was whirling about the showman's head. One of the apprentices tried to grab hold of them and almost fell out of the tree. The crowd clapped and cheered.

The showman lowered his flute and became as still as a triumphal statue in the midst of his birds. Tammo couldn't help noticing that one of them let drop the favoured gift of all birds to statues. A couple of people laughed, but most were still applauding. Several handfuls of coins clinked into the showman's hat.

"Thank you. Thank you, good citizens. But that is only the first part of the magic. Watch and be amazed as I play the song of captivity."

The feeble flute struck up a tune in the minor key. The birds swirled about the showman's head. There was a dip of bright ribbons, and the linnets flew back to their cage and, one by one, hopped inside. The magpie followed and closed the door behind them.

There was an explosion of applause, with hoots and cheers from the crowd.

"How d'you do that, then?" someone called out.

But the showman was in his element, and merely dipped his flute again with another breathy trill. The woodlark followed the linnets, then the starlings, and finally the magpie itself. It drew the bolt of its own cage shut and then let out a joyous "Clack, clack, clack!" More cheers rang out, along with several muttered speculations as to how the trick was done.

The show was over. Some of the cooks and housewives had already moved away, keen to find fresh entertainment or to take their wares home. But enough had tossed coins to the showman to justify his broad smile as he swirled his feathered cloak with a final flourish.

"Thank you. Thank you, good citizens! My birds and I will be here again on Friday."

It wasn't really magic, Tammo thought. He'd known these marketplaces well in the days before he joined the conservatorio. He'd been one of those little boys, dancing round the showman as he tidied away, asking if they could stroke his birds. There was always some sort of trick. The dipping of the flute probably had a lot to do with it, and maybe some carefully-laid trails of seed. As for the man's playing, Tammo could have given him a few lessons in that himself. Now he was playing that dark flute of Maestro Aquila's. That was a flute! If Tammo had played that in the marketplace, birds would have flocked to him just for the sweetness of his song. No tricks needed. No one would have noticed his scars then. They'd have been too busy gaping in wonder.

"Come along, gentlemen. Time to take these offerings home." Vice-rector Aprile spoke hastily as the great bell of the Sancti Michaelis sang out nine.

Tammo fell in step with the other boys, carrying his basket of coppers and silvers. They walked double file behind the vice-rector: across the market square, towards the bridge. Across the river, lines of freshly washed linen crossed and criss-crossed the skyline like carnival flags. Tammo shifted the basket to one hip and felt in his pocket. The paper was still there. Glancing around to make sure the vice-rector wasn't looking, he took it out and shook it open.

The words hadn't changed. Tammo had lost count of

how many times he'd read and re-read Carlo's letter. He'd even hidden in the confessional box for a whole five minutes after vespers, just to look at it one more time. He couldn't quite get away from the idea that the eunuch was laughing at him. He didn't want to think that. He liked Carlo—really liked him—and he wanted to meet him again. But what if the young castrato was waiting by the tree tonight just to make fun of him? Or wasn't waiting at all?

Paolo and Riccardo were waiting for him in the passageway. He'd been running. Since Maestro Aquila had promised him the dark flute, Tammo had been determined to avoid black marks with the other maestri. He wasn't going to let some stupid demerit get in the way of his one hour of happiness. He didn't notice the scowling tenors lolling against the wall until Paolo stuck out his foot. Tammo went sprawling onto the tiled floor, scattering sheets of manuscript everywhere.

"Clumsy, clumsy." Paolo wagged a finger. "Better pick them up, Crow. You wouldn't want to be late."

"Why exactly are you late, Crow?" Riccardo moved a couple of sheets away from Tammo with the toe of his shoe. "Been begging for your bread with the other little charity freaks?"

Tammo pressed his lips together until he could feel the blood blister burst. He licked the salty blood, snarling. He was so close to knocking Paolo into the middle of next week again. Was the dark flute worth the effort it took to stop himself?

"Why are you late yourselves?" he growled. "Or did your maestro throw you out again?"

Paolo narrowed his eyes and dropped a whole pile of papers to the floor, showing the palms of his hands.

"Now look what you've made me do. Pick them up, Crow. And don't get them dirty."

That was it, thought Tammo. He was going to shove Paolo into the wall now and hang the consequences. He tightened his fists.

A door opened just a little further down the passageway. A strident voice boomed out:

"And work on those appoggiaturas, Carlo. I want to feel you caress that closing cadenza."

"Yes, maestro." Carlo's delicate soprano was muted and respectful, as he came through the open door and into the corridor, his own sheaf of music tucked beneath his arm.

"Bloody ball-less warbler," Paolo muttered under his breath.

Tammo's temper flared in an instant. He was on his feet and within inches of Paolo's nose in a heartbeat. But Maestro Sarastro's agitated step had already moved in, bypassing Carlo, and bearing down upon the tenor boys.

"Paolo Agresto! Is that you, you hideous little toad? What is my recitative doing on the floor? Pick it up, boy, this instant. Have you no respect?"

"This boy from the bass class knocked me." Paolo sounded more sulky than cocksure now. Maestro Sarastro was well known for his intolerance of anything short of utter devotion to the art musical. Even boys who only knew him by sight feared to be at the sharp end of his insults.

"The bass class? You have no concern with the bass class, boy. You are with me on approval, do not forget. There are plenty of other tenors whose patrons have petitioned me long and hard. I may well choose to reconsider their cases. You will come and rehearse your aria to me in person. And it had better be more impressive than last week. You, boy!" He looked at Riccardo. "Stop cluttering up the passageway. This isn't the Marchese of Parini's gaming rooms. Boy with the fat lip! Is that your manuscript down there?"

"I tripped over, maestro. I was coming from the vice-rector's weekly charity collection at the fish market." Tammo looked at his shoes. There was no reply from the maestro. He squatted down and started trying to prise his papers from under Paolo's feet.

"You've hurt yourself." Carlo knelt beside him and dabbed at Tammo's bleeding lip with a handkerchief. "He was only doing his duty, maestro. The school does need the money."

"Damn right it does." For a composer of sacred music, Maestro Sarastro had no qualms about cursing. "Agresto, why are you still standing there? Move it, boy!"

With a practised eye, Carlo deftly separated the bass scores from the tenor, pushing the latter in Paolo's direction. Tammo's scores he neatened together before placing them into the other boy's hands.

"You'll come to the tree tonight, won't you?" he whispered in an undertone.

As the maestro swaggered off in a swirl of embroidered

coattails, a chastened Paolo at his heels, Carlo turned to Tammo and gave a wink.

A single point of yellow light bloomed and wavered in the darkness. It moved nearer. Nearer. The candle flame blew sideways in the wind. Tammo felt sweat prickle the back of his neck. The thought of all that dry tinder under the tree made him shudder. He squared his shoulders. No weakness. He wouldn't let the other boy see his fear. He blinked as Carlo held the light to his face. "You brought a candle?

"I prefer to see where I'm going. A strange fashion, but I hope it might catch on in time." Carlo wedged the candle holder between two protruding roots and squatted down next to it, his back against the lime's trunk.

"You know what I mean." Tammo squatted next to him, wondering if the eunuch ever answered a straight question. "Even I wouldn't steal a candle."

"Steal!" Carlo looked genuinely affronted. "I asked my housemaster for it."

"And he gave it to you?"

"Tammo, you do have an odd notion of social convention," Carlo said. "That is the way it generally works. One person asks and the other gives."

Tammo opened and shut his mouth.

"They let your class have candles?"

There was a moment of silence. Carlo flushed slightly and blinked his long eyelashes.

"Oh. Yes. I see what you mean." He gave a nervous

smile. "No, not the whole class. Just the prefects and...well... me. They're worried I might break an ankle."

Carlo was blushing so brightly, Tammo might have seen him without the candle. He really didn't like this "Nightingale" stuff, did he? It seemed strange for a student to be embarrassed by his good voice. A bad voice had been Tammo's bane since day one.

"So, what did you say you needed this candle for?"

"Nightingalising, naturally. You can't do it during the day. The name alone ought to make that clear. I sing in the dark, oh, once or twice a week. With a mirror, of course."

He looked so serious that Tammo was temporarily convinced the world had run mad. Singing into mirrors in pitch darkness?

"Seriously?" he said.

Carlo burst into girlish laughter and gave Tammo a gentle push.

"Of course not, you goose! I asked to go to the chapel and offer private devotions for my patron. Which I did, before you ask. Never lie, Tamino. The truth will find you out."

Tammo scowled. "And where do I come into all this?"

Carlo leaned his head against Tammo's shoulder. "You're so serious, Tamino. This is all about you. About you and me being..." He pursed his pretty lips and seemed to think for a moment. "Being friends. Best friends, if you like."

Tammo gave an involuntary shudder. He was no longer used to people touching him, unless it was to deal out a caning or a good right hook.

"Best friends?" he said, warily.

"If you like," Carlo repeated. Even by the dim candlelight, Tammo could see that the eunuch's eyes had gone wide. He reminded Tammo of a puppy, wanting to be stroked but afraid you might kick it instead.

"I've never had a best friend here." Tammo measured out his words. He'd never had a friend here at all. It meant trusting another boy, which was something Tammo had not done since he walked through the conservatorio gates, but he thought he could trust Carlo. He'd come to meet Tammo tonight, hadn't he? "All right," he heard himself say. "Best friends."

Carlo clasped both of Tammo's hands in his.

"Best friends. I swear, Tamino, I'll always be true. To the end of my days."

For a moment, Tammo was afraid the eunuch was about to kiss him or something. He put on the gruffest croak he could.

"What's all this 'Tamino' business? You can't pet-name me; I'm older than you."

"Says who?" Carlo's bright eyes danced with amusement.

"I asked around. You don't turn fourteen until after Epiphany. I'm your elder by nine months. You should look up to me."

In response, Carlo straightened his back, as if to emphasise his superior height even when seated, and stared down his nose with mock imperiousness.

"You were the one who named me a pet at our last

meeting. It's only fair that you should be one too. My dear Tamino."

Was he always like this? Tammo thought. He hated being called names, but it just wasn't possible to stay angry with Carlo when he was acting such funny poses and looking at him with such open-hearted affection. As nicknames went, Tamino—little Tammo—was preferable to Crow and infinitely better than Firebrand. He doubted he could stop Carlo once he'd started anyway. The eunuch seemed that type.

Tammo stood up and rubbed life back into his buttocks.

"I've got something to show you."

Tammo reached into the shadows and lifted his home-made birdcage to the light of Carlo's candle. The song thrush inside woke up with an angry twitter. Its specked chest was thrust out like that of a pompous virtuoso. Carlo's lips parted in wonder; his white fingertips caressed the outline of the cage.

"Be careful it doesn't peck," said Tammo. "It's hungry again and it wants water too." He watched with satisfaction as Carlo bent his head to the cage and trilled out a thrush-like phrase. "I told you I could get birds," he added.

"You did." There was genuine astonishment in Carlo's voice. Tammo felt a swell of pride.

"I got it especially for you," he said, awkwardly.

"Truly?" Carlo's eyes couldn't get any bigger. "Tamino, I'm so grateful! How did you catch it? You must tell me everything."

"It's not that hard, really," said Tammo. "You just have to be patient."

He told Carlo about twisting a cage, laying a trail of hairy fruits, being careful not to look the bird in the eye. It was good to be the generous benefactor for once. It sponged out the humiliation of all that begging for silver.

"So, he just hopped into the cage? Poor thing!" Carlo stroked the wilting leaves of the cage with tenderness.

"He was too greedy," said Tammo, blithely ignoring Carlo's sympathy for another caged singer.

"He was looking for a friend." There was a serious note in Carlo's voice. He gave the bird another tender look and made kissing sounds with his lips. "Thank you, Tamino. I can't wait to see the look on Maestro Sarastro's face. Nightingalising with a real songbird!"

Maestro Sarastro's name reminded Tammo of this morning's incident with Paolo. He traced patterns in the broken twigs with the toes of his shoes.

"Carlo. You know this morning? That boy with the bruise on his face..." He sniffed and cleared his throat.

"He gave you that fat lip, didn't he?" said Carlo softly.

Tammo managed to turn the curse on his tongue into a wordless growl. The mere thought of Paolo and Riccardo made him want to punch things. Carlo stiffened, his arms hugging the birdcage. Somehow, the castrato's fear made him more annoyed. What sort of monster did Carlo think he was? Hitting a eunuch would be like hitting a girl. He took out his frustration on the tree instead, punching it twice and making his knuckles split open again.

"I hate him," he said. "I hate them all."

"They're not worth it, Tamino." Carlo's voice was a nervous flutter.

"I'll hate who I like. They hate me."

"They hate us eunuchs worse."

Tammo huffed through his nose, clenching and unclenching his sore fist. It wasn't the same. Everyone said things about eunuchs. He half-wanted to ask Carlo the questions himself. *Does it hurt? Can you still straighten your stiletto? Are you all pretty bedfellows?* Except that he remembered how it had felt this morning when Paolo had said what he did about Carlo. It had felt like a knife wound.

"It's not the same," he said, but his words sounded lame and half-hearted.

"Not exactly the same, no." Carlo put down the birdcage and reached a tentative hand towards Tammo's shoulder. "But closer than you think, perhaps." He took Tammo's damaged fist in his other hand. "You're bleeding again. As a tumbler, you really should take more care."

Tammo put his fist in his mouth and sucked it. The blood tasted mossy.

"I can take care of myself," he said after a few minutes. "I just..." He picked at his scabs.

"Can't keep your temper?" Carlo suggested.

"If I can't, it's their fault." Tammo felt his blood get up again, remembering too late how his temper frightened Carlo. "Sorry," he croaked. "Look, you can't tell anyone this, but Maestro Aquila is letting me play this flute. It's... You've never heard anything like it, Carlo. I bet that even at the Teatro they don't have flutes like that. And I can handle it, you know...?" Tammo's voice trailed off.

"But that's wonderful," Carlo said. "I would love to hear you play the flute."

Tammo shrugged. "But the maestri are on my back all the time. If I'd hit Paolo this morning…"

"But you didn't." Carlo's features glowed with mischievous intelligence. "And you have me to watch your back now. You'll be a veritable Apollo in no time."

"I hardly look it," growled Tammo.

"Details, details." Carlo waved a hand. "Just picture yourself in a silk waistcoat and a white wig, playing with a quintet in some great lord's private chamber."

Tammo screwed up his eyes and made a vague attempt to see it, but even with the dark flute in the picture, he couldn't comfortably imagine himself playing gentle after-dinner music with a backdrop of curtains and gilt mirrors. The flute wanted to soar. It wanted to fly free. Its music wasn't the refined melody of a salon, but the wild song of hills and forests and the wings of the skylark. That was what Tammo yearned after: an escape from endless rehearsing and reciting. He thought again of the showman and his birds.

"Carlo, do you believe in magic?"

"I believe in miracles," said Carlo. "I think that's a kind of holy magic."

"The Archangel, you mean?"

Carlo nodded.

"But doesn't he just come to people who pray a lot?"

"We do pray a lot," Carlo pointed out.

Tammo gave a dismissive snort. Even Paolo Agresto

knelt in school chapel three times a day, and the Archangel definitely wasn't coming to him.

"I don't think miracles really happen," he said.

Carlo shook his head. "Oh, but they do, Tamino. I've prayed for the Archangel to take care of you. And he will."

"Not me," Tammo growled. He glanced at Carlo sideways. "I wager he smiles at you, though. You're one of the good people."

He blushed and cleared his throat. As an expression of friendship, it lacked a certain something, but it was the first Tammo had tried. He thought about giving Carlo a pat on the shoulder but decided to save that for another time.

"I wager he's smiling at you now," said Carlo. He touched a hand to his throat with a tiny frown. "I ought to go indoors. The night air is bad for my voice."

"Mine too," croaked Tammo.

Carlo's lips curved into a smile.

"Did you just make a joke, Tamino? I knew I could transform you." He looked at the song thrush, which had fallen asleep again. "Can you hide him until tomorrow after breakfast? I have my rehearsal with the maestro then."

"I'll bring him to your rehearsal room. Look out for me," said Tammo.

Carlo squeezed Tammo's arm before picking up the shortened candle and walking back into the gloom. Once or twice, he glanced back over his shoulder with a mischievous smile. Tammo's friend. His actual friend. Despite the near-autumn chill to the air, Tammo felt his heart warm at the thought.

He stretched and gave a yawn like the mouth of a cave

opening. The song thrush would need water if it was to survive the night. He picked out a couple of leaves that were covered with night dew and pushed them gently through the twiggy tangle. The cage could stay in the tree. It was well disguised enough. There; that was enough duty for one night. With a second yawn that could have been a groan, Tammo hauled his way up the branches toward a shared bed and a candle-less room.

4. Capons and Capers.

"Hush, Tamino! They'll hear you."

Tammo struggled back to his feet where he had slipped on the polished tiles of the passageway. The morning sunlight lit up arch shapes on the eastern side where the windows were, and made stripes across the earthy red of the walls. Tammo's shadow stretched and shrunk as he made an adjustment by his feet, then hopped and lurched after Carlo, trying hard not to laugh. Carlo bit the inside of his cheeks and giggled through his nose. His twin ran like he had gout in both feet, and his cassock looked like it had a lady's pannier beneath it. Tammo slid again on the floor. Carlo ran back and took hold of his wrist, pulling him to his feet.

"Come on. Hurry."

They bumbled together through the door of the rehearsal room. Carlo put his back to the door and slid to the floor, laughing until his sides hurt. Tammo knelt on all fours over the lump in his cassock, his hoarse guffaws reminding Carlo of a donkey's bray.

"Hush," he said again, held his breath, then snorted out more giggles. He took a clean handkerchief from his pocket and dabbed at his nose.

"How on earth did you manage to get through the whole of breakfast with that up your cassock?"

"The whole of breakfast *and* matins," said Tammo, looking up.

"What? No, you didn't!"

The two boys held one another's gaze, then burst out laughing again at exactly the same moment.

"Father Dominic asked if there was something wrong with me," gasped Tammo between laughs.

Carlo gave a happy sigh.

"Tamino, you are quite priceless. Where would I be without you?" He gave his eyes and nose a final dab and tucked the handkerchief away. "And how has our poor little friend fared? He needs a real cage. With scrollwork on top and a proper door and a perch and everything. I think he'd like that. We could give him a name."

"Dinner," said Tammo dispassionately.

Carlo drew himself up and took a prim stance.

"My fellow sopranist and I will pretend we didn't hear that, Tammo Capell. Don't you know it's dreadfully rude to devour a rival?" He gave an affected little sniff. "Hadn't you better go before you get into trouble?" he added in an ordinary voice.

"Yes, maestro." Tammo mock-saluted and pulled a face. "Pointless double-file walking along the riverside, here I come!"

The river would be at its best at this time of the morning. The reflection of trees in the water. Foam around the rocky falls. Geese bickering. Not too many insects.

"Swap places?" Carlo offered.

"No, thanks." Tammo grabbed his hat and headed for the door. "See you at the tree again?"

Carlo nodded.

"Take care, Tamino. And keep your temper."

The black look on Tammo's face as he went out of the door made Carlo think that might be difficult. His father used to have that look when he came home from the wine shop. His mother used to stiffen, and the little ones would cling round her skirts. And Carlo would stand in the middle of the floor and sing. Sing anything: psalms, ballads, lullabies. Impersonate the ancient soloist from the village church, or the strolling sopranist who competed with trumpeters in the tavern yard. Anything to make his father smile, to stop him from getting angry. Until his father had taken him to Signor Bernardi and said he needed lessons.

Little Carlo, alone in the empty church with the village choirmaster, his head barely reaching the keyboard of the organ. Signor Bernardi had told him to sing the *Kyrie Eleison*. He had done it all from memory, his eyes fixed on the wooden cherubs in the ceiling. He'd wondered if they were listening too. When he'd finished, Signor Bernardi had had tears in his eyes. After the choirmaster spoke with his father that night, his father had been the happiest Carlo had ever seen him. He'd kissed Carlo on the cheeks and called him a good boy, and everything had been peaceful and happy. For a while.

Carlo had never really asked what had made his father so angry. That was just the way he was. But he wondered about Tammo. It wasn't just the tenors' teasing that got him wound up. There was something else. Something to do with whatever had given him the scars and turned his voice to an old man's croak. Carlo wasn't stupid; he had a pretty good idea what sort of thing could do that. He shuddered again. He wasn't sure he wanted to imagine. He wouldn't ask Tammo about it. Not yet.

He walked over to the song thrush, still twittering crazily in its mess of twigs.

"I shall call you Orpheus. You will emerge from the underworld. To glory."

When Maestro Sarastro arrived, Carlo was standing with hands clasped behind his back, warming up his voice with scales and arpeggios before an open music stand. He looked completely baffled when his tutor tried to begin with the difficult middle section, and the harpsichord would only make odd, muffled sounds.

"Do you think there's something wrong with it, maestro?" he said anxiously.

And when the dancing nymphs were lifted to reveal what looked like an ill-constructed nest of broken lime twigs, the great Morestelli himself would have complemented Carlo's portrayal of wonder and astonishment as he exclaimed:

"Oh look, maestro! A bird. Can we keep him?"

The great Morestelli was on a number of minds that day. At recreation hour, when at the rector's insistence Carlo had taken time to relax with his fellow eunuchs, he found the whole castrato class gathered round an illustrated news sheet that plump Marco had picked up on the morning walk.

"Is it him? Who is it? Who's coming?"

"Stop crushing me, Giovanni. I'm trying to read."

"But I can't see."

"Well, take the veil off your hat, then."

It was always the same at this time of year. Carnival didn't begin for another two weeks yet. The Feast of Seraphim at which Carlo was to sing was its opening day. From that point, the street processions, balls, and masquerades began again, and wouldn't stop until Lent next spring. The Duke's opera house —the Teatro di Palazzo— shook off the dust sheets and got ready to open its doors for another season of magic.

And then there was always the question of which demi-god of song would undertake one of Angelio's most cherished carnival traditions: to sing the hymn of thanks to Michael at the singers' homecoming mass in the song chapel of the Sancti Michaelis.

"So, who is it? What does it say?"

Florid Giuseppe trod on Carlo's foot in his attempts to gain a better view of the news sheet. From where Carlo stood, the yellowish page showed a monochrome engraving of a man in a brocade waistcoat and coat, staring into the middle distance. His hand rested on what might have been a harpsichord, and several improbable cherubs fluttered above his head.

"Stand back, why don't you?" Francesco rustled the paper so the brocaded figure shuddered in grotesque postures. "Unless you all wish to be disciplined. I will read you what it says."

Several pairs of feet shuffled reluctantly backward.

"A number of notable sopranists have already arrived in

the city in advance of the carnival season. We are particularly pleased to announce that the Teatro di Palazzo has once again engaged Morestelli for the full season."

A babble of soprano voices started up.

"I told you it was him."

"No, you didn't. You said it was Parnasso."

"They always paint Morestelli with cherubs. Everyone knows that."

"Do you want to hear this or not?" Francesco scowled. "At the Duke's particular request, the Teatro has also engaged the talents of Il Cupide, along with the exceptional female vocalist La Bellina, and our beloved Figliolo, whose astonishing crystal tones will be heard at this Friday's homecoming mass, returning the traditional hymn of thanks."

"What? Isn't Morestelli doing it?"

"He just said that, you lackwit." Giuseppe snorted.

"Oh, and look here." Francesco ran his finger to the bottom of the sheet. "We are reliably informed that the coming Seraphim Mass will witness a performance by Maestro Sarastro's very latest protégé: an individual at this stage known only as the Nightingale. We can only hope this new, young talent is equal to the standard set by Sarastro's former pupils, Morestelli and Figliolo, who will doubtless be listening."

Carlo felt his face turn scarlet. Several of the other boys nudged him with comments like: "Nightingale's spreading his pretty wings already," or: "Remember me in your will, oh great one."

He made an exaggerated bow.

"Too kind, too kind."

The castrato class turned their attention back to the virtuosi in the news sheet. Voices rose higher and higher. The debate over Morestelli and Figliolo's comparative skills was now verging on a full-scale argument. Meanwhile, Giovanni was trying to wheedle the sheet from Marco's possession, on account of "that exquisite waistcoat".

Carlo walked away, not wanting to get involved. He strolled toward the shrubbery, humming snatches of his solo under his breath. He wondered what birds were hiding away in the evergreens. If they would fly away when winter came or protect themselves from the cold. Perhaps he would see them if he looked carefully, just as Tammo had. That was when he noticed it. A face. Staring between the rhododendrons that screened the eunuchs' private garden from the rest of the school. A cruel, calculating face with black eyes. Its owner held Carlo's gaze with the intensity of a hunting eagle, then turned on its heels and stalked away.

"No! No! No! Is this the Conservatorio Archangeli or the cattle market? It sounds like a load of heifers mooing!"

Maestro Allegri's voice screeched from the chapel as Carlo walked past.

"Stand still, I say! Stand still or I shall fetch the prefects. Intermediate choir: this is your last chance! I will have silence or it will be the birch rod for all of you!"

Carlo waited as the choirmaster was overtaken by a fit of coughing. Intermediate was Tammo's grade. Was he in there with the others or was this his time to play the dark flute? Carlo glanced over his shoulder. The courtyard was deserted. He pressed his body up to the plastered window frame and peered inside. His gangly height made for a better vantage point than many boys would have had. Despite the dimness of the chapel interior, he could make out Maestro Allegri in the pulpit, and lines of jaded boys standing in the first three pews.

"That's better. Now sit." A general mumbling and flapping of cassocks. "I don't recall giving permission to speak. Paolo Agresto. Sit down. Better. Now, I will hear each one of you in turn and you will sing like students of the art musical and not a herd of cattle. Bass line: stand up."

Bass line. His twin's very section. Carlo pressed his nose to the multi-coloured patchwork of glass, straining to make out Tammo's scrawny figure between the pews. Had Maestro Allegri forgotten the arrangement? Tammo was meant to be excused from singing solo in front of the other boys. If he was forced to sing now, the humiliation would be agony. But the choirmaster was in such a mood, he didn't seem likely to excuse anything.

"Uberti. Shoulders back, lad." The choirmaster hummed a note. "One and two and..."

There was Tammo. Just two places away from the boy called Uberti. Carlo pressed his lips together. Tammo's fists were tightly clenched and he was staring at the floor. He looked so tightly wound, he might bolt from the chapel at any moment. That wasn't right. His twin should be happy. And free.

"Claudio. See if you can do as well as Uberti. One and two and..."

A strong bass voice sang out the first line of the *Sanctus*. Carlo suddenly smiled to himself. The most delicious idea had come. He flexed his facial muscles a couple of times and hummed the tiniest of descending scales, like the mew of a cat.

"Tammo." Maestro Allegri gave a deep sigh. He sounded more than a little uncomfortable. "On the count of two. One and two and..."

"Sanctus, Sanctus, Sanc-tus."

Stifled giggles rose from between the pews. Carlo's flawless soprano tones came through the window in perfect timing with Tammo's lip movements. Maestro Allegri cleared his throat loudly. The giggling stopped.

"We'll have that again, shall we? One and two and..."

"Sanctus, Sanctus, Sanc-tus. Dominus Deus. Dominus Deus Sab-a-oth."

This time, the fragment of song ended with an ornamented cadence of such apparent piety that a couple of boys actually guffawed out loud, then hastily whipped out handkerchiefs in an attempt to disguise the sound as coughing or sneezing. Others were almost rigid with the effort of not laughing. Carlo moistened his lips, looking to see if his twin appreciated the joke. Tammo was looking toward the window, along with several others. But where the others were searching, surprised, Tammo's face had relaxed from its earlier death-mask of anticipation. Not exactly smiling, Carlo saw, but relieved. Grateful. His eyes darted to the gap where the window was open to the courtyard and, for a moment, caught Carlo's gaze. Carlo gave a superior smile and winked. Tammo gave the faintest of smiles back.

Maestro Allegri pulled out a silk handkerchief and scrubbed at his neck and forehead, tugging his cravat loose. Patches of sweat rubbed into powder that had shaken down from his wig, giving his face the look of an incomplete plaster cast.

"Whoever that boy is outside, can you kindly return to your own lessons? I am attempting to rehearse a choir."

"Maestro, it's the Nightingale," someone said.

"I don't care if it's Morestelli." The choirmaster was becoming frantic once more. "I will have this *Sanctus* rehearsed by the end of the lesson. "Luigi. Your turn. One and two and..."

A bubble of joy fizzed up inside Carlo's chest as he skipped away. He had done it! He had saved his twin from humiliation, and it had been such, such fun to do! Better even than the trick with the letter. Oh! How he loved his new twin! He was sure he could face the Sancti Michaelis and a hundred nobles with this much happiness inside him.

Tammo was delighted with what had happened too.

"You should have seen Paolo's face when you started singing through that window," Tammo said when they met at the tree that night. "When you hit that high note, I thought he was going to explode!"

Carlo shook his head. "I did it for you, Tamino. Not to annoy Paolo."

"Aye." Tammo shrugged his shoulders. "But you should have seen him!"

"I did see him." Carlo suddenly remembered. "He was

looking through the bushes into the eunuchs' garden the other day. He just stared and then walked off."

"Looking at you?" Tammo suddenly stiffened, his voice dangerously low.

Carlo gave an affected laugh and waved a hand. "Just looking. It's hardly a hanging offence, Tamino. Besides, what could he do? The prefects would have been onto him like a shot for trespassing had he come inside."

"I suppose." Tammo didn't sound convinced. "But I don't like it. He shouldn't be looking at you."

He should have listened to his twin a little more carefully. But the excitement of Mass and Carnival and the arrival of all those renowned singers in the city—not to mention the bubbling joy of friendship—had Carlo on a wave of enthusiasm that he couldn't imagine ever coming to shore. So, when he saw a handbill one afternoon, nailed to a wall on the side of the laundry house, he didn't dream there could be anything but goodwill in it. In the rough sketches of costumed players, he thought he recognised Morestelli, Il Cupide, and the rest. Someone's attempt at publicity, perhaps? It was only on coming closer that he realised his sad mistake.

It was Morestelli. Sketchily drawn but recognisable, if only by the name the unknown artist had scribbled on a plinth beneath the great man's feet. Similar plinths proclaimed the other two figures to be Figliolo and Il Cupide. But that was where the resemblance ended. All three men were drawn wearing a ludicrous extravagance of theatrical garments. Cloaks, high-heeled boots, bejewelled breastplates, feather head-dresses four feet tall. It was a wonder the grotesque figures could stand under the weight of the stuff. For grotesque they were. That was the truly sickening part. Their bodies were bloated, their heads tiny, their limbs more closely resembled those of spiders than men. In one corner was a fashionably dressed woman, small and dainty to the point of emaciation, turning to a companion and saying:

"Lah! How expensive capons have become!"

The companion—a rakish fellow carrying a walking stick topped with the most enormous brass ball—was replying:

"Indeed. One always pays more for cold cuts."

Carlo began to tremble. How dare they? Who would have the gall to write such things of the demi-gods of the opera? Morestelli was no capon! He was a primo castrato of the highest quality! Had someone placed this here deliberately for another student to see? He wouldn't let them. He tore at the handbill with his nails, ripping a hole through Figliolo's head.

"Carlo? Are you all right?"

The shock of Tammo's voice almost lifted Carlo bodily from the ground. He clutched at his breast with his left hand, blinking back the tears that had appeared in his eyes.

"I..." His voice cracked. He swallowed hard and held out the handbill.

Tammo scowled and grunted over the crude satire.

"Hmn!" He screwed up the paper and tossed it over his shoulder. "Lackwits write those things. And lackwits read them." He put out an awkward hand and patted Carlo's head. "Come on, Carlo. Let's go to supper."

Carlo sniffed and dabbed his eyes with a handkerchief. He put a hand on Tammo's arm and forced a wavering smile.

"Thank you, Tamino. My beloved friend."

A thump on his back almost winded him.

"You stick with me, Carlo my lad. We'll show them."

As they linked arms to walk away, Carlo looked back over his shoulder. A third boy had come to the laundry house and was bending down to pick up the crumpled handbill. He opened it out, smoothing it with his fingers, and then looked straight at Carlo with an evil smirk. Slowly, silently, without drawing Tammo's attention, the boy stuck out his neck, folded his arms like chicken wings, and flapped them up and down. A cold shiver ran down Carlo's back. But he would not be daunted. He blew a kiss at the boy, who scowled and turned away.

It was Paolo Agresto.

5. A Growing Threat

Maestro Aquila put down his flute and looked over his long nose.

"Excellent, Tammo. Now you see the benefit of application. The other maestri tell me you haven't been involved in a single fight since we began these lessons. Is that correct?"

"Maestro." Tammo lowered his head.

"You do yourself proud." The maestro had the hint of a smile in his features. "Keep this up and I must find you a public engagement. What do you say to the Cavalier Marchesi's salon? The cavalier takes a particular interest in instrumental students of the conservatorio and is himself a very talented flautist."

Tammo bit his lip and ran his thumb along the outline of a linnet carved into the dark flute. He knew what the maestro was trying to say. He wanted to put Tammo on the path to patronage and a secure future providing entertainment for the nobility. It was what everyone at the conservatorio was supposed to want. That was what they were here for, wasn't it? Lifted from poverty to a life of discipline and prospects. Given a trade and a future. But Tammo had had a trade once, back in that other life. His future had been snatched from him by an evil fate. He wanted nothing of the Cavalier Marchesi and his salon. He ground his teeth.

"Can't I...?" He heaved a frustrated sigh.

"What is it, Tammo?" Maestro Aquila tucked his coat tails out of the way and took a seat in the windowsill, narrowly avoiding a half-written score. "I am expending a great deal of effort on your behalf. For your benefit, Tammo, not for mine. Do you doubt your ability? Do you fear being overwhelmed by the splendour of a great man's hall? Speak to me, Tammo. There is nothing that cannot be overcome by hard work and preparation. But I cannot help you if you persist in silence."

"I..." It was pointless. Maestro Aquila was never going to understand. How could Tammo explain about the magic he felt in the flute, the longing to play it in the midst of nature? If only Carlo were with him! The eunuch had a way with words and a charm the maestri couldn't resist. Tammo turned people off him with a single glance.

"Maestro, can't I...?" A sudden thought came to him. "Maestro, may we do nightingalising? Like the eunuchs do?"

The maestro gave Tammo a quizzical look.

"Copying birdsong and...and writing it down. There is much to be learned from birdsong, maestro." Tammo began to babble, fearful of losing his audience. "And birds may be taught to mimic composed music also. There are bullfinches that..."

"I am well aware of the practice of nightingalising." Maestro Aquila massaged his chin. "Although I would be intrigued to discover how you came to learn of it. Not in the intermediate bass class, I'll wager."

Tammo felt himself flush bullfinch red.

"I...I have been studying. But studying is nothing without practise, is it, maestro? I'm sure the...the Cavalier Marchesi would approve."

Now he really was beginning to sound like Carlo. As long as that was all of the eunuch's personality that was rubbing off on him. Tammo didn't fancy himself fluttering his eyelashes and tittering like a signorina. Maestro Aquila nodded slowly.

"Very well, Tammo. We shall try a little nightingalising next week. Now, let me hear you on the sarabande."

The next day began as usual with the morning walk. Carlo and the rest of the eunuch choir had gone off to sing at the Michaelis Curationum convent, accompanied by Vice-Rector Aprile. According to Carlo, lauds at the convent was one of the conservatorio's longest-standing engagements. Although it was difficult to tell if the nuns enjoyed it, as they were always on the other side of a screen.

"How do you know there's anyone there at all?" had been Tammo's comment. "They might have all died a hundred years ago, and you're singing to a room full of skeletons!"

"Tamino, you are foul beyond belief." Carlo had looked down his nose with the imperious glance Tammo was expecting. "The nuns of Michaelis Curationum are this school's most devoted patrons. I am aware it may cause your head to erupt, but could you try to have at least some respect? Skeletons!" He shook his head with a smile, then rubbed his hands over his eyes. "Oh, I'm so tired! Why does there have to be such a thing as six o'clock in the morning?" He covered a yawn with his cuff. "See you at the tree. Yes?"

"I'm going to kill you, Firebrand!"

A violent shove to his upper back sent Tammo sprawling. Tammo flung himself round, snarling. Paolo Agresto was whispering in his ear, every word laced with hatred.

"How dare you humiliate me? You and that ball-less warbler."

"You leave Carlo out of this."

Tammo hissed the words with such fury that little bits of spittle appeared on Paolo's face. Paolo's eyes blazed cold fire. He wiped his cheek with the back of his hand and flicked it at Tammo.

"Yes, that's what I've heard about you, Firebrand." He waited until Tammo was shaking with suppressed fury at the word. "You've turned into a little capon-lover. I wouldn't have believed it until I saw it with my own eyes. Arm-in-arm with the Nightingale. Threatening my friends—my friends, Crow—over some talentless bread-stealer. And hiding behind Maestro Sarastro's pet to humiliate me in front of him!"

The last word came accompanied by another violent shove. Tammo's every bone was aching to rip Paolo to shreds. How dare he bring Carlo into this? How dare he?

But he mustn't. He mustn't. Not with his chance of nightingalising so near. He clenched his teeth together until they ached.

"You mock yourself, Agresto," he growled.

"Look at him: the little coward." Paolo sneered. "Too studious to fight back any more? I wager you'd fight if your paramour was here."

"He's not my paramour!" Tammo seized Paolo by the neck bands.

"Your pretty little songbird paramour," said Paolo. "How does it feel when he kisses you with his rosebud lips? Does he shut his eyes so he can't see how hideous you are?"

It would only take a slight movement of his hand to have a hold on Paolo's neck. One squeeze and he'd be in the sanatorium. Tammo clenched his teeth to the verge of breaking. His cheeks quivered violently.

"I'll not do it!" He pushed Paolo away so the tenor went down on his backside. "Get lost, Agresto. I'm busy."

Paolo picked himself up and straightened his clothes as carefully as a dandy in front of a mirror.

"Busy? Well, let's see how busy you are after Seraphim Mass when your darling paramour is getting his just deserts."

Tammo felt a cold chill grip his spine.

"You can't touch Carlo. He's the Nightingale."

"The Sancti Michaelis is a busy place." Paolo examined his fingernails. "Anyone might accidentally trip on a stair or bump into something."

"You wouldn't dare, Agresto."

Tammo felt sick. He should lay Paolo out now. Forget

the dark flute. Carlo's safety was more important. If Paolo, Riccardo, and the others ganged up... No, he couldn't let that happen. He clenched his fist.

"Gentlemen, this is a rehearsal room, not a salon. Kindly get off your backsides and apply yourselves to practise."

A senior prefect. Those fellows really chose their timing. Tammo scowled up. The prefect hardened his face and swished his birch rod.

"Signor," Tammo said reluctantly.

He put the flute back to his lips. Paolo picked up a viola and tucked it under his chin.

"Seraphim Mass, Crow," Paolo said as he strode away.

"You cannot fight him, Tamino. I forbid it."

Carlo's expression was as stern as was possible for his cherubic face.

"You can't lose everything you've worked for with the flute. You have to let him be." He folded his hands together and looked Tammo directly in the eyes. The faint spark of candlelight beneath the tree made lights dance in their limpid depths.

"He wants to hurt you, Carlo." Tammo fought to hold back the temper that was creeping into his voice. "I have to take him out now, before something happens."

"No." Carlo shook his head. Tammo could see the tension in his jaw, the pallor in his cheek. This frightened him. And with good reason. Why couldn't he see sense and understand that there had to be action? He thumped the branch so lichen flew up.

"Carlo, I have to fight him!"

Carlo gave a flinch so violent that Tammo feared he would fall out of the tree. The eunuch wrapped his arms around his chest, shivering. A look of hurt accusation was in his widened eyes.

"Stop doing that! I'm trying to help you." The anger Tammo felt with himself for losing his temper just made him angrier still. "Sweet Michael! What do you think I'm going to do to you? You think I'm just like one of them, don't you?"

Carlo drew in a ragged breath.

"I'm not going to justify that with an answer. Clearly, all semblance of intelligence has now left you."

"Oh, that's what this is about. You think me a dunce." Tammo's posture tightened to that of a hunting lynx.

"And you do very little to dispel the notion. There is nothing to be gained from fighting Paolo Agresto. If you love me, you will stay away from him." The hint of a challenge flickered in Carlo's eye.

"I'm not listening to this." Tammo jumped down from the tree. Yet he couldn't resist looking back up to see Carlo's reaction.

The eunuch had adopted his most imperious expression.

"Don't expect to find me here tomorrow, Tammo Capell." Carlo's voice had gone tight and high-pitched.

Tammo snorted. He turned and stalked toward the sanatorium, swearing under his breath in increasing degrees of profanity. Bloody stuck-up eunuch! Why did he have to be so pig-headedly stubborn? Tammo thumped every wall and tree he passed on the way, tripping on tree roots in the dark and cursing out loud. What was he supposed to do now? Fight Paolo and that would be the death-knell for friendship. He'd be back to being a black-marked charity boy with only bruises for company. But how was he meant to stand by and watch the blackguards beat the life out of his friend? Bloody Carlo! A pox on his stupid discretion! Did he want Paolo and Riccardo to beat him senseless?

There was blood running down his knuckles again by the time Tammo's temper wearied. Somewhere on the other side of the chaplain's house, a she-owl screeched to her mate. A light went out in an upper window as Signor Cavalli, the physician, went to bed. Tammo heaved a sigh. Should he seek his dormitory in case someone told on him? He didn't want to go back there. The silent backs of the other boys reminded him of his friendlessness. He slowly retraced his steps to the tree, scuffing the toes of his shoes along the cobbles with every step. His sore knuckles throbbed. In the moonlight, the shadows cast by the conservatorio buildings loomed long and eerie. They made Tammo feel very small.

Carlo was still there. The buckles on his shoes flashed in the wavering candlelight as they dangled from the low branch. As Tammo got nearer, he could hear a sniffling sound. A twig broke under his feet. Carlo started and looked down. Two shining streaks stood out on his cheeks. Tammo scraped his toe nonchalantly across a root.

"Can I come up?"

Carlo waved his hand vaguely over the branch.

Tammo cleared his throat and swung himself up into the tree. Carlo was busy with a handkerchief. Tammo looked the other way and took several deep breaths.

"I don't have to fight him—" he began.

"Please, don't let Paolo come between us," said Carlo, at the same time. His voice was as shaky as Tammo's was rough. He gave a little hiccup and swallowed hard.

"Go on," Tammo croaked. "You first."

Carlo took several deep breaths in and out.

"You're right, Tamino. We can't let this happen. But..." He held up his hand before Tammo could interrupt. "I can't let you fight Paolo either. I'd never forgive myself."

"Yes, but what else can we do?" said Tammo, as gently as he could. "I can't watch him hurt you. I just can't."

"We can pray."

Tammo looked at his eunuch friend, hoping there was more than this. Praying was all very well in its way, but this was a question of serious danger. It required action.

"Carlo..." he said, shaking his head.

"I'm serious, Tamino. To whom did the first Duke turn in his war with the Count? The Archangel. To whom does Morestelli turn to ask him to bless the season? The Archangel. To whom does every citizen of Angelio turn when in danger or need? To the Archangel, Tamino. I have prayed to him for you already. And he has answered. You have your dark flute, your nightingalising. If we both pray to him together now, he will hear us, Tamino. And he will answer."

Tammo gave a grimace. "I've told you before. The Archangel doesn't watch over me."

"I refuse to believe that." Carlo's face was now strong and determined. "Orphans are his special care. He has to be with you. Don't tell me you've never felt his presence, not even for a moment."

Tammo swallowed. A memory nudged his mind. The light in the sky when he'd caught Orpheus. But wasn't that just the sun shining on the dome? Carlo's eyes were aglow now, his face radiant with faith. Tammo let out a breath. He may not believe in the Archangel's protection, but he believed in Carlo.

"Very well," he said. "Let's pray."

"Let's, then," said Carlo, and crossed himself. Tammo did the same, suddenly feeling awkward and very self-conscious.

"What shall we say?" he whispered.

"I'll say it," Carlo whispered back.

"Very well."

There was another awkward silence. Carlo crossed himself again and took a breath.

"Beloved Archangel and patron. I, Carlo Bianci, do beseech you most humbly to come to my aid and the aid of my friend Tammo Capell, on the Feast of Seraphim. Protect us from harm, we pray, and keep us from violence. *In nomine Patris, et Filii, et Spiritus Sancti. Amen.*"

"Amen," said Tammo, crossing himself once more. He chewed his lip, wondering if he needed to maintain a meditative silence.

"Is that enough, do you think?" he said, with a glance at Carlo.

The eunuch reached out a hand and closed it round one of Tammo's. It was cold to the touch and girl-soft.

"All shall be well, Tamino," he said, squeezing harder. "All shall be well."

6. Michaelis Archangeli

St. Michael's Square was swarming. The whole of Angelio, it seemed, had turned out for the feast day. As Maestro Sarastro led the choir round the side of the cathedral to join the main procession, Carlo was met with a whole fleet of carriages and sedan chairs—not to mention horses, grooms, footmen, chairmen, and page boys—either discharging their owners to mass or awaiting their return. Beyond them, the ordinary citizens had gathered in huge numbers, trying to catch a glimpse of their betters, hoping to squash into the back of the nave, or picnicking round the smaller fountains and generally enjoying the festival atmosphere.

"Mind where the horses have been," barked Maestro Sarastro, swaggering expertly between carriages. "We join behind the standard- and torch-bearers. Aim for that cross."

The ornate gilded cross glittered above the crowd, held up with religious fervour by a boy whose hair his mother has apparently slicked down with enough oil to cook a family meal. He was surrounded by six other boys of precisely identical height, carrying torches that the dean's assistant was attempting to light. One of them kept blowing out again.

"Same bloody farce as usual," muttered Maestro

Sarastro. "Carlo, stay where I can see you. There are people I want you to meet."

Carlo took the opportunity to glance about the square. More and more people were arriving every minute. Families scrubbed up in their well-worn finest hurried along, trying not to lose children on the way. City militia in striped hose and doublet stood guard, ready to play their part in the pageantry. Barefoot urchins chased dogs and geese around. One or two enterprising souls had set up food stalls round the square's edge; the smell of savoury pancakes and sweet-sour sauce made Carlo's stomach complain. Others nearer the porch were selling religious wares: rosaries and miniature angels crafted from tin. They would do a good trade today. No one in Angelio wanted to be thought irreligious on a feast day.

"Monseigneur, this is Carlo Bianci, our soloist for today."

Carlo quickly drew his thoughts back together. The bishop, in full festal attire, was standing at Maestro Sarastro's side, regarding him with interest.

"I didn't expect him to be this young, Sarastro. It's to be hoped you've got a prodigy on your hands," the bishop said. He held out his hand to Carlo. Maestro Sarastro gestured sharply with his head.

"Monseigneur." Carlo went down on one knee and kissed the bishop's enormous ruby ring. It felt surprisingly warm. All in a rush, Carlo wished Tammo was by his side this moment. It wouldn't be the same to tell him about it later on.

The bishop laid a hand on Carlo's curls. "Bless you, my son. May the Archangel smile upon you."

Carlo was wondering if he ought to reply, when a cry went up from the crowd. "Long live the knife! The blessed knife!"

Carlo was left to struggle to his feet with the bishops' back turned to him. The back of his cope was even more heavily embroidered than the maestro's coat, and featured, among other things, an angel wielding a sword and a sunburst coming out of a moated castle. Was the man who had just arrived who Carlo thought he was? Was Maestro Sarastro really going to introduce him to…?

"Signor Morestelli. God bless you," said the bishop.

"Monseigneur." A gentle voice, self-assured.

"Now, monseigneur, if you will just let me through to introduce my former pupil to my present one," Maestro Sarastro was saying.

Carlo dropped to his knees without being asked. He took the scented hand that was extended to him and kissed it fervently. The great Morestelli. Taking notice of Carlo. Now he truly wished Tammo was by his side, if only to see him faint from happiness.

"Very well, Carlo. Very well." Carlo knew the impatience in his tutor's voice well enough to cut short his reverences. Geofre, this is my current pupil, Carlo Bianci. He has not yet taken a name. The boys call him the Nightingale."

"Ah, then I trust you sing like one." Carlo was far too awestruck to be aware of much more than a mellow voice, an alabaster cheek, and a vast quantity of lace and blue ribbon. "I shall listen to your performance with great interest. If you please the Duke today, Carlo, your maestro might see fit to introduce you at the Teatro. That idea you had about Hercules perhaps, Sarastro?"

"I'd have to get round the bloody rector first," grunted Maestro Sarastro.

"Ah yes. Dear, dear Rector Bartolomeo! How is he these days?"

"The same, the same. Has Count Pageno arrived yet? I wanted to speak with him."

"Ah." Morestelli dabbed at his beauty spot with a lace handkerchief. "I fear he won't be coming at all. They do say his son is very ill..."

The two men wandered deeper into the crowd, out of Carlo's earshot.

"Parade! Parade: attention!" yelled the captain of the Duke's personal guard.

In front of Carlo, the boy with the cross and the torch-bearers hastily formed rank. Maestro Sarastro hurried back to take his place alongside the bishop and cathedral dignitaries. Up ahead, Carlo saw the Duke's personal standard raised high: a silver fountain with a crown on a blue background. Other standards rose in response at various points down the line. It was too late to worry about Paolo now. This was it. The Feast of Seraphim was about to begin.

Once Mass began in earnest, time seemed to take wings and stoop like a falcon toward the last benediction in an unreal blur. From his seat in the choir stalls, Carlo watched, half in a dream, half in stark alertness, as the celebrants moved around the high altar: purifying the congregation, blessing the bread. The air was sweet with incense from the great winged censer. Its perfumed clouds billowed out into the white-and-gold cathedral, reducing the congregation to a blur of hats, wigs, and veils, which stood and knelt and stood again as the celebration proceeded. In only one area, to the right of the altar, was anyone seated. That would be the ducal family in their private pew with its ornamented canopy. They would be the first to receive the sacred bread too, but Carlo would be singing by that point. Much as he longed to see the most powerful man in Angelio, he had his own sacred duty to perform, and there could be no room for distraction.

The moment arrived with a literal fanfare. From a gallery in the dome, trumpets blared out a triumphant summons. The guards and militia—to that point standing to attention in the north and south transepts—dropped to their knees as one man. The bishop stood and pronounced the angelic blessing on the city's defences, his voice booming up toward the scenes of heavenly splendour cascading from the dome. As if answering from above, the organ thundered into life. Maestro Sarastro was working the stops with every ounce of his celebrated passion. Carlo stood, suddenly beatifically calm. The Archangel was with him. He opened his mouth. Sublimity burst forth.

The six minutes of Carlo's song felt simultaneously like half a second and fifty years. He leapt. He trilled. He gently caressed one phrase, joyously declaimed another. The modulation, the da capo, the soaring finish: each followed the other within a capsule of control and purity. It was as if Carlo stood for those six minutes outside time and the Sancti Michaelis itself, somewhere only angels and sopranists trod.

When the song came to an end, he found he had tears in his eyes. He looked up. In the centre of the dome's fresco was the Archangel Michael himself, descending in an arabesque, wings outstretched, sword poised to smite his enemies. As Carlo gazed through his tears, the Archangel seemed to pause for a moment amid the fiery clouds and turn his eyes on Carlo. The look was tender, fatherly. Then the tears dropped to Carlo's cheek; and the Archangel went back to being paint and *trompe l'oeil* once more.

There was one more part that Carlo had to sing, a solo section within a choral piece during Holy Communion. But that passed with nothing like the emotion of the grand solo. Before he knew it, torches were being extinguished round the altar and the choir were standing to begin the slow procession back through the congregation and into the west porch once more. Carlo could feel eyes burning into him as he walked past. There was no hiding now. By tomorrow, every last child in Angelio would have heard his name. A twinge of loneliness plucked at his heart. No; he must ignore that. Today was a festal day, a day of celebration. He had done what his maestro believed he could do. He had touched the heavens with his own voice.

"Carlo! Carlo!"

Now, there was a voice he would recognise anywhere. He spun on his heels to see Tammo pushing his way through the crowd at the back of the cathedral. It looked like his hair had been forced to succumb to the same severe oiling as everyone else's this morning. It was plastered round his temples, apparently much against its will.

"Tamino! What are you doing? The maestri will whip you black and blue if they catch you out of place on a day like this."

Tammo grinned. "Don't fret so much. They've given us all ten minutes to buy angels and light candles for our parents and stuff." He heaved a happy sigh. "Carlo, you were magnificent! Even Vice Rector Aprile was speechless when you'd finished. And I heard a woman behind me say you were better than Il Cupide."

Carlo felt a delicate warmth spread over his cheeks. "I doubt that."

Behind Carlo, the cathedral choir had bunched to a halt. There were one or two shouts of, "What's the hold-up?" and "Keep moving." Carlo's neck felt hot and sticky. He glanced round the crowded cathedral and grasped Tammo's wrist.

"Come on. Let's go somewhere quiet. Just us."

Tammo followed Carlo's gaze, dwarfed by the press of hats and veils. "Where?"

"The roof, the gallery, anywhere. Come on."

"And what about Sarastro?"

"Now who's fretting too much?" Carlo lifted an eyebrow. "Come on, Tamino. I can scarcely breathe in here."

Carlo began forcing a passage, dragging Tammo after him. Every soul in Angelio appeared to be coming in the opposite direction, or having a conversation with their neighbours right in the most inconvenient spot. Carlo was forced to execute a minuet of politeness in order to avoid treading on toes. Every step was punctuated with, "pardon me, signor", or "excuse me, mother abbess", and he was beginning to lose count of the varieties of fine cloth his cassock had crushed.

"This is ridiculous," grunted Tammo. "Just go through that side door."

"I don't think that one leads the right way, Tamino," Carlo panted. Sweat was starting to form beads on his forehead.

"So what?" Tammo yanked Carlo's arm and opened the door. A blast of cold, stale air rushed up to greet them.

"That," said Carlo, trying for an imperious tone, "is the crypt."

"Who cares?" said Tammo. "At least it's cool."

"And what if someone's praying down there?"

"What if they're not?"

"Tamino." Carlo wagged a finger. "What have I told you before about respect?"

Tammo threw back a look that was half smile, half grimace. Carlo touched a finger to Tammo's lips, to cut off whatever his friend was about to say next.

He would never find out. Something sharp and cold touched the side of his neck. Tammo's expression changed to pure murder. Then came Paolo's voice, hot and venomous in his ear.

"Let's hear you squeal now. Castrato."

For a second, Carlo's heart seemed to stop altogether.

He sought deep inside himself for every breathing exercise Maestro Sarastro had ever taught. This couldn't be happening. The Archangel was on their side. They had prayed. Carlo had seen him in the painted dome. Halfway inside the crypt, Tammo was straining against Carlo's grip like a bulldog, teeth bared. Carlo pushed against his friend's wrist, praying that for once his greater stature would prevail. Tammo mustn't pounce. They mustn't make any sudden movements.

A second voice buzzed against his ear from the other side. "Think you're so high and mighty, don't you? Why don't you sing to us now?"

Riccardo. They must have both followed Tammo as soon as the maestri let them loose. The cold blade pressed against Carlo's sweating neck. Cold like ice. The worst ever memory. He locked eyes with Tammo, his arm shaking with the effort of keeping his twin at bay.

"No pretty song for us, Nightingale? You sang prettily enough through the chapel window for your paramour."

The blade pressed harder.

"We could cut you right now, castrato. But you've already been...cut."

Tammo growled, his nails biting Carlo's wrists. Carlo shook hard. He couldn't hold this any longer.

"Run, Tamino," he mouthed. And when Tammo scowled, uncomprehending, he raised his voice and yelled, "Run!"

He jerked his head back, and spun away from Paolo and Riccardo. He didn't consider whether or not the blade would cut him. He simply threw his whole weight down the stairs of the crypt, dragging the breathless Tammo after him. The heels of their shoes made echoes bounce off the narrow walls. Close behind them, more echoes followed.

"Ball-less knave! I'll make you pay!"

"This way." Carlo gasped, hauling Tammo after him. The passage had opened out into a series of low, vaulted chambers with chequered flooring. A few dim flares hung in cages amid carven pillars. Their light showed eerie glimpses of marble sarcophagi and reliquaries behind wrought-iron fences.

"Quickly."

Carlo dragged Tammo into the largest chamber. An extravagant amount of candles at varying stages of melting lit up an ornate ceiling and a huge sarcophagus in opalescent marble and gold. It wore an ancient armour and had in one hand a sword, in the other a rosary.

"The first Duke," breathed Carlo. "Quick. Get down and hide."

He flung himself to the floor behind the sarcophagus, forcing Tammo down with him. They both hit the floor hard. Carlo's knees jarred with pain. He pressed his lips together. His neck itched, he suddenly realised, and something liquid was trickling down it. Tammo battled his way out of Carlo's grip. His well-oiled hair now had rogue tendrils that had an anger all of their own.

"I am not hiding from those blackguards!" His cheeks were flushed with fury. He rose to his hands and knees, ready to pounce. Carlo began to shiver. He grabbed hold of Tammo's cuff.

"Please, Tamino," he begged. "For me."

"We know you're in here, lovebirds." Paolo's voice echoed from one pillar to another. "And we're going to get you good and proper this time."

"You have to let me protect you," croaked Tammo. Veins were standing out on his neck.

Carlo shook his head violently. Whatever happened, it mustn't come to that. Not after so much.

Footsteps paced round the side of the Duke's sarcophagus. Stopped.

"Well, what have we here?" Paolo's satisfied voice. "The Crow and the Nightingale. Got you at last."

Behind him, a sound of laughter echoed. Riccardo. Carlo looked up. The two tenors had smug grins on their faces. Paolo spun the knife round his fingers.

It was too much for Tammo. "Filthy blackguards! I'll—"

The light in the chamber suddenly changed. From wavering candlelight, it flared in an instant to something white and pure that showed up every carven leaf and tendril on the vaulted arches. Paolo and Riccardo's eyes went like dinner-plates. They dropped to their knees and started crossing themselves frantically.

"Mighty Saint Michael, Prince of Seraphim. Weigh us not in the balance of your justice. Mighty Saint Michael, Prince of Seraphim..."

The light seemed to flare—if anything—still brighter.

Riccardo gave a yelp like a puppy. Paolo ran for the stairs, barely troubling to get off his knees first. Riccardo— only seconds behind—practically pushed Paolo, flying in his desperation to be out of the crypt first. In less than the time it took Carlo to pass a hand over his face in relief, they were gone. The light faded until there was nothing but burning candles again.

"What was that?" Tammo's voice was little more than a hoarse squeak. "Do you think it was...?"

Carlo staggered to his feet, shivering. Any strength he has left in his legs had deserted him. He wished he was lying on his pallet bed in the eunuchs' dorm.

Still holding hands, they crept back the way they had come. But when they reached the chapel-like chamber, it was no longer deserted. A man was standing with his back to them, gazing at the reliquary behind the fence. A rich man. Carlo counted at least three rings on his fingers, and couldn't have estimated the price of the lace tumbling from the man's gold-buttoned cuffs.

"We beg pardon, signor," he said with a bow.

"Signor," Tammo said, following suit.

In response, the man turned and smiled. He had a kind face, well-proportioned and large-eyed, and extremely clean-shaven. Or was it simply that he didn't need shaving? The more Carlo looked, the more he noticed the tenderness of the man's lips, the softness of his skin. He was beautiful. This wasn't a nobleman; it was a fellow eunuch. But not Morestelli or Figliolo or anyone whose picture Carlo had ever seen. Could there be eunuchs who made a living some other way than singing?

"Forgive us, signor. We had no idea this chapel was taken," he said.

The man inclined his head.

"This whole area was taken some time ago, as I recall.

By prayer and by cold steel. Neither of which are things to be treated lightly, as well you know, my sons. There were far less buildings then and a great deal more trees. But many would argue that the architecture has improved since then." He gazed up to the stuccoed ceiling.

"Still, music lives on here. Music and the singer's art. And there are still those who love the forest and its winged inhabitants."

Carlo wondered whether the man was a eunuch after all. He was no sopranist, that was for sure. His voice was a rich tenor, clear as a clarion. And there was something almost terrible about the man's beauty; it would hurt your eyes if you gazed at it too long. His body was no eunuch's, either. This man had no chance of deteriorating to a capon. From what Carlo could make out from the cut of his clothes, the man's physique stood every chance of rivalling that of the statues on the portico roof. He was certainly not a person any man would wish to call out in a duel. And he did bear a sword, Carlo noticed. A beautiful basket-hilted rapier. It must have been worth a fortune.

"Excuse me, signor," he heard himself saying. "Were you in the mass just then? I was the soloist. I hope my performance pleased you."

The man smiled at Carlo, and then at Tammo, with a look Carlo could only think of as fatherly.

"I have paid attention to both your performances, in public and in private. That is why I am come, my sons. You imagine you called on me, but you could not have done so had I not already decided to call you."

Carlo felt his legs go liquid. His heart was hammering

louder now than it had when Paolo had put the knife to his neck. Beside him, Tammo—still holding his hand—was stark white and shaking violently.

"Who are you, signor?" Carlo said.

The man leaned closer. "There is nothing to fear. An Angelian need never fear his protector."

The man's eyes looked into Carlo's. They were burning with a fire brighter than a thousand suns, a thousand stars. A myriad points of light and colour spiralled deep in infinite blackness. A myriad spirals drifted away to the bounds of infinity. Carlo dropped to his knees. Tammo dropped with him.

"Archangel!"

"Get up, my sons." Michael put a gentle hand on each of their shoulders. "I am merely a soldier of heaven, though you know me as patron and protector." He smiled. "Don't be afraid. I know you, Carlo Bianci and Tammo Capell. You are true sons of Angelio. That is why I have decided to bless you. Now, what was it you were so desperate to ask of me when you were sitting in the lime tree?"

Carlo turned and looked at his twin. Tammo was biting his lip so hard it had turned white. In his eyes was the very question in Carlo's mind: what do we say now? In the tree, they had been thinking only of a way to avoid a confrontation with Paolo. Even Carlo had not expected the Archangel to come in person. Those burning eyes seemed to look right into his soul. The Archangel had said he had called them. Whatever that meant, it made this day special, holy. Something for himself and Tamino. He would not sully it by praying for harsh vengeance on Paolo. Carlo had seen the terror in the boy's eyes as he ran. No gentle soul could pray for an increase in that.

Should he say nothing, then? He looked at Tammo again. Suddenly, he knew what it was he should ask. He may never get the chance again.

"I wish to ask..."

Of all the ridiculous things, Tammo began with the exact same words at the same time. Both broke off and looked at each other. The Archangel raised a perfect eyebrow.

"I wish to ask you something for my friend Tammo," said Carlo quickly, before Tammo destroyed his chance by praying for something else. "Please will you let him be able to charm nature with the dark flute; the one you let Maestro Aquila give him? For the sake of our friendship?"

The Archangel's androgynous face took on a look of severity.

"I already placed a bird in Tammo's hand for the sake of your friendship. The one you call Orpheus. And you would ask for more?"

Carlo felt his eyes begin to prickle. He blinked. Tears would be terribly inconvenient just now.

"Can't there be any more, signor? It's all he wants."

Michael gave a long sigh, like a breeze through the forest.

"You ask for your friend to be gifted beyond what nature has provided. I am merely a servant; I have no power to create. From where would I get this gifting?"

"Take it from me." Where had that come from? Carlo so badly wanted this favour for Tammo. For him to know he was not abandoned by the Archangel. The words had simply spilled from his mouth. "I have natural gifting; everyone says so. Take some out of me and give it to Tammo. I'm sure I must have enough."

Tammo finally snapped out of the trance of awe he'd been in since the Archangel's appearance. He caught Carlo by the sleeve.

"You can't ask that. Are you insane?"

"Not insane." Michael's voice spoke into the gloom of the crypt. "But you do not know what you ask. I could take gifting from you to craft something new in Tammo, but it would weaken you, Carlo. You would be reliant on your friend to support and protect you. Your friendship would have to stand firm, come whatever."

"It would," Carlo said. But Tammo had clearly decided the eunuch had spoken long enough.

"He doesn't know what he's talking about, your highness." Tammo cleared his throat, trying to avoid looking the Archangel in the eye. "He's just showing off; you know what castrati are like." An unconvincing attempt at a smile. "Don't listen to him. But just hear me for a moment, signor. Because I was going to ask—for the sake of our friendship—for Carlo to be seen by just one person for who he truly is when he becomes a real sopranist. So he won't, you know, be alone out there. I doubt there's anything you can take from me, signor, to make that happen. I probably am the wastrel everyone says I am. But if there is something you can use, then go ahead. He's my best friend, you see." Tammo's voice faded down to a whisper. "In fact, my only friend."

"Oh, Tamino!" Carlo's eyes were distinctly moist now. He squeezed his friend's hand.

Michael folded his hands together and touched a finger to his bee-stung lips.

"Both boys ask for the sake of friendship. How do I weigh this in the balance?" He shook his head, making the curls of his white wig bounce. "For friendship I called you, but not to make you suffer. You are both so very young..."

"I'm fourteen. I'm a man. Carlo's the one you should protect," said Tammo stoutly.

The Archangel made a sound that might have been laughter, if it wasn't sacrilege to think of a seraph prince laughing.

"Ah, the sweet children of Angelio. You're enough to melt the heart of a granite statue. Was it not always thus; or else why did the seraphim swoop to your aid in the beginning?" He sighed. "Oh, my dear sons! I wish I could spare you the pain you wish upon yourselves with these requests; but there is no friendship without pain, not even among angels."

He reached out and laid a hand on each of the boys' heads in blessing. Carlo felt the warmth and lightness of his touch.

"For the sake of your friendship, I grant your prayers. But be warned of the consequences. Carlo, you will be physically weakened by this transfer of gifting. You must take care of yourself. And Tammo, by this gifting of a friend to Carlo, you have sacrificed something which as yet you know nothing about. I say again: your friendship must hold fast. For the sake of friendship these gifts have been granted, and only through friendship shall any good come of them. That is my warning as your patron and guardian. Now, go in peace, my sons."

The Archangel smiled. Carlo once more got a sense of that devastating beauty, which could transform the darkest place to a district of heaven, and yet could raze a city to the ground with a single glance. Instinctively, he bowed and crossed himself. St. Michael reached out one finger and touched the side of Carlo's neck. There was a searing burst of heat, and then nothing. Carlo put his own fingers to the spot to see what had happened. There was no blood. No wound. It was only after touching and re-touching smooth skin that he remembered to look back at the Archangel to thank him.

He was gone. Carlo and Tammo were alone in the crypt, holding each other's hands and gasping in wonder.

7. The Bird-Catcher's Song

"Very well, Tammo. I want you to stand by this window. There. Turn your shoulders. Better. Posture is everything in a good flautist. Now." Maestro Aquila gathered up a pile of half-written manuscripts from the table, looked about for somewhere to put them down, and eventually settled on a tray containing an empty coffee dish and a half-eaten pear. "I have procured this bird from Maestro Sarastro's possession under strict instruction regarding its care. So, you must do nothing to startle it."

With two hands, the maestro placed a birdcage on the table. There was nothing shoddy about that workmanship, thought Tammo with approval. The cage was finely crafted from wire mesh, with a domed top and a clasp to fasten it. Inside was a cocksure specimen of bird-kind that shivered its wings and trilled out the same flourish over and over again.

"Hello, Orpheus," said Tammo.

Maestro Aquila cleared his throat.

"You will listen to one short phrase of birdsong at a time and repeat it back to me on the flute. This is an exercise in listening and pitching. I expect this to be simple for you, Tammo. I know you have a good ear."

Simple? Ideas about logs and falling off them crossed

Tammo's mind. He breathed into the dark flute. As ever, something seemed to yearn toward him the moment it touched his lips. But whereas before it had been a vague feeling of connection between the flute and him, now it was something more definite. A call. A summons.

Orpheus twittered. Tammo ornamented. Orpheus whistled. Tammo held the note clear. He had done this sort of thing before a hundred times. Calling birds. Copying their song. But this time he could feel a sense of energy, something filled with potential. Was this the ability Michael had taken from Carlo to make him a bird-charmer?

It was definite now. Something was calling out, saying: *follow, follow*. He could feel it in the music. Only he couldn't tell whether the call was addressed to him, or if he was the one calling out. It was all mixed up somehow. And there, at the back of it all, was a strange feeling that Carlo was there in the room with him. Not standing beside him, but somewhere closer than that. In his fingers or his breath. It was odd and disorientating. He was almost scared to play. At the same time, he wanted never to stop.

"What on earth is wrong with the creature?" Maestro Aquila scowled over his beaked nose. Orpheus had ceased his cocksure trilling and was throwing himself at the mesh of the cage, wings whirring. "It's going to do itself an injury." He stooped so his face was close to the mesh. "Damn bird. Sarastro will have an apoplexy if it takes harm here."

"Open the cage lid, maestro." Tammo's heart was beginning to pound. The dark flute was calling Orpheus.

The bird could feel its summons. And Tammo could make him come. He could show the maestro, if only...

"When I want your opinion, Capell, I'll retire." Maestro Aquila breathed heavily through his nose. Orpheus was calling and flapping in a frenzy. Tiny feathers were flying everywhere. "Open the lid, indeed! We'd never see the creature again."

"Maestro, we would." Tammo stared fixedly at the sanded floorboards. His cheeks burned. "He wants to come to the music. To the flute. Let me show you, maestro. Please."

"Tammo..." The maestro's tone had the beginnings of a lecture in it. Orpheus whirred like a madhouse creature against the mesh. "Oh, very well. Anything to stop it from beating its brains out. But you will be the one to catch it again."

"Maestro." Tammo grinned.

He put the dark flute back to his lips; began the tune he had been playing moments before. Orpheus whirred and twittered. Maestro Aquila released the clasp on the cage, swearing under his breath as Orpheus's beak caught his finger. Tammo could feel the summons now: almighty, irresistible. Orpheus flew up toward the ceiling of the maestro's parlour. For a moment he seemed to hover there; a tiny buff and brown angel amid the falling dust motes...

...then he flew to perch on the end of the dark flute, as calmly as if he had been flying to a branch of the lime tree.

Maestro Aquila gave a low whistle. "Egad! Who would have thought it?"

Orpheus tossed his head and let out a shrill flourish. He

looked very much at home on the instrument: one of the carven birds come to life and enjoying a song. The look in his beady eye seemed to say to Tammo: *There. We showed him, didn't we?* Tammo couldn't say he felt anything like the same confidence. His fingers were trembling over the holes of the flute; he had to tense everything to keep them still. It had worked, it was happening. Their prayer to the Archangel. Everything. He wanted to run back to Carlo right now and tell him. The excitement was fit to burst out of him. But he would be hanged if he would let a maestro see.

"He's tame now, maestro. Look."

Tammo lowered the flute and gently cupped his hands around Orpheus. The song thrush nestled into Tammo's palms, apparently quite satisfied with the arrangement.

"No pecking this time, hey? You little blackguard," he whispered.

Maestro Aquila lifted the lid of the cage, and Tammo lowered Orpheus back in. The bird hopped from one perch to another, setting off a chime of miniature bells, then began eating seed as though nothing had happened.

"Remarkable." Maestro Aquila scratched his chin. "What a curious little bird. No wonder Maestro Sarastro is so particular about it."

"It's not the bird, maestro." Tammo was determined to speak while conditions were favourable. Never mind that it had all happened in a blur of surging sensations he didn't really understand. He might never get such a chance again.

"It's the flute. I mean when I play the flute. Let me show you, maestro." He blushed as Maestro Aquila turned a questioning eye on him. "When I nightingalise, it makes birds come. I swear on Michael's sword. I could show you. Outside. I could do it again."

Could he? Was that how it actually worked? Tammo imagined the shame of looking a complete fool in front of his maestro. Of the other boys getting to hear of it. No. This was his and Carlo's prayer. It had to work again. It must.

"May I, maestro?"

Maestro Aquila sucked his cheeks. His gaze travelled from the wire cage to the dark flute and back again. His fingertips drummed a gavotte on his thigh. He took a deep breath.

"I'll think about it. Now. The minuet we looked at last lesson. From the second movement. And let me hear every one of those semiquavers. One. Two. Three."

Tammo lifted the flute to his lips with an inward smile.

The pear tree in the maestro's garden had been harvested with meticulous care. There wasn't so much as an undersized yellow pear left to pilfer. A couple of half-rotten ones lay on the earth beneath it, rapidly being claimed by slugs and beetles. Had Maestro Aquila not been watching, Tammo might have pocketed one for the sake of its good side. He'd eaten worse. But there were other things on his mind just now beside food. The maestro had relented. On Tammo's arrival at the house, he had given the sigh of a man ground down by circumstances beyond his control, and said:

"You have ten minutes, Tammo. I shall count them on

my pocket watch. Show me what it is you think you can do with your flute and the birds, and then let me hear no more about it."

Ten minutes. Tammo blew air into the dark flute, testing his fingers on the holes. Already it was calling to him, eager to begin its work. There were three finches in the olives outside Maestro Mancini's house. Two sparrows were hopping from ledge to ledge on the chapel. He played a scale, letting the music flow up and down. He felt the surge of power instantly. All the birds stopped singing and turned to look at him. Maestro Aquila cleared his throat, his gaze intense. Tammo took a deep breath. Even without sound, the flute was singing to him. A faint echo of the Archangel's voice. Finches. He would concentrate on the finches. Send them a message in their piping song. *Come to me. Stay with me. I am your master, your protector.*

Tammo turned a phrase on the flute. Another. Another. Mimicking finch song. There was a returning call from the olives. A jubilant reply. Wings shivered.

Maestro Aquila gasped aloud. Not one but all three finches took flight and came to alight on the dark flute, balancing on carven leaves and flowers as naturally as if they were the real thing. Tammo gently lowered the flute from his lips and let the tips of his fingers stroke their feathered backs. So light, so tiny. It was a wonder such dainty creatures could have life in them at all.

"Do you want to keep them, maestro? They're quite tame." Tammo turned to look up at tutor, standing silent beside him.

But Maestro Aquila seemed to have lost the power of

speech. He opened his mouth, closed it again, stretched out his fingers to the complacent finches, held them back in mid-air.

"I..." His voice came out half an octave higher than usual. "Set them down, Tammo. Set them down for now. Tell me, pray: can you do that again?"

The pocket watch was quickly forgotten. The bell in the campanile chimed a quarter, a half. The finches, and then the sparrows from the chapel roof were joined by a linnet, starlings, and—with twisted irony—a crow. The latter overbalanced the flute, making Tammo drop his arms with a jerk, but it wasn't scared away. None of them were. They clustered around Tammo: on the ground, on his shoulders, on low branches. Maestro Aquila was a baffled statue, staring and scratching at his chin with wary caution as bird after bird joined the growing flock around Tammo's flute.

"This is a rare gift." His voice was low, fearful of scaring away the chirruping crowd. "Have you been able to do this all the time you have been learning the flute?"

"Not all." Tammo hunched his shoulders. He was not going to mention the Archangel to a maestro. "It's come on more...recently."

"Remarkable." The maestro shook his head. "Tammo, you should not keep this gift to yourself. It is...it is an incredible talent. It's like a gift from heaven."

"Is it, maestro?" Tammo's tone was pure innocence.

"You should...you ought to..." Maestro Aquila glanced around the courtyard for inspiration. The tap of a cane rang out on the cobbles from the direction of the porter's lodge. With majestic stride, Maestro Sarastro swaggered into view. His embroidered coat skirts swung in rhythm; his hat sat on his wig with the authority of a papal mitre. Sweet Michael! That man always looked as though his business of the day relegated everyone else's concerns to insignificance.

"Maestro Sarastro!" Maestro Aquila managed to call out while still keeping a muted tone. "God save you."

"Aquila!" Sarastro's familiar boom resounded from the plastered facade. The flock of birds took off as one, flapped about Tammo's head, reluctantly settled down. "Starting an aviary, man? I only loaned you the use of my song thrush yesterday. Now I see a veritable enthusiast before me."

"Ah, no." Maestro Aquila tugged at his neckerchief. "In fact, maestro, might I trouble you for a few moments? I have a demonstration that will interest you greatly."

Maestro Sarastro settled with both hands atop his cane.

"Interest me greatly? Go on then, Aquila. I shall indulge you."

"Show the maestro, Tammo," said Maestro Aquila under his breath.

Tammo showed him. First with a flock of starlings. Then with a pigeon that was strutting close by the rector's house. Then—at Maestro Sarastro's insistence—with the linnet he had already caught, stepping back from it as far as the rector's garden and playing its song again so that it followed after him, singing and whirring its wings.

"This is a timely discovery, Aquila." Maestro Sarastro didn't waste time on things like awe and wonder. He turned to Tammo. "Can you do this to order, boy?"

"Yes, maestro." Tammo had no idea whether he could or not, but he wasn't going to waste his big opportunity.

"Good. Come with me. Bring the linnet. The rest are useless. Aquila, I'll send him back when I've spoken with the rector."

"As you wish, Maestro Sarastro." Tammo spotted a tightness around the flute master's mouth as he spoke. No one at the conservatorio would gainsay the Duke's Master of the Art Musical, but they didn't have to like it.

Maestro Sarastro swaggered out in the direction of the rector's house, cane striking the ground with stern purpose. Tammo looked back for a moment, then ran after him, the linnet cradled between his palms. He wasn't sure what would happen to the other birds now they were called. The crow in particular seemed to be following him. Maestro Sarastro glanced over his shoulder and looked Tammo up and down.

"You're the boy Bianci wanted to help back to his classroom. The one with the fat lip. It's gone down."

"Maestro." There wasn't much to say to that.

"Hmm."

The maestro's tone gave nothing away. He said nothing more until they reached the rector's door. The rector... Tammo's backside began to smart of its own accord at the sight of the familiar tiled lobby with its miniature waxwork portrait of the Sacred Heart and pale wooden bench for waiting penitents. This was the first time he had been inside the rector's inner sanctum without the added accompaniment of: "And let that be a lesson to you, Capell."

He couldn't help thinking the rector might whip him anyway, for tradition's sake.

A manservant in livery crossed the lobby with a salver of letters in his hand. He pulled up short at the sight of Sarastro.

"Maestro. Forgive me for not noticing you. Is the rector expecting you this morning?"

"He will be when he hears what I've got to say. Well, then. Hurry up and announce me, man. The letters can wait."

The manservant bowed. Power, thought Tammo. It was a useful thing. People respected you for it. No one told Maestro Sarastro to wait his turn or to consider whether his behaviour was fitting for a gentleman of the conservatorio. Beneath Tammo's palm, the linnet quivered. He stroked it gently.

The manservant flung open the study door.

"Maestro Sarastro to see you, rector."

Sarastro sailed in with Tammo at his heels.

"Ah, rector! God save you. I believe I have found a solution to a mutual problem."

The rector looked up from the small volume he was reading, a sugared almond part-way to his mouth. His features tightened.

"Maestro Sarastro. How thoughtful of you to call so promptly. A lesser man might have waited on my convenience." He emphasised the last word with undisguised irritation.

"Oh come, rector, there's no need for that." Maestro Sarastro swept his coat tails aside and took a seat on one of the rector's chairs, leaving Tammo standing by the embarrassed manservant. "You need money; I need students trained in nightingalising. Only consider Carlo Bianci. He has made his début now. He needs more than the meagre resources this priest-hole can offer."

"We've had this conversation before." The rector turned another leaf of his book.

"Indeed. But Maestro Aquila has just acquainted me with a pupil of his who seems to have developed a gift for bird-charming." His gaze slid toward Tammo.

"Tammo Capell." The Rector seemed about as pleased to see him there as he had been the last time Tammo had stood in this study. Tammo stared stolidly at his hands.

"Is that the boy's name?" Maestro Sarastro's tone suggested he found the detail unimportant. "At any rate, he can capture wild birds to order. I have just been given a rather impressive demonstration. So: a supply for the training of castrati. A surplus to sell in the marketplace. I think we have the beginnings of a profitable arrangement, rector."

The rector closed the book with a snap.

"You wish me to use the boy as a huntsman? In order that we two may begin a business venture?"

"In so many words." Maestro Sarastro looked highly pleased with himself.

The rector turned his full attention on Tammo. Tammo shuffled and stroked the linnet. Something momentous was hanging in the balance here. Something that could alter his whole life. He let out a ragged breath.

"Boy's a troublemaker," said the rector. "A charity case.

I let Aquila train him in the flute because he thought it would tame him."

"And now you see the benefits of your wisdom." Maestro Sarastro leaned back in the chair. "The boy uses the flute to charm birds and repay the charity you were so forward-thinking as to bestow on him."

The rector knit his brows.

"What's that in his hands?"

"A linnet. I'm taking it for my collection. Waste not, want not. His next captures would naturally go to you."

No mention of the flocks of other birds he'd already charmed, Tammo noted. The Duke's maestro was nothing if not wily.

The rector steepled his fingers to his lips. They still had a crust of sugar round them.

"Dismiss the boy. Let's talk business."

Maestro Sarastro turned to Tammo, a gleam of triumph in his eye.

"You heard the rector. Take the linnet to the porter's lodge. I'll collect it later."

Tammo made an awkward bow, mindful of the tiny life in his palms. His neck flushed. The rector and the maestro were about to discuss the first step on the road to his future career. Not the way he would have had it, with so many interfering maestri, but he could think on that later. The Archangel's gift had begun to bear fruit.

"By the way," Maestro Sarastro said as Tammo scuttled out of the doorway. "Have you heard the news? Count Pageno's son has died. Only eight years old, they say."

"Really?" The rector's voice rose with interest. "Do the family require a cherub child for the funeral?"

"It will have to be an exceptional one. The Countess is deeply religious and, I hear, quite heartbroken by her loss. I thought I might call to offer my condolences..."

Tammo didn't stay to hear any more.

"I shall only accompany you this first time. The rector needs his report: proof that you have not abused our trust and failed to deliver. After that, Pietro will go with you."

Maestro Aquila nodded towards his manservant, who was toiling up the rocky hill behind them, a rectangular birdcage slung across his back like a satchel. The maestro himself was dressed in stout boots and a wide-brimmed hat, swinging a staff he'd cut down from a nearby ash tree.

Just as if we were going on a fishing trip or a holiday picnic, thought Tammo, tightening his grip on the dark flute. It was hard to force his feet to keep the slower pace of the older men. He wanted to run, to jump and swing in the trees for the joy of being alive. Freedom! He could feel it calling to him from every leaf, every stone under his shoe. He was outside, away from the conservatorio, away from rules and lessons and other boys. And no prying housewives, either. No humiliating charity collection. No stink of fish. The air around him was vast and expansive. It smelled of autumn, of crisp leaves and earth and a faint wisp of wood smoke coming from deeper along the path into Angel's Wood.

They were climbing the road out of town, away from

the streets and piazzas. If he looked back, Tammo would be able to see the silver dome and the statue of the Archangel, now shrunken to the size of a waxwork miniature, watching over the valley beneath him. Silently, he made a prayer to Michael. *Thank you.* A smile twisted the corner of his mouth. How many other people pictured their city's patron in a gold-buttoned coat and white wig? For all the fine words of maestri, he and Carlo were the ones who had seen the Archangel face to face. They were the ones he had blessed with this magnificent gift.

He had hardly believed his luck when Maestro Aquila told him the news. It couldn't be real; something always went wrong. The rector would go back on his word. Maestro Aquila would forbid him to go. But it hadn't happened. He had permission to go to Angel's Wood once a week to charm birds for the rector and Maestro Sarastro. The more valuable orioles and bullfinches would not come so close to the city with its noisy streets and markets. Nor would the nightingales. He must get nightingales. There would have to be dawn and dusk trips for those. He would be able to look down on sunsets reflected in the silver dome. How long since he had been able to dream of such a thing? The very idea was magical.

"It must be the dark flute, maestro," he had told Maestro Aquila. "It won't work with the others. Just that one."

It was warm in Tammo's grip now. Its carven leaves and vines sang to him even in repose. This was what it was made for. This was what they were both made for.

"Crow's following again, signor," said Pietro.

Tammo turned. He had hoped over the past few days that it was just his imagination. The other birds had scattered—well, not completely. He could hear them waiting at a distance when he crossed the courtyard or sat in the tree with Carlo. But the crow was tenacious. It followed him everywhere. As if the stupid creature knew what the other boys called him and was determined to remind him of it. He'd just gotten rid of Paolo and Riccardo, for sweet Michael's sake! He didn't need taunting by a poxy crow.

"Shoo! On your way!"

Maestro Aquila clapped his hands and brandished his staff. The crow gave a harsh caw, flapped toward a branch, and looked down with the superior stare of corvid-kind. It would wait a few minutes, then hop after them, just as it had done the previous three times. Tammo shrugged his shoulders and trudged on along the path.

"Are you not able to...um...un-charm the creature?" Maestro Aquila glanced down at the dark flute.

"Don't know," Tammo said to his shoes. The flute yearned beneath his fingers, calling, calling. It sang nothing about sending away. Carlo hadn't prayed for that. To charm nature, he had asked. And that was what Tammo had done. If there was more to it, that would take time to learn. Time to experiment. Away from maestri. When would that chance ever come?

"It's all right. I don't mind," he said.

The smell of wood smoke grew stronger. They had reached the top of the hill now, and the trees were closer together. The earth beneath them was sandy and still dry from the long summer. On their right side stood a ruin: stairs and an archway in sand-coloured bricks. Something from an earlier Dukedom, abandoned and forgotten. An ash tree was growing through its centre. Built onto the side of it was a rustic hut, a simple thing in wood and thatch. Smoke rose from a shelter opposite, along with the rhythm of iron striking iron. Blacksmiths often chose to set up business outside city walls, taking the irritation of smoke and risk of fire along with them. Tammo felt his muscles go taut as the smell filled his nostrils. Sweat prickled his armpits. Away from the city was not far away enough. For the length of an eye blink, he pictured all the trees ablaze. He gave a muffled cough.

"God save you citizen." Maestro Aquila gave a superior nod. The grizzled blacksmith glanced up from his forge with the look of a badger baited in its hole. He tugged uncomfortably at his forelock and went back to hammering.

"Queer fellow," said Maestro Aquila. "Touched in the head, I should think. They say he never comes down to the city." The maestro swished his staff. "Looks like a wild beast himself."

The blacksmith put down his hammer and limped toward the back of the forge. His left leg dragged behind him. There didn't look to be any apprentice in there to help him. As Tammo watched, the man glanced again, furtive under his shaggy tangle of hair, and looked straight at Tammo. His eyes were bright as a bird's. He didn't look touched, Tammo thought. Perhaps he just liked to be alone. Perhaps he appreciated his freedom.

The crow cawed again and flapped down from the tree.

Tammo gave it a hard stare and fingered a carven wing on the flute. Then he followed Maestro Aquila deeper into the wood.

8. Celestina

Carlo knelt in a candlelit chapel, robed in white with swan-feather wings on his back. He had been kneeling for around half an hour and his legs were beginning to go dead. But not as dead as the poor lad in the coffin. *His* legs would never trouble him again, nor any other part of his body. He was now in the arms of Seraphiel, whose portrait—illuminated by a great rack of candles—cast reflections of Michael's subordinate upon the coffin's glass lid, making it look as though its inhabitant had joined the seraph in this world as well as the next. Or he was with the Virgin Mother, a rather more shadowy figure at Carlo's left-hand side, whose likeness had been painted directly onto the wall, and who appeared to Carlo as a startling white face looking out of different shades of blue and black.

"The Pagenos are among the very first Angelian families," the rector had said, just before he set off. "Count Pageno is considered by many to be the Duke's right-hand man. The Duke himself is said to be heartbroken over this boy's death. I assure you, it will be felt most deeply that I send Maestro Sarastro's protégé to stand cherub for him."

He looked at the boy in the coffin. They had tried to lay him out peacefully, but he still looked more like a shrunken waxwork than an actual boy who had once laughed and played. He was even smaller than Luca, and much thinner too. His face was screwed up as if he was trying to keep something away. Pain, Carlo decided, looking more closely. The boy was covered with raised spots, which someone had tried to disguise with powder but which were still pitifully obvious. That explained the glass lid on the coffin; the spots were probably contagious.

Carlo stepped back. His breath was steaming up the glass. He had seen his share of dead children, and the sight didn't frighten him. Once before, when he was only nine and had stood cherub for some poor child, Carlo had been so sleepy and the child he was guarding so apparently peaceful that he had climbed into the coffin, put his arms around the chilly shoulders and gone to sleep. He had woken in the night thinking he was back in bed with his younger brothers in the country village. Carlo wasn't sure he could fully recall all his siblings any more. At least three of them had the baptismal name Michelangelo, but whether that was two girls and a boy or two boys and a girl he couldn't think now. Were they all still alive? Perhaps the older ones would be married and have children of their own. Maybe he would have even younger siblings he knew nothing about. Or maybe his mother had been through many funerals like this. Carlo might be her only living child. He would never find out.

A sound he couldn't place jerked Carlo out of his gloom. It was something like the turning of carriage wheels, the cranking of a handle such as might draw a bucket from a well, and the whirring that went on inside a clock case. He stepped away from the coffin in a hurry and placed his hands together in an attitude of prayer. He daren't look to see what was making the sound.

"I saw you move, Angel-boy," aid a feminine voice. "So, you needn't pretend to be a statue now. You were looking at my brother, weren't you?"

Carlo looked at his hands and tried to think of a suitably deferential answer. One that wouldn't lose him the patronage. The strange noises had stopped now. The voice spoke again, very young, with a tone somewhere between curiosity and command:

"Oh dear. I've made you blush. Won't you turn round and look at me? I won't bite."

Carlo turned. The speaker was not positioned quite where he expected her to be. From her face, she looked about eleven years old; all pink lips and soft eyebrows. Her hair was piled on her head in the fashionable style and decorated with black feathers. The bell sleeves of her white frock had ribbons on. Black ribbons. And there was a brooch pinned to her chest with a picture of a weeping angel, done with pearls and worked hair. She held her head in a way that suggested she was a lady already, and had been since the day she learned to talk.

But her head only came to a level with Carlo's waist. She was sitting in a brocade-upholstered chair with two wheels at either side like carriage wheels. The skirts of her frock were neatly tucked under a sort of cabinet, supported by a third wheel. The cabinet was lacquered and decorated with gilt flowers. Two brass handles were fixed to either side of it. As Carlo watched, the girl turned the handles and the chair rolled nearer, making the strange sound he had heard earlier.

She drew level with the coffin and looked at the shrunken waxwork inside.

"Poor Orlando! He wanted to go and ride on his pony." She pulled a lever so the chair turned toward Carlo, then looked up, a frown of concentration puckering her baby eyebrows. "I haven't cried, not even once. Does that make me bad, Angel-boy?"

"Of course not, noblesse." Carlo gave his very sweetest smile. "You are the model of sisterly devotion." He glanced in the direction of the door, half-expecting a nurse or governess to appear at any moment. Children of great families did not attend funerals, much less girl children. As for girl cripples, it was unheard of. This tiny countess in the making had come to her brother's vigil of her own accord. Carlo couldn't help but admire her spirit, for all she was so sweet and doll-like.

"I knew it!" The child clapped her hands. "You're a cast...cast..." She screwed up her face, searching for the right word.

"Castrato." Carlo lowered his eyes, uncomfortably aware of the shortness of his robe.

"Castrato." She spoke the word carefully, committing it to memory. "I knew it when you talked. Papa makes cast...rati famous. He made a boy famous once before, and he went all over the empire, singing to princes and cardinals. Then he died." She ran a finger up and down a pearl crescent on the cabinet. "I like Il Cupide best, though. Have you been to the Teatro this season, Angel-boy?"

"I fear not. We castrati must attend to our studies if we are to become famous." Dear God, she had a mind like a butterfly! Carlo wished he had just a little food inside him, to give him the strength to keep up.

"Oh." She looked disappointed. "Papa always takes box forty-three, every year. Pompey carries me up the stairs. I have caraway comfits and a small glass of Madeira, and I beat Teresa at piquet."

"Indeed?" Carlo raised an eyebrow. His new companion had managed to breeze through the delights of the opera, which Carlo so longed to experience, with the briskness of a housewife running off the daily chores.

"Yes. But we shan't be able to go for a while now, because of Orlando. Mama says she shan't ever go again, but papa says we must. The Duke needs him. Papa is indis..." She screwed up her face again.

"Indispensable?" said Carlo.

"Yes." A look of satisfaction. "You know things, Angel-boy. What's your name?"

"Carlo Bianci, noblesse."

He made the same bow he had made to Tammo when they first met, adjusting the balance slightly to bring out the full effect of the wings. His eyes sparkled with amusement. She was like a self-assured kitten that confidently walks along the back of an old hound, knowing itself to be the true mistress.

The girl drew herself up to her full seated height of three feet.

"I am the Noblesse Celestina of the House of Pageno. But you may call me Celestina in private. Until I'm sixteen.

Then you must call me Noblesse Celestina at all times. That will be in five years' time. How old will you be then, Angel-boy Carlo Bianci?"

"I will be eighteen years old, noblesse. And your devoted servant if the Archangel permits"

Carlo sniffled. The cold air was making his nose run, and there was nowhere in a cherub's robe for a handkerchief. Celestina tilted her head, Orpheus-like, and pursed her pretty lips.

"You're shivering, Angel-boy. You're going to catch a chill, standing there all night. And you haven't had enough sleep. Your eyes are all shadowy."

"I am happy to serve your poor brother in this last office." Carlo produced a warm smile while inwardly cursing her astuteness, tensing the muscles in his back to try and halt the shivering. Unfortunately, this moved his stomach to make a loud complaint. He blushed.

Celestina gave a little toss of her head, and turned one handle of the cabinet until her chair was facing the chapel door.

"Come along," she said. "I will take you to the music room. Pompey always leaves me some fruit and biscotti in there. We'll be quite alone."

"Ah." Carlo gestured towards the coffin. "My engagement is in the chapel. To stand watch at your brother's side and to sing him on his way in the morning." He sniffled again.

"You won't be able to sing if you're all sniffly and shivery, silly." Celestina sounded as though she were stating the painfully obvious. She looked back at the coffin. "Orlando won't mind you having a little rest."

"But your father might." Carlo's body was crying out for food and a warm fireside. Much longer in this chapel and he wouldn't be able to keep memories of the ice at bay any longer. And Celestina was right about his voice. He had no hope of patronage if all he could manage tomorrow was a strangled squeak. But surely, he couldn't leave the duty he had been engaged to perform? To watch and pray the young nobile into paradise. He turned serious eyes on Celestina. "I cannot afford to lose the Count's good opinion. I must stay."

Celestina looked at Carlo as if he were simple.

"Of course, you mustn't stay. Papa won't mind. Not if I tell him I advised you to come out, so your voice would be stronger in the morning. Papa always listens to my opinion."

I'll bet he does, thought Carlo, as the chair cranked and whirred across the marble floor. He had met very few girls since he had been at the conservatorio, but he didn't think any of them were like Celestina. She could probably stand up to Maestro Sarastro in an argument, and still make him feel like he'd done her a favour in conceding. And yet she was so dainty and frail. And at such an obvious disadvantage in the world.

"Are you coming, Angel-boy?" she said from the door. "Oh, and watch out for Giacomo. He doesn't understand why Orlando doesn't come to play with him anymore, and sometimes he tries to bite."

Carlo's gaze flickered back toward the shadows. Michael himself would watch over Orlando. The Archangel never forgot his own.

He leaned over the coffin one last time, watching the brave, pained face disappear behind his breath-mist.

"You have an interesting sister," he told the dead boy. "I think I should like to know her better."

The music room was a comforting round space—the friendlier twin of the chapel—with large mirrors and classical scenes of Apollo, Orpheus, and Pan on the walls. Carlo stoked the fire, taking great care not to get soot on his white robe. Celestina wheeled about, selecting dainties from two low tables. The handles and levers on her cabinet allowed her to weave her way between the obstacles with impressive elegance. A harpsichord, adorned inside and out with the most exquisite decoration, stood opposite an arched window. Carlo longed to try the sound, even though he felt weaker and wearier now than he had with the cold air of the chapel to keep him awake. He lit three candles on a stand with a light from the wall sconce and watched the room blossom into colour. Soft greens and golds flickered in the firelight.

"I always come in here in the evenings. To play on the harpsichord. My chair fits under it exactly. Look." Celestina demonstrated the snug fit before wheeling back to the fireside. "But I can't play tonight because of Orlando." She sighed then smiled again. "Maestro Loreto teaches me. Do you know him?"

"I do indeed, noblesse." Carlo tipped a drop of wax into the wall sconce and stuck the candle back in place. "He is harpsichord master at the conservatorio. A fine tutor. I'm sure you are quite his favourite pupil." He sniffled.

Celestina finished with the confectioneries and sat back with satisfaction.

"Would you like a handkerchief, Angel-boy? I have one spare."

"Yes, please," said Carlo.

The handkerchief was of soft cotton-lawn fabric, and had a golden pheasant embroidered in one corner. The sigil of House Pageno. Carlo's prospective patrons. He dabbed his nose daintily, afraid to spoil it.

"You can keep that if you like," said Celestina, airily. "Now, lift me onto the sopha and we'll have some supper."

Carlo wasn't at all sure he could manage that, with the way the room was swaying at the moment. His stomach was hard with hunger and his arms felt more like water than actual arms. What if he dropped Count Pageno's only daughter on the music room floor? If she was used to being lifted by those god-like footmen, the efforts of a thirteen-year-old eunuch were going to seem pathetically feeble. Sweet Michael, but he was weary! Had he always been this weak, or was this the reverse side of the Archangel's bargain? If only he could swap places with Tamino for a moment. His twin could have lifted the young noblesse without a thought.

Carlo put his arms about Celestina as gently as possible. He had never been this close to a girl before, and fire touched his cheeks as his hands closed around her frame. She was so fragile, like a little bird. And so pretty. Her hair smelled of rose oil and fine linen. He breathed in the scent as he braced his legs to take the strain. His cheeks quivered with effort. He didn't think he'd ever seen anyone so pretty. Like a wood-nymph in a painting. Like a song.

"I like your wings." Celestina reached out to touch the swansdown as Carlo set her down on the sopha.

"Thank you, noblesse." Carlo managed an even tone, silently thanking his musical training.

"Now sit beside me and eat. There, next to the fire. Oh, your poor feet are blue! Here." She pulled a crocheted blanket from inside the cabinet and tucked it over Carlo's legs. Now eat. And I told you: you may call me Celestina."

Carlo smiled. It was pleasant, being cosseted by a girl. He wished Tamino would cosset him a little sometimes. Play fights were all very well, but Carlo liked the tender things in life. An arm round the shoulder. A chaste kiss on the forehead. Sometimes Carlo wondered if his twin would ever stop acting the cornered beast and notice Carlo's sighs and silent pleas. The little noblesse did it all so naturally, and she and Carlo had only just met.

The almond biscotti and squares of pineapple were not the fish stew and bread Carlo longed for, but he ate them gratefully, taking dainty bites, although his stomach was screaming for him to cram as many into his mouth as possible. Two dishes of warm cinnamon water and several biscotti later, the pains in his belly had disappeared along with the lightness in his head. Celestina smiled triumphantly between spoonfuls of chocolate cream.

"Now you look better," she said. "I knew you would. Your cheeks are all rosy like a proper cherub."

Carlo dabbed his mouth with the handkerchief and lowered his eyelashes.

"How do you know I am not a cherub? I may unfold my wings and fly away at any moment."

Celestina squealed with laughter and clapped her hands.

"I knew you would make a merry companion!"

"I aim to please." Carlo made a slight bow. She was remarkably easy to please, he thought. He hadn't known girls would be so simple to charm. He and Celestina had more in common than he would have guessed. A love of music, for one thing. A tender heart. The fact that neither of them were complete as the rest of the world saw it. He found himself looking at the wheeled chair.

"You want to know how I lost the use of my legs, don't you, Angel-boy?"

Celestina was looking at him with the victory of having caught someone out.

"No, no, noblesse. Not at all." Carlo would never have dared ask such a question. Such things were private. He certainly didn't want anyone to ask how he had lost that which would have made him a man. Except, Tamino. Sometimes he almost wished Tamino would ask. But he never did.

"It's all right. Everyone in Angelio knows." Celestina settled her hands in her lap. "I caught a fever when I was seven, and when I got better, I couldn't move anything below my waist. Papa had my house carriage designed specially by a clockmaker from Festeburg. It's the only one like it in the world."

"It is ingenious." Carlo inclined his head.

"Papa says I may have everything I need to live the life of a lady." A cloud passed across Celestina's face. "Since I will never be able to make a marriage alliance and have babies. And neither will you."

Carlo blushed at her pointed look. Did this child consider no topic too delicate for discussion? What did an eleven-year-old noblesse know about making babies anyway? What did he, come to that? It wasn't a topic he liked to dwell on, although there was enough discussion and experimentation in the dorm to join in with, had he wished. Carlo preferred to sit with the younger boys and tell stories, or go out to the tree to be with Tammo. Why take an interest in something you weren't made for? Surely song was the greatest pleasure a eunuch could hope to know.

"People call me a cripple." Celestina scowled, her baby features distorted. "I may be a cripple, but I'm a noblesse of House Pageno. They call you cripples too, don't they? What do you say to them, Angel-boy?"

"I..." Carlo hesitated.

The awkward moment was abruptly broken by something leaping on Carlo's back and pulling at his hair with tiny fingers.

"Oh!" he exclaimed with a cry that went up into the third octave.

Celestina laughed.

"Giacomo, there you are! Come here, naughty boy and stop pulling Carlo's hair." She held out a sugared almond. "Come on. You like these, don't you? Yes, you do. Yes, you do."

Carlo was relieved to discover that his assailant was none other than a monkey in a red waistcoat. Once it had discovered Celestina had a considerable supply of sugared almonds, it became content to cling to her chest like a baby, occasionally darting out a paw to snatch an almond and then eating it in a succession of furious nibbles.

"Naughty Giacomo," cooed Celestina. "You frightened Carlo. Don't you like monkeys, Angel-boy?" She twinkled.

"Giacomo is my first," Carlo admitted, catching his breath. "I think I prefer birds."

"Oh, but I have ever so many birds," Celestina said. "Would you like to see them?"

Carlo tried to frame a polite refusal before Celestina had him wandering all over the house. An unexpected yawn came out before he had the chance to stifle it.

"Oh, Angel-boy! You're sleepy." Celestina hugged the monkey. "Why don't you put your head in my lap? I promise Giacomo won't grab you."

"I should get back," Carlo said, trying to prevent a second yawn. That was the trouble with being well-fed and warm again. It was so hard to stay awake.

"Just for a little while. You'll feel much better." Celestina patted Carlo's curls. Her tiny fingers were gentle. He decided that just two minutes wouldn't hurt, so long as he didn't actually fall asleep. "Your hair is so pretty. Like a curly puppy. We should be friends, Angel-boy. I have no friend left now."

"Rector Bartolomeo and Carlo Bianci!"

The liveried manservant bowed them through double doors and retreated with silent grace. Carlo took a deep breath and brought to mind his rehearsals in front of the mirror. Heroic posture. Self-assurance. He was the Nightingale, the talk of Angelio. He deserved this position. He was ready.

Rector Bartolomeo paused to catch his breath, leaning for a moment on Carlo's shoulder. There had been a flight of stairs to climb from the portico to the grand entrance hall, and another from there to the Count's reception room. The fierce angels and illustrious ancestors that glared down on them as they walked through the petitioner's gallery were enough to take anyone's breath. This was as much an occasion for the rector and his tight waistcoat as it was for Carlo. There must have been arguments with Maestro Sarastro over who got to present the young prodigy to the Duke's right-hand man. Carlo wondered how the rector had managed to triumph over his bombastic tutor. Perhaps the opera was taking up enough of Sarastro's time.

Carlo's and the rector's footsteps echoed as they crossed the tiled floor. The reception room was bright with tall mirrors and an elaborate ceiling with golden pheasants in the four corners. Swathes of black crêpe hung from picture-frames and curtain-rails. Orlando was clearly not forgotten.

The man himself was sitting behind a lacquered and gilded desk, sorting through sheaves of papers. Two dark lines under his eyes spoke of grief. He touched the large mourning ring on his left hand to his lips, an absent-minded gesture.

"Your lordship." The rector made a bow and Carlo

followed suit. The Count folded his hands and acknowledged them with a nod of the head.

"Gentlemen. God save you. I trust you understand why I have called you."

"Indeed, your lordship." The rector tried to bend his seal-like body into a second bow. "May the Archangel smile upon you and comfort you in your hour of need. You have always been a magnificent patron to the Conservatorio Archangeli and the art musical. It is keenly felt, I assure you. May I introduce to your lordship our finest student, Carlo Bianci, in whom you have been so kind as to take an interest?"

Carlo thought he saw a flicker of a smile break through the Count's mask of grief.

"By your good leave, rector, I prefer to speak to the boy himself." He turned his head. "Carlo. I believe your fellow-students call you the Nightingale?"

"I believe they do, your lordship."

Carlo wasn't about to begin grovelling like the rector. Looking into the Count's grey eyes, he could tell this man was far too intelligent to be fooled by nonsense like that. An honest answer, and a plain one, would suffice.

"But that is not my name of choice. I will take my artistic name when I come of age. Or when my patron suggests it. Until then, I shall remain Carlo to your lordship."

"Very well, Carlo." The warmth in the Count's eyes told Carlo he had made the right answer. "And tell me, Carlo, what patronage have you had to this date?"

Carlo looked steadfastly into the Count's face. A good

man, he decided. Decisive. Caring. And Celestina's father. That had to count for something. He would make a good patron.

"Ser Julianus of my home province pays my school fees. And I sing for some of the smaller churches in the city, and the convent."

"He's a very good boy, your lordship." The rector interrupted. "We have taken great pains to ensure he is not corrupted by the opera or worldly temptations."

"Most laudable. Your care does your institution credit," said the Count. Carlo recalled Celestina's description of box forty-three and her assertion that the Count was indispensable at the opera. "Well, Carlo, a boy of your talent needs exposure at a higher level. Maestro Sarastro did well in securing you a solo at Seraphim Mass..." The rector ballooned with repressed indignation. "But you need to be heard by the right people, and more frequently."

Carlo's heart hammered in his chest. This was the moment.

"You will come and sing for me in my chapel once a week. To begin with. And partake of a little company— suitable company—while you are here. It will help prepare you for the world you are to enter. That should suffice for a boy of your age. I do not wish to take you from the training Rector Bartolomeo is so assiduously putting you through."

A nod to the rector, who responded with an awkward bow.

"Thank you, your lordship." Carlo made his own bow, his mind racing. Suitable company? Did that mean he was to spend time with Celestina? Perhaps the little noblesse had spoken up for him after his departure.

"You are a member of my household now, Carlo Bianci," said the Count. Remember, you represent the honour of House Pageno wherever you are and whatever you do. To that end, I would like you to receive this token."

The Count opened the strings of a velvet bag that had been lying on the desk and took out a ring. The centre stone was of black enamel surrounded by gemstones. It was decorated with smaller gems to create a little face, disguised for Carnival, in a black mask with red lips. It was a jolly little thing, out of place in this house of mourning.

"I had this made for my son, Orlando." The Count's voice went husky as he tried to pronounce his son's name. "He was so sad to have to miss Carnival. I thought at least he could go in spirit." He pressed his lips together and took a deep breath. "I think another boy should have it now, one who has not yet experienced *Carnevale* in all its mirth and excess. Nor will, for some years to come."

"You do me too much honour, your lordship," Carlo said.

The Count placed the ring on his finger. His smallest finger was the one it fit best; it must have been made for Orlando's middle finger, before he shrank to the waxwork in the box. Carlo ran his fingertips over the raised gems. This was a significant moment, he thought. A bond of honour and responsibility had been formed. Whatever came next, he must not let Count Pageno down.

The Count and the rector spent further minutes arranging the exact terms of Carlo's patronage. Or rather, the Count dictated the terms to the rector, who punctuated them with sycophantic phrases. Carlo looked up to the golden ceiling, trying to pace his breathing. His dream was coming true. It was beginning right in front of him. Thanks to the blessed Archangel! Carlo put his hand in his pocket and touched the corner of a handkerchief, his fingertips meeting the same golden pheasant that crowed down at him from the ceiling. Celestina! Thanks to the Archangel, indeed. Now he would not have to enter this new life alone.

"You prayed this for me, Tamino," he said silently. "I'm sure you'll see that soon. Celestina is the one."

And when the rector and Carlo finally bowed their way out of the reception room and descended the intimidating staircase once again, Carlo was certain he heard the cranking of a wheeled chair and caught a glimpse of white lace between marble banisters.

9. Ice and Fire

There were masks everywhere. Black masks on ladies' faces, tied with matching ribbons. White masks staring from cloak-and-tricorn disguises, giving their wearers an inhuman look. Dazzling masks like suns and moons. Crossing the busy piazza, Tammo blushed at the nakedness of his own face. The old scar snarled up at his right ear like a burning flame. He pulled down his hat and tried to be inconspicuous: a boy in an indigo cassock with a crow on his shoulder.

Duke's Day had come. The boys had been given a half-day off to celebrate. Most of the intermediates had rushed out of the school gate, whooping and jangling purses of small coin. Now that Carnival had begun in earnest, you could try your luck at cards, or fencing against professionals, or take part in eating and drinking contests. The cards were a dupe's game—Tammo knew from experience—and the sword masters were unlikely to take on anyone less than a senior. Eating contests weren't such a bad idea, provided you didn't vomit, but it was no fun being at Carnival alone. Easier simply to relieve a stall of the odd cheese or fig-cake and eat it in private. Then get up a tree and watch the sideshows unseen.

It would have been different with Carlo. But the eunuch was singing at St. Remiel's and then paying a visit to the Pageno mansion. Chattering with that baby noblesse, no doubt. Funny, he hadn't had Carlo down as one with such infantile taste. The sopranist was more girl than Tammo had realised.

Anyway, Carlo wasn't there. Pity. He longed to see Carnival so much. Tammo didn't really have the heart to enjoy it without him. He would fill his belly, then look for the bird sellers. He'd like to see where his conquests ended up after Sarastro had concluded business.

It was drizzling slightly. The winter mists hadn't set in yet, but it was feeling distinctly like the November day it was. Cloths and banners flapped wetly on stalls. A performing dog in a collar shook its muddy fur on Tammo's cassock. Tammo growled at it and pulled his cloak about his shoulders. The crow cawed in sympathy.

For all his practise negotiating "the swell" at school, it wasn't easy getting through the crowds. All it took was the sound of a drum and trumpet across a piazza, or the rumour of a puppet show down a particular alley, and a crowd that had been inexorably moving one way could turn tail and surge back the way it had just come. Tammo recalled a way to the bird-sellers' porticos from St. Uriel's Bridge, along the riverside. He just needed to ride the crowd making for the clockwork automata. The harpsichord-playing mannequins were an old established favourite in Angelio. He couldn't imagine them failing to draw a crowd.

He hadn't bargained on the giraffe. A sea captain had

put in with it at Fair Havens and sailed it up the river in a barge. No sooner was Tammo within sight of the porticos when there was a cry of "The beast! The marvellous beast! I saw its head!"

Tammo found himself being forced a way he didn't want to go. He wanted to hit out at the popinjays who would rather ogle a giraffe than let an honest citizen pass, but some of them wanted to take it out directly on, "that ill-omened bird." Reluctant as he was to call the crow his pet, he wasn't having anyone abuse a creature he'd summoned with the Archangel's gift.

"Fie on them, Coronis!" he growled, shielding the bird with his arm. "And stop shoving!" he yelled at a man sporting the face of a fox.

Tammo was jostled down narrow streets. The grubby faces of children peeped between the slats of balconies. Everywhere, there were coloured awnings, hanging trinkets and tables groaning with bargains. A chandler's, where drying candles hung as conjoined twins from their wicks. A potter's workshop, where plates engraved with fountains and crowns took pride of place to honour the Duke. A wood turner's, a soap maker's. A basketry shop... Tammo's legs suddenly grew heavy. His heart was a crushing weight, too big for his chest. Not this street. Of all the places in Angelio where he didn't want to come... He couldn't turn the corner. Yet his feet kept moving, one and then the other. He wouldn't look up.

He looked.

The timbers round the door had been replaced, but a

black shadow still licked its way up the stonework, from where the forge had been. Charred shutters hung slantwise, clinging on by Michael-knew-what. Someone had hung a tin angel in one of the empty spaces. Tammo blinked hard, trying not to see wooden dolls ranged along the windowsill. Trying not to smell frying mushrooms and molten iron and hear the laughter of childish voices.

"Damn Carnival," he muttered under his breath. "Damn poxy freak show. What did you bring me here for?"

A couple in matching velvet masks made a hasty side-step round him and glared back, fans fluttering.

"What are you looking at?" Tammo snarled.

He stared at the shop, breath hissing between his teeth. The crow flapped anxiously.

"Damn house. Damn street."

Something was fighting to get out of him. He couldn't stop it. He pushed past the stalls and beat on the charred walls with his fists. His feet kicked at the timbers, over and over again.

"Stupid damn bloody house! It wasn't my fault, do you hear?"

The crowd had begun to murmur now. At the basket maker's, a woman in a cap and apron came out of the doorway.

"Surely that's not the Capell boy, is it?" She leaned back into the workshop. "Augusto, come here!"

Pain was searing his knuckles now. Good. He kicked harder and heard a satisfying crunch.

"It wasn't. My. Fault."

"Oi!" A voice came from inside the shop. "What do you think you're doing? Clear off or I'll send for the city militia!"

At the same time the woman called out, "Tammo Capell! Is that you?"

"Blackguards!" Tammo croaked at no one in particular. He gave the boards a final kick and ran off down the nearest side street, the crow clearing a pathway for him with beak and talons. Everything was blurry and there was saltwater on his face. And his heart ached for Carlo.

"Won't you tell me?" Carlo said.

His friend had found a stocking to bandage Tammo's swollen knuckles. He tied the ends off with a knot, then took the bandaged hand in both of his and gave it a gentle kiss. Tammo winced.

"I told you, I got in a fight at Carnival." It didn't sound convincing, even to him.

Carlo's jaw tightened. "What about?"

"Nothing. It doesn't matter. I don't want to talk about it."

"But it does matter. You're meant to be staying out of fights. What if the rector got to hear?"

"All right, I didn't get into a fight." Tammo shrugged. "Are you happy now?"

Carlo pursed his cupid's lips. That sad look was in his eyes again. Tammo growled in the back of his throat. Why did that look always make him feel so guilty?

"Are you happy, Tamino?" Carlo said.

"I'm fine," said Tammo, for the umpteenth time.

"How's Count Pageno? Does he have you sing to the sound of a golden harp, knee-deep in turkey carpets, or what?"

"You can tell me anything, Tamino." Carlo's eyes were liquid pools of emotion.

"I'm telling you I want to hear about the Pagenos." Tammo chewed at the knot Carlo had tied. "So, tell me, then? Has the noblesse had you playing at dollies today?"

Carlo gently extracted the stocking bandage from Tammo's mouth.

"You'll make it come undone," he said. "If you must know, Noblesse Celestina has been showing me her toy theatre. The Count had it made in the exact likeness of the stage at the Teatro di Palazzo. Curtains, moving scenery, a ramp to the stables for the horses to come up and down. Everything. And she has two little dolls for it called Morestelli and La Bellina. You move them from above by wires. Celestina's governess helped her stitch the costumes, precisely as they wore them in *Oriolanda* last season. Morestelli's head-dress—"

"So, you were playing at dollies," said Tammo dispassionately.

"I was entertaining a lady of quality." Carlo looked down his nose. "And a monkey." He held the pose for some minutes, then slowly fluttered his eyelashes.

Despite the misery buried inside him, Tammo felt the urge to laugh. How did Carlo always manage to do this to him? He prodded Carlo in the ribs, making the eunuch squirm and giggle.

"So, Count Pageno keeps an opera-singing monkey?" he said, scratching his neck. "Oh, wait. That's you, isn't it?"

The leaves Carlo pushed down his neck were mouldy and wet with rainwater, but the liquid emotion that remained in the singer's eyes was of another source altogether. And, in spite of Carlo's shrill giggles, it didn't disappear.

"Hurry, lad, or we shall lose our footing," said Pietro.

The birdcage bumped against his buttocks as he walked. The three nightingales inside flapped and huddled together, as if for comfort. Tammo wanted to play a few bars on the dark flute to calm them, but he was walking too quickly to breathe evenly. The ground underfoot was muddy, a mass of fallen leaves and exposed tree roots. And, as Pietro was so keen to point out, it was getting dark. One more chime of the clock and the sun would sink behind the horizon. Pretty as Angel's Wood was, Tammo didn't fancy having to grope his way through the trees in the dark. It would be all too easy to twist an ankle. Or get lost. And although no one had seen wild boars this close to town, there was always a first time.

"We should have asked Maestro Aquila for a lantern," said Tammo.

"And lit it with what?"

The sharpness in Pietro's voice suggested he had already thought of this possibility.

"We could go to that blacksmith's forge," Tammo said. "He might have a lantern to spare."

Pietro grunted. "Madman. He'd just as soon hit us over the head with his own hammer."

"He didn't look mad to me." Tammo stumbled over a root. The crow complained and flapped about on his shoulder. "We can't risk anything happening to the nightingales. What if you tripped and fell on the cage?"

"Suit yourself then, young know-it-all." Pietro hitched the cage higher on his back. "Don't blame me if we're bludgeoned to death as we stand."

The glow of the forge was easily visible through the trees. Tammo stumbled along, with Pietro following, to where the ruined whatever-it-was towered gloomily over the thatched hut. The blacksmith was working with his back to them, sparks flying up from the anvil with each strike. The sound put a queer feeling in Tammo's stomach. What was he doing, coming to a forge again? He should turn back. No, he shouldn't. Yes, he should. The blacksmith turned and pushed something into a pail of water. There was great hiss and a cloud of steam. Tammo jumped back so that the crow squawked. Forget the lantern. This was too much. He had to get out of here. Right, and who was acting like a baby now? It was just a forge. Just a forge. Like the forge that had blackened the walls at—

"Excuse me, citizen, but we were wondering if you could spare us a light this dark night."

Pietro's voice. The maestro's manservant had apparently overcome his fear of madmen. The blacksmith looked up, his head a wild tangle of hair and beard.

"Not dark yet," he muttered. "And I don't spare nothing for free."

"Be a bit more civil and we might think about opening

our purses." Pietro summoned up all the dignity he could muster.

"Got a lantern in that purse?" The blacksmith gave a throaty chuckle.

Tammo rocked, agitated, his fingernails biting his palms. The smell of hot metal in his nostrils... He mustn't think about his father. Not his strong, smiling father. Nor his mother. Nor his little sisters.

The blacksmith caught his eye. "You afraid of me, boy? Afraid of an old man? You look like you've seen a ghost."

"I'm not afraid of you," Tammo croaked.

The blacksmith narrowed his eyes and looked Tammo up and down. He nodded his head, slowly. The crinkled eyes glittered.

"Then you won't be afraid of this, will you?"

Afraid of what? Tammo wanted to ask, but the words stuck in his chest. He was afraid. Afraid of the forge. Afraid of his memories. Afraid that the reason the Archangel never saved the others was that he—Tammo—ought to have done it instead. Only he hadn't. He'd tried to go back for his sisters, but the door was too hot. It had hurt his hand, his face. He'd pushed against it but the pain was too much. And the smoke...

The nuns hadn't told him what happened to the others until he'd been in the infirmary a fortnight. His throat had hurt too much to cry. He'd thought he might die too, but his body had gone on stubbornly living. He'd slept there for weeks, sweaty with pain, until they told him to get up and start doing light chores. No one took him to say prayers for his family. No one even asked their names. Instead, a steward had arrived from the conservatorio to offer him St. Michael's charity.

They'd hauled him up before the rector and told him to sing. That had to be the single most humiliating moment of his life. The frowns. The exchanged glances. But then someone had handed him a flute and told him to have a try. That had been the beginning. The prelude to everything that happened next.

The blacksmith had been bending over the forge fire, tinkering with something. He came back with a torch in his hand, fashioned from an ash bough wrapped in oiled rags. A naked flame. A firebrand.

"For the boy who isn't afraid. To see him down the pony path." There was a look in his face, half-hidden by hair though it was, that made Tammo feel as if the old man was appraising him. "That'll be two centesimi," he added, holding out his hand to Pietro.

Pietro paid up, grumbling. Tammo stood rooted, his hair sweaty under his hat. The blacksmith was waiting for him to take the torch. Its flickering light shone on his face. He would bet any amount it showed the old blacksmith his scar, that mark of another fire. His hand shook. He was going to be sick.

"Hurry up, Master Capell. We need to be back by evensong." Pietro fussed with the cage of nightingales. "Thank you, citizen."

Tammo snatched the torch and turned from the forge before the blacksmith saw any more of the horror threatening to tear him apart. He no longer cared about tree roots or twisted ankles. The pace he set down the hill had

Pietro cursing and stumbling. And the torch shook in his hand every step of the way.

He was sitting huddled beneath the tree when Carlo found him. His head was down, his arms round his knees. He had stopped noticing the damp leaf litter seeping into his cloak and cassock, into his breeches. The crow was dozing in a roost above him. Some of its mess had dropped on the edge of his cloak. He had stopped noticing that, too.

"Tamino?" Carlo's voice was hesitant.

Tammo raised his head, a boy in a dream. A bad dream.

"Can I help?"

Carlo held out his hand. The soft hand of a eunuch. A hand that had never known searing flame, licking up its perfect whiteness. And yet, Carlo had known pain. Pain and fear. Suddenly, the keeping of secrets no longer seemed important. What was important was to have a friend. To no longer be alone.

He took Carlo's hand.

"Let's go to the chapel," he said.

There was a warmth in the chapel. A musky closeness of incense and dying candles. The smell of prayer, as every boy in Angelio knew. Before the portrait of St. Michael, a few votive lights still flickered in the long stand. The Archangel in the portrait was golden-haired with enormous wings, and clad in armour. It didn't look terribly like Michael as Tammo and Carlo had encountered him, but the sight of it gave Tammo heart all the same.

The boys reverenced the portrait and altar, and slipped

into the pew usually reserved for soloists. Above them, the dying flames made stars glitter in the dark ceiling. Years ago, some patron had put constellations of silver leaf there, to shine down on the boys as they sang. Tammo watched them wink one by one as the tiny lights shivered. Beside him, he felt Carlo shiver in sympathy. Without a word, he unfastened his cloak and tucked it round Carlo's shoulders, on top of the one the sopranist already wore.

Carlo turned to him with a sad smile.

"My dear twin. What is it that upsets you so? Cannot you trust your truest friend? I swear by the Archangel himself that I will never betray a secret of yours, no matter what befalls."

"I know." Tammo squeezed the icy hand next to his. "It's just that...I've never told anyone about...well, about things that happened to me before."

He chewed hard on his lip. It felt like it was going to burst. Carlo had gone as still as the statue of the Saviour above the altar.

"There are things I have never spoken of either. Dark things." A shadow passed across his face.

It was beginning to feel like some sort of dangerous game. Tammo felt the pulse beat in his neck.

"I'll speak if you will," he said.

"Very well." Carlo looked as sepulchral as was possible for such a cherub. "Who will go first?"

"I will." Could Carlo hear his heart trying to escape from his rib cage? "It's about what happened before I came to school."

"Mine too." Carlo's voice was high and tense. "But go on."

"I..." Where could he possibly start? He was no good at this kind of thing. "It wasn't my fault."

"I'm sure it wasn't, dear Tamino."

"There was a fire."

There, he'd said it. After all these years, he'd finally said the word. Carlo waited, a warm presence by his side.

"At the metalworking shop. That was where we lived. My father..." His voice trembled on the word. "My father was a coppersmith. He made kettles, candlesticks, birdcages sometimes. We all used to help. Me. Mother. My little sisters..."

A candle on the votive stand flickered and went out. Tammo took a deep breath.

"I smelled burning one night. I wasn't asleep. The others were. I went down to see what it was, but then I couldn't get back up. I tried but...the door burnt my arm. I couldn't breathe. It hurt so much..."

He was breathing hard now. Tiny puffs of steam came out in the dark of the chapel. Carlo put a hand on his shoulder.

"I didn't get them out, Carlo. They were all just sleeping in their beds. They didn't even wake up."

"They woke up in paradise," said Carlo. "It wasn't your fault, Tamino. It was an accident."

"I went there the other day," said Tammo. "Duke's Day. I just ended up there. It was all different. Someone else was living there. Selling things from my father's shop. Like they just didn't care."

His choler was beginning to rise now. He kicked at the back of the pew. Carlo flinched.

"Forget them, whoever they are. They don't matter." He hesitated, his hand caressing Tammo's shoulder. "I care, Tamino."

Tammo clenched and unclenched his fists. "I know."

They sat and watched another votive candle quiver and go out, sending a thin column of smoke up toward the Archangel's breast.

"Did you love your father?" Carlo said eventually.

Tammo scowled.

"What do you mean? He was my father."

Carlo took his hand from Tammo shoulder and clasped both hands together, looking down at them as if they'd suddenly become fascinating.

"I hated my father."

"What?"

Tammo's raised voice echoed round the deserted chapel. Had he heard that right? It seemed impossible to think of gentle Carlo hating anyone.

"Have I shocked you now, dear twin?" Carlo sounded sad and hurt. Tammo put back his shoulders, like a guardsman.

"No." He was a citizen, a man of the world. Why should anything shock him?

"You would not be shocked if you knew him. He was a cruel, violent drunkard. If he lives still, I hope never to meet him again."

"Did he hurt you?" The anger that had begun to build

welled up again. If anyone had laid hands on Carlo, he would lay them out with his bare fists, father or no.

Carlo gave a mirthless laugh.

"Who do you think had me cut? He said it was necessary; that I was growing malformed ever since a pig attacked me when I was an infant. But he only said that after Signor Bernardi at the church had heard me sing. I don't know if he was telling the truth. My mother said he was, but..."

Tammo swallowed hard. He felt sick. He'd always thought that castrati had some kind of call from above, like nuns or priests. Not one they necessarily wanted to obey, but something that made their sacrifice somehow holy. Meaningful. He hadn't imagined that boys could be treated cruelly by their own families. By their own fathers. The world was cruel. Boys were cruel. Family was...refuge.

"He cut you himself?" Tammo said.

Carlo gave a short shake of the head.

"He took me to the barber-surgeon. To a horrible room at the back. It smelled of... No, I can't say." Carlo shuddered.

Tammo scrabbled in the dark for Carlo's hand and held onto it.

"The surgeon put his fingers on my neck. Two fingers. He kept on pressing and pressing. I thought I was going to die, Tamino. Everything went white and swirly. Like fog."

"Then what?"

He had to know now. It was foul, and it made his blood boil that anyone could do such a thing to Carlo, but he had to know.

"I woke up thinking I was in the midst of some dreadful nightmare. I was in a bath of ice, Tamino. Great chunks of ice were floating about me. The water was pink. And the pain, Tamino. The cold and the pain..."

There were tears in his voice now. Tammo could hear him sniffling and fumbling for a handkerchief. This merry, caring boy. His friend. Subjected to such awful torture. Without a second thought, Tammo put both arms round Carlo and held on tight. The eunuch sobbed and shivered in his arms. Tammo stared at the portrait of the Archangel and held on grimly until the sobbing ended. Hang what anyone would think who saw him! There was no going back to the days before. He and Carlo were each other's family now. Together, they would shield each other from the ice and the fire. Nothing would separate them. He'd vowed it to Michael himself, and no one called a Capell a liar.

Carlo sat up and started blowing his nose. Tammo released him, his arms feeling strangely cold without his friend inside them. Carlo turned towards him, a shaky smile lighting up his cherubic features.

"By the way, what were your sisters' names," he said.

"Maria and Angela." The words hung in the air: a long-lost confession. "Did you have brothers or sisters?" he said to Carlo.

Carlo lowered his gaze.

"Yes. But I no longer remember their names."

Part II

10. Epiphany at the Pagenos'

A carriage arrived at the porter's gate at six by the clock on the Feast of Epiphany. It was deep blue and drawn by two bay horses. Tammo stared in awe as they snorted and pawed the cobbles. He'd never ridden in a carriage in his life. The feeling of power and speed must be tremendous! There was no fog tonight, only glittering frost and stars. The cobbles sparkled like they'd been strewn with silver dust. Well, he was going to see plenty of silver before the night was out. Tammo made up his mind now that he would not be over-awed. He would pretend silver and gold were as common as trees and water. No one was going to catch him off his guard.

Two years had passed since that night of secrets in the chapel. Two years of catching birds in Angel's Wood. Two years of returning to the Cage of Nightingales, which felt more and more like a prison every time. Carlo tried to encourage him with dreams of the life they would share on graduation—an apartment by the opera house, good food, cages of singing birds. But Tammo was done with the city. Walls stifled him. His body was surging with humours a eunuch couldn't understand. Sooner or later, he would have to break free.

The porter came out and began scattering straw so the

horses wouldn't slip. Tammo adjusted the straps of the birdcages hanging from each of his shoulders. He'd been given velvet cloth to cover them with, and the birds within were eerily quiet. From the roof of the potter's house, Coronis gave a sharp caw.

"Not tonight," hissed Tammo, turning his head in its direction. "You stay where you are if you don't want to end up in a pie."

A muffled laugh rose up beside him. Tammo had to assume that Carlo was somewhere underneath the exuberance of scarves and shawls to be seen. There was no mistaking the figure of a eunuch. In the past two years, Carlo had grown until he now towered over Tammo. His chest was becoming a barrel, made to contain the finest pair of lungs in the Conservatorio Archangeli.

A footman leapt off the plate at the back of the carriage and opened the door. Carlo was ushered inside by a coughing Rubin.

"You next," said the footman. "I'll take those," he said, making to store Tammo's bird cages under the driver's seat.

"No, no!" a voice bellowed from inside the carriage. "Put the birds in here with me and the boy up with the driver. And be quick about it! It's like the steppes of Tartary in here with that door open."

"Maestro."

The footman dispatched the birds and gave Tammo a leg up to the driver's seat. Tammo had never been up so high, except in a tree. You could look down on the world from here! It was like being a king, an emperor. The driver cracked his whip and the horses set off walking. Tammo could see the muscles in their backs, moving in tandem. They snorted out steam, the bells on their harness jingling. The carriage bumped over the cobbles.

"Easy now," said the driver.

They were heading towards St Michael's Square. Tammo could hear music and see the lighted torches of revellers. Carnival would go on until dawn tonight. Tammo wondered if Maestro Sarastro might allow Carlo to raise the blind and look out the window. It would do him good to have just a little peep. However luxurious a great man's banquet, it couldn't compare to the thrill and festivity of Carnival on the open streets. What could?

The wind flew in Tammo's face. The driver's whip cracked; horseshoes sparked on the cobbles. They were leaving the cathedral precincts behind now, crossing the river at St. Seraphiel's Bridge. Tammo could see the gold and marble magnificence of the Ducal Palace at his left-hand side. They were coming to a part of the city Tammo didn't know. Away from the cheerful chaos of the old town, this was a modern artist's fantasy of tree-lined avenues, gardens, and huge, imposing facades. Great palaces of houses put forth belvedere towers, loggias, and balconies wherever you looked. Torches burned at regular intervals along the walls, lending the streets a theatrical brightness. Smart carriages and well-groomed horses drove past, alternating with laden carts and torch-bearing boys. The carriage drew up opposite a mansion rising three storeys high in burnt umber, with white floral decoration round the windows. A golden pheasant spread its wings above a portico engraved with classical scenes. Maestro Sarastro's footman leapt down to open the carriage door and let down the steps. At a nod from the driver, Tammo began to clamber down too.

"Give the boy his birds."

Maestro Sarastro's collar was turned up to cover half his face, his hat pulled down over his eyes. He peered through the space that remained with the look of a hunting hawk.

"Round the back, boy! Report to the major-domo. Ah, Pompey, my good man. Will you be so good as to take Master Bianci's things from my man there?" Another hawk-like glare at Tammo. "Well, what are you waiting for, boy? Do you want those birds to freeze to death?"

A red-nosed gatekeeper let Tammo into a courtyard with a well at the centre, overlooked by stables, coach houses and buildings of that sort. The kitchen door opened, causing heat and the flavour of roast goose to surge out. A maid came running out, a silver tray in hand. She was even shorter than Tammo but looked a little older and certainly stouter. She was the sort one more often saw at Carnival than elsewhere— all head and torso, and not much in the way of legs—although Tammo wouldn't have said so to her face. She looked the type who could turn a tray to a handy buckler should the need arise, and be none too gentle with it.

"Hoi! You forgot this!" she called after a footman.

"Excuse me. God save you." Tammo trotted out from the shadows and ran after her. "I need to report to the major-domo with these birds. Do you know where I can find him?"

The girl gave a screech and turned on Tammo with a

look of fury. "Don't you ever do that to me again! I could have dropped this tray of oysters and then where would I be? Out on the street, that's where, and just when I nearly got my promotion. Who in Michael's bootstraps are you anyway?"

Tammo could feel a blush rising to the roots of his hair.

"I...er...I have to report to the major-domo with these birds." Tammo lifted the flap of the cage. "I have to make than fly from behind a screen when Carlo—I mean Master Bianci—sings." He tapped the flute, which hung in a pouch at his hip. "I'm a bird-charmer. Well, sort of."

The maid looked at the birds with interest, while skilfully balancing the tray.

"Sweet little things! But it's the rehearsal room you want. Signor Plattini won't have time for you on a night like this. And you still haven't told me your name."

"Tam...er...Tammo Capell." Tammo blushed.

"Shy one, aren't you? We'll soon coax you out of that; don't you worry, Tammo Capell." She gave a smile that made parts of Tammo feel distinctly odd. "Come on, then. You stick with Fenice. I'll make sure your little birdies don't get cold."

Count Pageno's resident musicians were all clad in salmon pink, with lace and powder aplenty. They gave Tammo the unfortunate impression of an overdressed fish dish. There were five of them, all warming up with scales and dexterity exercises on a variety of instruments—recorders, flutes, viols of different sizes. He was pleased to note, however, that none of them compared with the dark flute. He tapped his hip again, reassuring himself of its presence. For a New Year gift, Maestro Aquila had given him a special leather case, like the sheath of a stiletto, which fastened to his belt, to keep it safe when he went abroad with it. Not that he would ever let any harm come to it, case, or no. The flute was part of him now. Nothing was going to separate him from it.

"What's this?" One of the musicians loosened his touch on the harp strings and jerked his head in Tammo's direction. "*Commedia dell'Arte* eat in the courtyard. Or did his pretty face drive it from your mind? Hey, Longshanks?"

Fenice gave him a look worthy of an Amazon.

"Does he look like *Commedia* to you? He's with the maestro."

The musician barked a laugh, then scowled. One of the other overdressed salmon passed him a cup of something that steamed.

"A brave soloist he'd make! Why isn't he dining with the maestro and all his *primo* singers, then?"

Fenice whipped the velvet cloths from Tammo's cages.

"These are the singers, you lackwit! Do you think his lordship wants them pecking on his table? They'll stay here until it's time for them to perform, and their tamer will stay with them. Would they like some birdseed brought, young citizen?" She turned to Tammo with a smile he was sure was intended to make him blush again. He lowered his gaze.

"Thank you. And maybe a little water."

"Well, hark at him now!" One of the salmons sniggered. "Such a face, and a voice to match. What do they call you, boy? Apollo?"

"Ignore him." Fenice hissed. "May I take your empty plates from you, gentlemen?" She wove her way between the music stands. Tammo watched with a mixture of awe and horror as pieces of bread, whole pilchards and slices of goat's cheese were tipped as scraps from one plate to the next.

"They're ready for you in the great ballroom now."

An Afric-featured footman stood like an idol in the doorway. The musicians hastily gathered their instruments and papers. Four more footmen came and carried off extra instruments and stands. How many people worked here, Tammo wondered? Did his lordship keep a limitless army of maroon footmen about him, summoning them through the floor by magic whenever another task needed doing?

"Here." A prod on his backside made Tammo flinch. "Take this and don't tell anyone."

Fenice pushed the plate of scraps into his hand behind his back.

"Ah, Pompey, you stud," she said, turning to the footman. "Where were you last night when poor Fenice was waiting?"

"Wait again tonight and you'll find out," said Pompey, in the deepest bass Tammo had ever heard. "You little vixen."

Tammo didn't look to see where the footman put his hand next, but from Fenice's squeals, it certainly wasn't the door handle.

The fish and cheese were delicious, and the fireside was warm. Once he was alone, Tammo dared sit in a chair to keep the draughts from his back, although he didn't quite have the courage to do more than balance his nether regions on the part nearest the fire. Fenice returned at one point with birdseed and water. She cooed to the birds, especially the pretty orioles, and asked Tammo if they had names.

"They're not even mine," he said with a shake of his head. "By rights they belong to the maestro. Say, is Carl...Master Bianci truly eating with other soloists?"

Fenice put her hands on her ample hips.

"Only Morestelli and La Bellina! You don't know much, do you, Tammo Capell? The maestro and his singers are always served in the small library on feast nights."

Morestelli and La Bellina! Carlo would be in the seventh heaven! Tammo hoped it didn't put him off his song.

"What about the opera?" He scowled. "Won't they miss their primo acts?"

Fenice swept up birdseed with her apron.

"They'll put on the ballet and the lesser serenata. Anyone who's anyone will be here tonight. You really are green." She sashayed past him and smiled mischievously. "You know the young mistress's angel-boy. He's a little sweetheart, isn't he?"

"Don't know who you mean," said Tammo through a mouthful of goat's cheese.

"Why are you so bothered who he dines with, then?" She took a piece of cheese and sucked it from her finger before hip-swaying out the door.

Tammo pushed the cheese away from him after she had gone. The young mistress's angel-boy? He'd remember that one for Carlo later. What was she like, he wondered? This Noblesse Celestina. Might he catch a glimpse of her after all? Did nobles allow their children to balls and banquets? He didn't know. Maybe he would see her going past with a nurse. He pictured her in the firelight: a pale, sickly child hugging a doll to her chest, ringing a bell for Carlo to feed her sweetmeats and catch her escaping monkey. What on earth could his eunuch friend possibly see in her? Sometimes Carlo was simply impossible to understand.

A log cracked. Tammo realised with a jerk he had been dozing. The footman Pompey stood at his shoulder, waiting.

"Gather your birds," Pompey said. "The maestro needs you below."

Tammo had never seen such a chamber as Count Pageno's music room. He hovered by a curtain at the room's entrance, a hand on each birdcage for comfort. It looked nothing like he had imagined from Carlo's descriptions. Every candelabra in every wall sconce was lit, making the mirrors dance with a myriad lights. A great chandelier, wrought to look like forest flowers, shone down from the ceiling. The lid of the harpsichord was thrown open, revealing a dramatic landscape of a castle by the sea and soldiers approaching on horseback. Gilt-edged screens, similarly illustrated, had been set up at points to keep out draughts and—Tammo realised—to conceal him and his birds from public view.

"Don't just stand there cluttering up the place, boy!

Bring those birds over here this instant and stop gawking. This isn't a carnival sideshow."

Sarastro was sitting at the harpsichord, his brocade coat almost an exact match for the curtains behind him. His sleeves foamed with lace. His shoe buckles shone with intimidating brilliance. A man paced the alcove behind the maestro, humming something that sounded like "Me, me, me, ma, ma, ma." He wore shoes of blue and green cloth tied with ribbons. He was incredibly tall, with a wig like lamb's wool and a beauty spot on his left cheek. He walked like an emperor on parade. That had to be Morestelli. And he supposed the woman with the tight waist and a row of bows down her dress, surreptitiously checking her appearance in the mirror, must be La Bellina. Tammo had to admit that he'd expected her to be more "bella" than that. She was squat and sallow with a masculine chin, hardly the stuff of sonnets. As Tammo watched, she grimaced and rubbed her front teeth with a finger.

"You look delightful, signorina," said a familiar voice.

Tammo gasped. He would hardly have recognised Carlo. He, too, had a lamb's wool wig, and was dressed in a suit of blue velvet lined with fur. It looked as if someone had made up his face as well. Tammo was sure his face had never been quite so pale, nor his lips so red. His friend looked as if he really did belong in another world now. Count Pageno's own tailor must have provided that outfit. At least Carlo would be warm, Tammo thought. There must be no thought of ice tonight.

"The birds, boy!" Maestro Sarastro snapped.

"Yes, maestro."

Tammo was relieved to get behind the screen after seeing Carlo dressed up like that. He himself had grown since September, and his school cassock was looking short in the sleeve and mossy. He wondered what sort of state his hair was in. He hurried toward the screen, avoiding the mirrors.

"Are you all right, Tamino," Carlo whispered under his breath. "Do you know what you have to do?"

"I think so." Tammo struggled to arrange the bird cages in convenient positions, while Morestelli paced up and down behind him like he didn't exist. "You start singing; I release them one at a time. Then I make some bird calls so they circle you and eventually come back."

"Did I give you leave to speak to the singers, boy?" Maestro Sarastro's voice boomed from the harpsichord. "Out of sight, out of hearing, except for your flute. If Count Pageno's guests see so much as a toe, you shall feel the consequences of it in the morning.

Carlo leaned in where no one else could see and pulled a face that strongly resembled the maestro. Tammo suppressed a giggle.

"Carlo Bianci. Are you warming up?" Honestly, did Sarastro leave no one in peace?

Carlo bowed and began with the same sort of *me, ma-ing* as Morestelli. Meanwhile, experienced castrato plucked a cut crystal vial from his waistcoat and took the tiniest sip from it. He raised the vial to Carlo.

"Good fortune, son."

From where Tammo squatted, it looked as though Carlo would burst with pride. But what Carlo didn't see was the look on the two adult singers' faces at that point. It looked something like jealousy.

Tammo's fingers trembled as he gently stroked the last nightingale and fastened the cage door. The last chord on the harpsichord faded and the guests applauded.

Tammo heard the voice of one elderly, and presumably deaf, lady say loudly, "I must say, that's the first time I've seen birds fly back. I remember one season at the Teatro. They released a flock of doves every night, and never caught them all. There were doves fluttering everywhere for weeks. The seats in my box have never cleaned up properly since."

Tammo smiled to himself. The stagehands at the Teatro had never possessed the dark flute! Tonight, he and Carlo had performed what the showman at the fish market had only pretended to do. He was sure Angelio had never known such a recital. Only friendship and the Archangel could do this.

Morestelli had begun to sing now. He was standing in that heroic pose Carlo had demonstrated in the dormitory. One arm was extended out before him, one leg bent slightly, as if he was about to step forward. With surprise, Tammo noted that not all the guests were attentive to the castrato's song. Two ladies were making suggestive movements across the room with fans. One man was taking snuff; another was actually asleep in his chair.

A man dressed soberly in an expensive cut of grey had a hand on Carlo's shoulder. He heard the words, "Master Bianci," spoken, and Carlo made a bow. A pregnant lady by the man's side, also in grey, did not seem to be enjoying the concert at all. In fact, her face looked thoroughly disapproving, and she glared at Carlo in a way that made Tammo's stomach turn.

When Morestelli had finished, La Bellina sang. Then they sang a duet together. Then one of the guests got up to play the harp. Tammo's legs and bottom became sore as he tried to sit comfortably in the cramped space. He couldn't see Carlo any more. Where had his friend gone? Tammo wished he knew what he was supposed to do now. Maestro Sarastro was drinking and chatting with Morestelli and another man. Two o'clock, he had told the coachman. Surely, he didn't expect Tammo to squat behind a screen the whole time?

"Oi!"

Someone poked Tammo in the back, almost making him knock the screen down. He jerked his head round. A door that had previously been disguised as part of the wall had opened a crack. Fenice, the maid, was glaring through it.

"Through here. Sharp! Leave the birds, lackwit," she added when Tammo made to pick up the cages.

"Why? What is it?" Tammo's voice was no more than a dry rasp as he struggled to squeeze through the gap without being heard or seen.

"Someone wants to meet you. That's what."

Fenice turned her back and began hip-walking as briskly as her short legs allowed. Tammo looked about him before following at a pace to match. They strode through a gallery, watched by the eyes of ten score gods, heroes, saints, and wood nymphs. Then through the vast marble expanse of ballroom, where footmen were snuffing candles, yawning, and exchanging jokes as they worked. At the other end, a door opened into a library, a long room lined with bookcases, all full of matching volumes of gilt leather. Only a couple of candelabra were lit in here. A round table still held empty glasses and decanters, the remains of Maestro Sarastro's dinner. Marble busts of Pageno ancestors cast shadowy glances from high above a glowing fireplace.

A sound of giggling and whispering from the far end of the room caught Tammo's attention. There was Carlo! He was leaning over to say something to what looked like a very small person sitting on a lacquered box. Both of them held sequinned eye masks to their faces and burst into laughter at every other word. A stab of jealousy piqued Tammo's vitals. Carlo had spoken of the noblesse many times over the past two years, but Tammo had always considered their friendship a sort of joke. He teased Carlo about dressing dollies and exchanging hair ribbons with his playmate. Now it struck him that there was a serious rival for Carlo's affections. What if Carlo preferred the little noblesse to dull, old Tammo? What if, when schooldays were over, Carlo dropped Tammo altogether for a friend more suited to his new social circle?

"Noblesse Celestina." Fenice's voice recalled Tammo to himself. "I've brought Tammo Capell like you asked, noblesse."

"Tammo!" A voice that, to Tammo's ears, sounded like silver bells rang across the room. The person on the box had put down her mask and was leaning forward. "Oh, Angel-boy, he's just like you said! Come closer, Tammo, so I can see you."

"Well, step up then, sluggard!" Fenice hissed, when Tammo hesitated.

For some reason, his feet seemed to have grown heavy. The wall candles only cast a flickering light, but Tammo could see the noblesse a little more clearly now. A dainty figure—a sylph, a dryad—sitting ramrod-straight in the fantastical house carriage Carlo had described. A shimmering grey dress and a grey ribbon round her neck to match. And the face! Tammo couldn't take his eyes off that face. The sweet lips, the arch of the eyebrows, the look of spirited queenliness. Tammo felt himself growing warm all over. It was a bit like when he faced Paolo in the courtyard, only it wasn't. He wanted to run fast, to kill giants, to scale impossible mountains. He wanted to flee this library as quickly as possible, and he wanted to stay forever.

"Noblesse Celestina." He forced out a croak.

"Tammo Capell. At last," the vision said.

She smiled. In that moment, Tammo knew that smile was just for him. And that his heart belonged to Celestina always.

11. To Fly the Cage

"You've changed your tune, oh Master of Birdsong. I do believe springtide has come early."

Carlo tweaked his twin's hair. It had grown longer over the past weeks and was bristling out in all directions. The housemasters were less keen with the scissors during the winter months, allowing the boys a little natural protection against the cold. Anything to save on fuel, Carlo assumed.

"Not one mention of dollies, nor of needlework. Do I take it that your encounter with the noblesse finally showed you the error of your ways?" He raised an eyebrow, slyly.

Tammo picked at a scab on his knuckle. The tips of his ears had gone scarlet.

"She's a nice girl. That's all I said." There was an edge to his croak that said *stay away*, but Carlo couldn't resist the chance to tease a little.

"So, you bow to my superior judgment, Tamino?"

"I said it, didn't I?" Tammo twitched and shuffled.

"So, you admit I was right?"

"Leave it out, Carlo!"

"The Cavalier Marchesi was very impressed with your performance at the Pageno mansion," he said, with a sideways glance.

"I told you Carlo: that's not what I... Hold on. How did he know it was me?"

Carlo laughed, a stream of silver bubbles. "Oh, Tamino! You walk into the snare every time." He reached over and patted Tammo's scabbed hand. "I suppose the nightingales have gone to market now?"

Tammo gave an affirmative sniff.

"Maestro Sarastro will be wanting you for the opera next," Carlo said.

Tammo turned around with a scowl.

"What do you mean?"

Carlo returned his hands primly to his lap.

"It's not everyone who can return birds to their cage once they've been released. Just imagine the scene, Tamino. Flocks of white doves released into the auditorium of the Teatro as the primo castrato is freed from his golden chains. They swell to the roof with his song, then fly back to roost in the safety of the wings, as the audience gasp and throw roses. And there you are behind the curtain, the dark flute at your lips, directing the whole spectacle."

"No thanks," Tammo growled. "You can sing in golden chains if you like. I'm going to make my music in the free air."

Carlo lowered his eyes and swallowed. Golden chains. That was exactly what life had in store for him. He would forever be a nightingale returning to its cage, a glamourous prisoner singing in golden chains. Tammo could choose such thoughtless words sometimes. Words that set him bleeding in parts no one could see.

"Besides, you're the one they'll want for the opera."

Tammo went on, regardless of Carlo's sudden withdrawal. "You said Morestelli was keen, didn't you?

"Mmm." Carlo willed a smile to his features. "He told Maestro Sarastro I ought to have a small part as Victory in *Hercules*. He said I have a heroic throat."

Tammo snorted. "What in a cherub's eye is that supposed to mean?"

Carlo shook his head. "I don't know. Anyway, Maestro Sarastro and the rector never agree over the opera. They're meant to be discussing it today. Pray that the rector says yes, Tamino. Just one glimpse of Carnival, that's all I want. I'll study like a slave for the next two years if I can have one week in the Teatro."

"And what of the rest?" said Tammo. "The automata and the acrobats and the coloured fountains?"

There was that pain again. The golden chains. The price of success. Of never being an ordinary boy. Carlo closed his eyes and put a hand to his temple.

"Don't tempt me, Tamino. There are times when I think I would sell my own voice for a night of Carnival."

Rays of winter sunlight shone coldly on the coloured marble of the Pageno chapel. Count Pageno liked to hear mass early in the morning. Candles and incense did not suffice to warm the room, and Carlo's breath came out in clouds as he sang.

The whole of Count Pageno's household was present for mass, as ever. Household staff were ranked around the walls, in strict order of precedence. Carlo had been secretly informed by Celestina that the day he came to sing for them was the highlight of their week. Whether this was true or not, Carlo didn't know. It was a embarrassing question to contemplate.

The part Carlo looked forward to most was breakfast with Celestina in the music room. The coffee and white rolls. Celestina's deft touch with the sugar tongs. And the conversation. Ah! After a week of hearing nothing but boys and maestri, how refreshing that was!

Today there was apricot jam in a china dish, and a jug of fresh cream. Celestina filled Carlo's coffee dish with a flourish, swirling the cream into a spiral that slowly disintegrated. Her governess sat in a nearby alcove, sewing silently. Pompey was a silent statue by the door, waiting to lift his little mistress at a moment's notice. Carlo did his best to pretend they weren't watching. A servant saw nothing until you told him to. Celestina had taught Carlo that on his second visit.

"There you go, Angel-boy." Celestina held out the dish and smiled. "Your nose is pink. Better drink up and get warm."

"Thank you, noblesse." Carlo took the dish between finger and thumb and sipped with a delicate turn of the wrist. "No Giacomo this morning?" He couldn't say he was sorry about that. The monkey was the only thing in the Pageno house that Carlo did not like.

Celestina leaned forward, confidentially. "He's in disgrace. He bit the mother superior when she came to give me Scripture lessons. On the bottom!" She giggled.

Carlo glanced at the governess and smoothed over a smile. "And how are Carlino and Carlotta?"

"Carlotta has been a little sick, but she seems better this morning. She can draw up her pail ever so quickly now. You should see her. And Carlino ate from my hand yesterday."

"I'm pleased to hear it," said Carlo.

Carlino and Carlotta were two goldfinches that Celestina had been given for a New Year's gift. They lived in a cage that resembled a palace, with turrets and a front door done in gold scrollwork, and they had a trick of pulling up a tiny gold pail on a chain to get at their drinking water. Carlo was unsure whether to be flattered or embarrassed that Celestina had named the birds after him.

"Oh, but I'm so glad you are come, Carlo," Celestina went on. "It's terribly dull here since Mama went into her confinement."

"Confinement?" For a moment, Carlo imagined the Countess in prison.

"For the baby, of course." Celestina threw Carlo a look of exasperation. "Don't boys know anything? She has to stay in bed until the baby comes, and of course Papa is dreadfully worried, and all the servants are creeping around telling me to hush all the time. And now even Giacomo has gone away."

She pouted. Carlo felt a stab of pity. She looked so small and lonely. He reached out his hand.

"And how are you, noblesse?" he said gently.

Celestina blinked hard and swallowed. When her voice came out, it was barely a whisper. "I miss Orlando."

Carlo nodded. "We pray for him every day at the conservatorio."

Celestina looked into the coffee dish and said nothing.

"And I hope I can always serve as a friend to you. Along with my dear twin, Tamino. I'm so glad you could make his acquaintance the other day."

A faint smile returned to Celestina's lips.

"He's not much like you, Angel-boy."

"He is a true Angelian. The salt of the earth. I hope we may all meet again very soon."

"At Carnival!" Celestina clapped her hands.

Carlo sighed. "I told you, noblesse. The eunuch class is forbidden to attend Carnival. But you may see me at the opera. Signor Morestelli has recommended me for a part in *Hercules.*"

"Then I shall tell Papa to make sure you get it." She took a sip of coffee as if that settled the matter. "But couldn't you go to Carnival just once? On St. Michael of Justice they have an orchestra with fireworks that go right over the river. Last year, they looked like flowers in all different colours, and the year before that they had flying angels and a dragon. It was so pretty. Couldn't you go even if I asked Papa to speak to the rector?"

"I think your Papa has other things on his mind," Carlo reminded Celestina. "And, no, I don't think the rector will change his mind. It's a school rule. Besides, I don't have time for Carnival. I need to study and rehearse. And if I get the part in the opera, I'll be working even harder." He put a spoonful of jam on his bread roll.

Funny, though, thought Carlo, as Celestina moved

onto the topic of an automaton in the form of a fashionable lady that could play eight different tunes on the dulcimer. St Michael of Justice was the night on which Carlo had been born. That date would be his sixteenth birthday.

"Who's a lucky boy, then?" Giuseppe nudged Carlo in the ribs as the eunuch class made their way from the rehearsal room to the joys of classical poetry.

"You sound like a parrot, Giuseppe." Giovanni twisted his ringlet round his little finger with a languid sigh.

"You sing like a parrot, Giovanni." The florid boy glared back.

"And soon I shall look like a parrot, so we shall all be equal," said Carlo.

He hugged the manuscript to his chest with pride. Written across the top sheet in Maestro Sarastro's dashing hand were the words: *Recitative della Vittoria.* The recitative of Victory. He had the part. He had been cast as the allegorical figure in *Hercules*, singing the lines that would open the entire opera. And—more miraculous still—Rector Bartolomeo had allowed the engagement. Carlo was to perform in front of the Duke himself.

"Thank you, Archangel," Carlo whispered.

Celestina had done this. He was certain that was what had made the difference. Celestina and her winning ways. It was happening at last. He was going to the Teatro.

"I can't wait to see him," said Giuseppe with a grin. "Just imagine how pretty he'll look in his girl's clothes. I hope they give you a golden wig." He leered at Carlo.

"Don't forget to make the most of your cleavage," said Giovanni, with a flutter of eyelashes.

Carlo looked down at his chest, his cheeks reddening.

"I don't have one," he managed to say. Would that count against him? Would the manager of the Duke's theatre complain that Maestro Sarastro's choice didn't look sufficiently buxom? He fanned himself with the manuscript paper and tried to think of other things.

"Marco wouldn't have had that problem." Giuseppe guffawed.

Marco and Francesco had graduated last summer, and Giuseppe and Giovanni had taken their place as prefects. They were now the senior students, and yet it was Carlo who had been offered a part in the opera.

"You make it hard on all of us, Nightingale." Giovanni said that night in the dorm. "Some of us have been working day and night for years, and then you just open your mouth and make us sound like ravens." He held up his hand. "Yes, I know you don't mean to. And I know you work as well. But the rest of us have to make a living too. I graduate in two terms and I haven't even found a decent patron yet."

"I'm sorry, Giovanni." Why did it always come to this? Friendship turned to rivalry and competition. It made his stomach hurt. "I believe it was Signor Morestelli's suggestion. I could speak to him for you."

Giovanni stretched out on the bed and cupped his alabaster cheek in his hand. On the next bed, Giuseppe was shuffling a pack of cards. Luca and Antonio—no longer the infants they had been—were begging to be dealt in with the bigger boys, while the latest recruit, sparrow-limbed Dante, was clutching a pine cone doll to his chest with wide-eyed fervour.

Giovanni sighed.

"I wouldn't waste your breath, darling. There's only one Nightingale around here, and it's not any of us."

Carlo opened the mesh door of the cage, hardly daring to breathe. His hand trembled slightly as he held it flat, the brown crumbs tickling his palm.

"Come on, Orpheus," he cooed. "It's your favourite."

Orpheus cocked his glossy head, looking at Carlo with one eye. He shivered his wings, a flurry of nutmeg and cream. His voice sounded, stilted and shrill.

"Take your time, Carlo," Tammo whispered in his ear.

Orpheus' head cocked toward Tammo, then back to Carlo again. Carlo pursed his lips in silent urging. He was going to come. He was.

With a musical twitter, Orpheus hopped from the cage to curl his tiny talons around Carlo's finger. His pecks at the crumbs made Carlo want to wriggle and laugh. He stretched out his fingers flatter and breathed deeply.

"Now then, lads." The porter came down the shallow steps from his desk by the open hatch into the tiny parlour, trying to find a place for his hands under the tails of his shabby greatcoat. A red muffler round his neck trailed about his knees and added to the general tangle. A tiny fire in a tiny grate did little to keep out the damp mist. Carlo felt deeply grateful for his school cloak and seat by the hearth. The porter scratched his head against the lie of his hair, making it burst free of its leather thong and stand up on his head like a brush.

"Don't you be troubling that there bird," the porter said. "Any harm to him and it would be more than my life's worth with the maestro." He stretched a grubby finger toward Orpheus, who scolded and flapped his wings. Carlo shielded him with a hand and returned him gently to the cage. Tammo fastened the door behind him. "You know, I shouldn't even be letting you boys in here together. Don't you have lessons to be about?"

"It's recreation," said Tammo, gruffly.

Carlo turned on the brush-haired porter with a smile that would have melted stone.

"Besides, it's an honour for you to entertain a darling of the Teatro di Palazzo. You are looking at the figure of Victory herself. You may kiss my hand if you like." He held out a white hand.

Tammo snorted.

"That's all right, Master Carlo." The porter fumbled in more pockets than it was likely the greatcoat possessed. "I'm sure you'll be a great success without the likes of me kissing your hand. Nobiles and marchesas and Lord-knows-who will be lining up, I'll warrant. You won't have time for old Pascual then."

"I shall have all the time in the world for you," Carlo assured him. "And for darling Orpheus." He twittered at the bird.

"You'll be lucky if you have time to use the close-stool," Tammo said under his breath.

Carlo cast a rebuking glance at his friend. He knew

Tamino was proud of him really. It had been there in his eyes when Carlo had told him he'd got the part.

"Tamino..."

Carlo glanced back to make sure the porter wasn't listening, but their host had decided constant vigilance against crows was the order of the day, and was scowling out of the hatch, keys in hand.

"Tamino, I need to ask you something."

Tammo took his hands away from his head and looked up.

"I want to go to Carnival. On Justice Night. Can you get me out?"

"What?" Tammo looked at him as though he'd just asked for a unicorn's tongue.

"I want to go. Before I have to start at the Teatro, and it all gets too busy. I want to spend the night with you." He blushed. "It will be my sixteenth birthday."

"You want to go to Carnival at night?" Tammo still had the "unicorn's tongue" look on his face. "Carlo, that's insanity. You think no one is going to notice you've gone? What if someone recognises you?"

"I'll wear a mask."

"And you shouldn't be out in the night air. What about your voice?"

Carlo frowned. "I thought we were best friends. I thought you would want to go with me."

Tammo scratched his neck and pulled at the bands.

"I do. I am. I can get you out as easy as that." He snapped his fingers. "But you've never even broken one school rule before, Carlo. What if you change your mind at the last minute?"

Carlo huffed out a sigh.

"How long have I wanted this, Tamino? How hard have I worked? Surely no one will begrudge me one night of freedom. Celestina says it's one of the most magical nights of Carnival. Allegorical displays. Orchestras on the river. Don't you think I should see it just once?"

"Celestina?" Tammo's face immediately changed. "Will she be there?"

"In her family's barge. Provided all goes well with the countess. Oh, imagine it, Tamino! The lights, the music..." He pulled at Tammo's sleeve.

"And do these barges dock?" Tammo's mind seemed to be on other things.

"All barges dock, Tamino. Oh, just think," he said, a delightful thought striking him. "We could go to the waterfront and see her. You, me, and Celestina. Wouldn't that be marvellous?"

"Marvellous," Tammo agreed. He coughed and cleared his throat. "All right, Carlo, we'll do it. St. Michael of Justice. For one night, the songbird flies the cage."

Orpheus shivered his wings and twittered in agreement.

"I have a new brother, Angel-boy. His name is Rinaldo."

Celestina made the announcement as calmly as if she had been reciting instructive verse. Giacomo ran up her arm and curled his tail about her neck. She raised a hand and moved it to her back.

"I know, noblesse. Was not mass this morning a celebration of his safe arrival?"

"Oh, of course. How silly of me! But you know so much, Carlo. You're far cleverer than I am."

"Nonsense." Carlo took Celestina's tiny white hand and kissed it. Giacomo gave a jealous chitter. "Although, I do know one thing. But it is a great secret. You must promise not to tell."

"A secret!" Celestina clapped her hands. "How delightful." She looked round at Pompey and the governess, then opened a fan to shield her face.

"Let's go into the cabinet of curiosities. Then we can speak freely." Her eyes sparkled with excitement.

"And our chaperones…?" Carlo also had one eye on the governess. She looked to be busy threading a needle, but you could never tell.

"Fie on them!" Celestina said in a whisper. "They made me kiss Rinaldo this morning, although he is red and wrinkly and not a jot as pretty as Orlando. And when Mama asked if I did not love him more than anything in the world, I said I was sure I would love him one day, if only he would leave off crying so much. So Mama told Teresa to spank me on the hand. And it hurt, Carlo." She held out her palm. Carlo bent over it and nodded sympathetically, although there was no mark to be seen. "So I told Mama that I liked you better than Rinaldo; and she said it was neglectful of Papa to give favour to a gelding when he had his son and heir to consider, which was a cruel, horrid thing to say. So,

I don't care what they think now." She suddenly put her hand to her mouth. "I didn't mean to say the gelding part."

The cabinet of curiosities was a tiny chamber off the billiard room, barely Large enough to accommodate Celestina's house carriage and Carlo standing up. But what it lacked in size, it made up for in fascination. From the black-and-white tiled floor to the panelled ceiling, every inch of it was shelf upon ornate shelf of wonders. Mounted birds and animals, foreign clothes and weapons, forks of coral, goblets of shell. Miniature worlds under glass, so dainty it was inconceivable they were formed by human hand. Giant teeth so monstrous it terrified Carlo to imagine what creature might have bitten with them.

"Look, Angel-boy!" Celestina said. "A perspective viewer. It shows the Passion, very lifelike and affective. It's just as if you're there."

"Indeed?" said Carlo.

His attention had been attracted by a piece of quartz, as big as his fist. How had such a thing been prized from the earth, and how did anyone know it was there to find?

"And just by your hand is the sandal of St. Sebastian."

Carlo stepped back and crossed himself, for fear of disturbing more holy relics. He clasped his hands behind his back, just in case.

"Perhaps now we can discuss our secret, Noblesse Celestina?"

Celestina put down a shrivelled, green thing labelled *mermaid's hand*, and beamed up at Carlo.

"Our secret, of course! Do tell!"

"Well..." Carlo felt the faintest spots of a blush begin

on each of his cheeks. "I am to visit Carnival. In secret."

"Travelling incognito? How thrilling!" Celestina fluttered a fan on a level with her throat. Giacomo removed his tail from around her neck with an angry chitter.

"Yes, but you must keep this absolutely private." Could the little noblesse keep herself from chattering until St. Michael of Justice? Carlo hoped he was doing the right thing in trusting her. "Tamino, my beloved twin..." He felt his blush deepen. "Tamino is helping me escape the conservatorio on Justice Night. We are to go masked and enjoy all the delights of the city. Fireworks, music, street players...everything!"

"But that's wonderful, Carlo." Celestina seemed as excited as he was. "I do so long to see you cloaked and masked as a reveller. And shall you meet me? Please say you shall."

Should he meet her? Perhaps it would be best to stay away from the barges. And the dragons. And the flowers. And the heavenly music...

"Where do you disembark?" he heard himself say.

"We reach the Teatro at eight by the clock," said Celestina. "Will you be there?"

"We shall be on the Bridge of Glories," said Carlo. "Look out for us. But make no sign," he added, as Celestina began to squirm with delight. "None but our friends must recognise us. And tell no one."

Celestina pouted. "Who is there to tell? Apart from Teresa, and I'm never speaking to her again for what she did this morning. And Giacomo already knows. Don't you darling?" She caressed the monkey's ears. Carlo tried to stay well back in case the little creature decided to rebel against his mistress's affections. She gave a pretty little sigh, a dryad's sigh. "It's so lonely here, Carlo. I wish I could come with you."

Despite the monkey, Carlo came and leaned over the house carriage, laying his hand on Celestina's shoulder.

"You are always with me, dear noblesse. How could you ever suppose otherwise?"

He tickled her on the neck until she laughed. Giacomo slunk away to the mermaid's hand.

12. *Carnevale*

He had gone over the plan a hundred times. Evening walk for the main school began at five by the clock. Tammo would slip out of rank as soon as they reached the busier streets, and double back to the conservatorio. Carlo would be waiting under their tree. Tammo would help him into the branches and over the wall. They would keep under cover for a while, confusing their tracks to avoid detection. And then they would be free, alive, and running for the piazza under golden torchlight on one of the most magical nights in the calendar.

So where was he? Tammo chewed at his lip, his back to the tree, trying to pull his hat yet lower over his eyes. The eunuch had better not have let him down. Not on this night when Celestina was going to be out there. Celestina! Tammo's pulse quickened just at the thought of her name. He had thought of girls as a necessary evil before he met her, like the laundry girls with their incessant giggling and teasing words. Or as infants incapable of facing the world on their own, a handicap to serious activity. Now he wondered if the other girls he had seen were of the same progeny as Celestina. Her hair was so soft, her skin so white. Was it white all the way down, he wondered? He blushed furiously as urgent sensations made themselves known in his body. Celestina was a lady. Crude thoughts did not belong near her. And yet Tammo couldn't help but wonder just how her skin would feel under his fingers. Was it the same as other people's? It looked just like porcelain. How would it feel if he and not that Black footman was carrying the little noblesse in his arms?

"Tamino?"

Carlo's whisper brought Tammo back to reality with a jolt. He glared at the swathe of cloaks and shawls hurrying toward him through the thickening mist.

"Where have you been? Someone's going to see us if we hang about too long."

"Forgive me." Carlo's voice sounded muffled and a little softer than usual, as though he were trying to comfort himself. "I got away as quickly as I could. It took me a while to get everything from my trunk." He looked around at the mist and shivered. "It was finer weather last night."

"It can't be helped." Tammo took a firm hold of the lower branches, scouting for the best footholds. "Have you got the masks?"

"In my breast," said Carlo, tapping the place. "Do you want them now?"

"No. I've got to get you up this tree first. Come on, Carlo. Take hold here and see if you can swing yourself up to that fork."

He had never seen his friend's face light up the way it did under the torchlight of the acrobats. Even veiled by the glitter of the mask, Tammo could see the softer, wondering light in Carlo's eyes. He was like a little child. His body swayed with the rhythm of the drums and bells. His hands were clasped tight before him, rising at intervals to touch his lips, as if music might escape from his mouth and gavotte down the street. A painted performer in greaves and helmet, like the fins of a sea creature, leapt inside a man-sized cage, clanging a heavy bell. With a flourish, he swung himself round the bars and onto the cage's exterior, balancing on top with a gesture of bravura.

"*Voila!*" he exclaimed.

"*Bravo! Bravissimo!*"

Tammo thought Carlo was about to leap on the cage with him. He pulled his friend away, as a woman in a dress too low-cut for the weather came flirting round with a basket for coins. Carlo would never last the night if he wasted his money on the first thing he saw.

"Come on, Carlo. Let's see more."

"But see how he leaps, Tamino. Have you ever seen such a thing?"

The acrobat began to caper around the roof of the cage, clanging his bell, now high, now low. It was all too close to the torches for Tammo's taste.

"I see him," Tammo said. "But let's see some other things too. We only have one night."

He wanted to go to the Bridge of Glories now, straight away, even though he knew Celestina wouldn't be there for hours. He had to get there. He had to find the right spot where he could see her. Carlo had said they would only look down and signal with their hands, but anything could happen in a night. Tammo had heroic visions of her servant stumbling on the wharf side, of himself seeing from the bridge and running, pushing other people out of the way, diving to catch Celestina before she could be harmed. Then of dusting himself down and retreating into the crowd, while all the high-born and well-to-do revellers asked each other who the brave rescuer could have been and how he ought to be rewarded.

"Where shall we go?" Carlo gave a longing glance back at the acrobat.

"This way."

Tammo pulled at Carlo's sleeve. Carlo prized away the clinging fingers and linked his arm through the crook of Tammo's. They made for an uneven match in height, and Tammo might have minded the familiarity of it at another time. But in the mist and crowds it was all-important that Carlo not be lost. Even through the thickness of gloves and cloak, Tammo could feel how cold Carlo's hands were. He was still trembling.

"Are you cold, Carlo?" They could get some punch, some hot food.

"A little." Carlo drew closer.

"Well, then, let's go through the candlelit market."

One step nearer the river. One step closer to Celestina.

They got some spiced wine and a helping of fish stew in a kind of shell called angel wings. Carlo said the wine was watered, but Tammo could feel the burr in his chest, the warm fuzziness in his head. It made him feel bold and adventurous, a cavalier fit to rescue a noble lady. Around the market stalls, buyers leaned close with baskets on their arms to examine piles of winter vegetables. Tallow dripped from candlesticks onto the rinds of pumpkins. A mottled dog ran to and fro, sniffing and licking at table edges.

"Listen. Someone's singing down there," said Carlo.

It was hardly to be called singing compared with what Carlo could do, a rough and roisterous voice, closer in tone to Tammo's sad efforts. The words were scarcely cleaner and made Tammo want to blush and snigger. But the tune was merry, a dance that set feet tapping and hands clapping. Over the masks and hoods, Tammo could make out the flapping backdrop of a makeshift stage. A man in patchwork was juggling while another played a small guitar.

"Strolling players," said Tammo.

They wove their way through the crowd to get closer. A giant face on stilts loomed close, then wobbled away. A dog in cap and bells danced around on its hind legs, holding out a box for coins. Nearer the stage, revellers in the crowd were dancing, capering hand-to-hand, many with bottles in their hands. One well-made girl was being swung round and round by an apprentice, her hair billowing out behind her.

"They're certainly lively," said Carlo.

He was talking in that self-comforting voice again. Tammo wondered if the boisterous crowd frightened him. He remembered what Carlo had told him in the chapel of his violent father. Carlo's world nowadays was sedate, a world of books and vocal exercises, and coffee with Celestina. Did this crowd take him back to things he hated? They would be better off on the bridge.

"Do you like this?" he said to Carlo.

Carlo nodded, eyes on the stage. He was quiet tonight, unusually quiet. Often Tammo couldn't shut him up. The constant flow of teasing and witty banter from the eunuch wore him out. There was none of that now. Carlo was muted, unreadable behind the golden mask. Did music and theatre really mean so much to him?

The harlequin had now finished juggling and was engaged in a conversation with a character Tammo presumed was meant to be his master. Master and servant argued back and forth, as the servant tried to persuade the master into a ridiculous disguise in order to court his lady love. A cloak was brought out, then a mask with a great hooked nose, then a rolled-up bundle of cloth to give the master a humped back. The audience laughed and pointed and swigged on their bottles. The patchwork harlequin capered about, commenting on how well the master now resembled his rival in love.

"Tell him to give her one!" someone in the crowd yelled out.

They were drunk, the lot of them, swaying into each other, bottles clinking. All the easier to persuade them to part with their coin. Tammo felt the same easy warmth, a pleasant mist to match the mist in the winter air. They should get some more wine. Keep warm. Find Celestina.

The harlequin was now pushing the master behind a pole held up by the guitarist, which was meant to resemble a tree. Every time he pushed his master one way, a different part of him stuck out the other way. The master broke off a branch from the pole and beat the servant on the backside.

Tammo tapped Carlo on the shoulder.

"Shall we get some more wine?"

Carlo shook himself as if he'd been roused from sleep.

"What? Oh. No, thank you. That last cup made me queasy. I think it had soured."

He wrapped his arms about himself and turned back to the stage. Tammo tried again.

"Come on, Carlo. We haven't seen half there is to see yet."

"I'm happy here, Tamino. That soft voice, still. "Unless we're going back to the torches again. It was warm there."

Too warm. Tammo didn't like the way the fish-finned man pranced around those naked flames. In his mind's eye, he could see those flames licking higher and higher, swallowing up the giant birdcage, the man inside still clanging his bell like a death knell.

"If you're cold, you should move about," he said.

Carlo tightened his arms about his chest. "I'm happy here."

The play eventually came to an end. The lovers were finally united, the grotesques suitably put out by the state of affairs, and the harlequin delivered an epilogue to the sound of the guitar, while dancing with the dog. Carlo put three coppers in the box, which Tammo thought was far too generous, and turned to Tammo, shoulders up to his ears.

"Is there anywhere indoors?"

There was something else about his voice now, something Tammo couldn't place. His head felt too fuzzy, blurred by the swaying of the crowd and the twanging of the guitar.

"This is *Carnevale*, Carlo. Only the rich go indoors. And even they stay out tonight."

His feet were impatient, twitching in his shoes. Get to the river now.

"Come on, Carlo. Let's go."

Away from the crowd, it was colder. Tammo could see the mist settling as dampness on Carlo's cloak and hat, clinging like glass beads to his curls.

"That second cup of wine will warm you," Tammo said. It had certainly warmed him. His heart was burning for Celestina now, a strong, pure flame. She would see him from the barge, he knew it. She would look him in the eye and know that he was her cavalier. He would lay all the birds of the forest at her feet. He would carry her over mountains. He would face down any foe that stood in her way. All they had to do was get to the river. All they had to do was stand on that bridge.

"This way," he said to Carlo.

He knew his way round Angelio like he knew his own hands. He was an Angelian. A born-and-bred citizen. One who had spoken with the Archangel. Every little crook and alley was a childhood friend to him. This was his city, alive under his feet. A twist this way, a tuck that way. Dodge the crowds and avoid the militia. Ghost under the gilt paper noses of the revellers. Out-slink the city cats and come to the river by ways no one else knew. Quick and nimble on his feet. Lighter than the most graceful tumbler.

But that was without Carlo at his heels. Carlo didn't

slink and twist. He dragged. He stumbled. Tammo's itching feet pulled him toward the river. Carlo fell further and further behind. Tammo twisted round, impatient. He should have seized the eunuch's hand and tugged him along.

"What's wrong with you tonight, Carlo?"

Carlo wrapped his arms round his chest again, shoulders to his cheeks. "Forgive me, Tamino dear. I just need a moment to regain my breath. This mist creeps inside me so."

Tammo knew what was wrong with his voice now. He was losing it. From a clear soprano, he had gone to a cracked reed, squeaking, and stopping unexpectedly. Tammo felt a tug of misgiving.

"Are you all right, Carlo?"

Carlo took out a handkerchief and wiped his nose.

"Yes. Yes, I'll be fine. Let's get onto the waterfront. I feel I will be warmer there."

"Very well."

There were nearly there now. This was what they had come for. He could keep an eye on Carlo, thought Tammo. He could keep an eye on Carlo and watch for Celestina at the same time. He was a citizen. A cavalier of Angelio. One who had spoken to the mountains. He burped and tasted wine. It felt warm. He reached for Carlo's hand.

"This way."

They had to pay to get onto the waterfront. Men in thick cloaks and tricorns stood at every available entrance. Some revellers were handing over pre-paid tokens. The crowd on the quayside already looked thick. Lanterns and braziers burned. There was a smell of garlic sauce and black powder. Tammo strained his eyes to make out the Bridge of Glories through the mist.

"Two lira six. Each," said the man.

Tammo choked with outrage, but Carlo calmly handed over the coin. How much money did he have? They ought to have asked for a bigger helping of fish stew. He had been seriously ignorant of just how well castrato singing paid. That apartment Carlo kept talking about, with the flowers and the cages full of songbirds: he was going to be able to afford that when he graduated. He would glide into Celestina's world with ease, and no one would suspect him of having been born a peasant. It was Tammo, the citizen, who would be left on the outside.

"The bridge is that way, look," he said in Carlo's ear. "We'll have to step lively to get a spot. Everyone and their dog is here."

Despite the crowds, it was no warmer by the river. If anything, it was colder still. White mist swirled on the surface of the water like grasping fingers. At the water's edge, ferrymen poled off with stiffened hands and drink-reddened faces. There was a scaffold on the other shore. It was a little hard to see through the mist, but it looked something like a triumphal arch or palace. Tammo thought he could hear a sound of flutes and fiddles drifting from that direction, but the wind kept blowing it the other way.

"This is where the barges will come." He made a sweeping gesture over the ferrymen. "Straight down here. The Teatro is just past that bridge. That's where they'll all get out. Look at the crowds, Carlo! Do you think it will cost extra for a spot on the bridge?"

Carlo shrugged and wiped his nose again. It occurred to Tammo that Carlo had not actually spoken for some time.

"Carlo? Did you hear me? That's where Celestina will be."

"Yes, Tamino. That's where she'll be."

His voice cracked again. Somewhere deep inside, Tammo knew he ought to be worried about that. But there was too much else going on. The crowds and masks and burning torches. The snatches of music from across the water. A sudden breeze sent feathers flying from someone's disguise. One of them fluttered into a torch and sizzled to ashes. The people nearby screamed and giggled. It was all so unreal. So many paper faces, white as parchment or gilt like manuscripts. The heady scent of wine in the back of his throat. The vision of Celestina, sailing down that river like a queen.

They reached the Bridge of Glories. The riverside walkway rose to become a staircase with a decorated balustrade, then turned a corner to rise still higher, coming to a peak at the bridge's apex before descending to the further shore. Stone cherubs cavorted on every available projection. Their bare backsides seemed to wink at Tammo. He had never been on this bridge before, and the sheer weight of it might have over-awed him, if not for that cheeky touch.

"We'll be all right here, Carlo," he said. "It's all under cover. Nice and warm."

It was true. Once you got up the first flight of stairs, the main body of the bridge looked more like a cloister or the nave of a church. High arches like windows rose on either side, and a vaulted roof completed the splendour.

"We'll go to one of those windows," he said to Carlo. "If we get right to the middle, we won't be able to miss her. I'll wager you can see for miles up there."

It would be like the carriage ride, like the top of the tree, like being a bird in flight that could look down and see the world all flattened out and silent. Where was Coronis, anyway? Ha! He'd finally given the wearisome crow the slip. No black reminder of courtyard taunting tonight! He was Citizen Capell. Cavalier Capell. He was...

"Tammo...?"

"In a minute, Carlo."

They fought their way to the apex of the bridge. A gust of wind howled through the tunnel of arches. Someone's mask blew off and was carried down the river, an empty-eyed face drifting with the current. Tammo pushed past a portly man in leopard breeches and leaned out over the water. Was that the flotilla of barges on the horizon? Wasn't that a gilded prow stabbing a hole in the fog?

"Tammo...?"

He could see the scaffold thing more clearly from here. Its plastered façade—the front that faced the river—was painted to look like a palace. It had rows of pretty windows with roses climbing round them. From the back, Tammo could see it was supported by wooden structures and ropes. A row of spiralled cones stood on a platform just behind the painted turrets. In front of the palace were what looked like metal trees and giant metal flowers. Men in woollen stockings were going around it, adjusting, examining, patting things into the ground. Some had shovels, others were measuring lengths of fuse. One man carried a fire pot. It suddenly struck Tammo what it was they were about to do.

"Tammo...?"

Carlo's voice was a mere thread. He took a feeble hold on Tammo's sleeve.

"Tammo, I don't feel very well."

"What?"

He tried to focus on Carlo, but the activity of the men tugged at his attention. Fire pots. Fuses. They were going to let off fireworks. Hundreds of fireworks were going to go off right over his head. Tammo felt his neck getting hotter. He tugged at his collar.

"I don't feel well, Tamino. My throat hurts."

Carlo swayed as someone bumped into him from behind. Tammo saw for the first time how hard he was shivering. He reached behind Carlo's muffler and unfastened his mask.

"Let me see."

The mask had left a faint pink outline on Carlo's skin. The rest of his face was white as ash. His eyes were unnaturally bright with deep shadows underneath. His nose was running. Tammo pulled off a glove and touched the back of his hand to Carlo's forehead.

"Damn."

He yanked harder at his collar and scratched his neck, nicking the skin with a broken fingernail. He was supposed to be taking care of Carlo, not getting him sick. From somewhere beyond the wooden palace, a trumpet fanfare sounded, causing the crowd on the bridge to erupt into cheers. Bodies, cloaks and paper faces pressed closer. Someone tossed a rose into the river. Tammo's head fuzzed with wine. In the corner of his eye, he saw one of the firework men light a length of fuse. He scratched harder; his fingernail had blood on it. His collar was too tight. He couldn't breathe.

"I'm so cold." Carlo shivered and gave a loud sniffle.

The barges were coming. Prows like swans, angels, Death's heads. Rows of liveried servants rowing. Canopies draped with velvet. From the shore, a sound of fiddles and oboes sang out. Trumpets flourished. Drums beat a tattoo. The shadow of a man with a fuse ran along the row of spirals.

Fire.

Explosions corkscrewed into the sky. Orange. Yellow. White. A communal *ooh* went up from the bridge. Fire was falling. Drops of fire. Over the bridge. Over the water. Coming down on their heads.

Ooh! Aah!

A forest of fire appeared in front of the wooden palace. Burning trees reflected on the water. It looked like the whole river was on fire. The ferrymen. The approaching barges. Everything.

Ooh!

Tammo hadn't noticed the platform in the river until the last minute. The ferrymen had rowed one of the fuse-lighting men out to it. There was an almighty flash. An enormous column of fire shot up. The blast of its heat singed their faces.

"Holy Michael!"

Without thinking, he grabbed hold of Carlo. Carlo winced and moaned, but Tammo had no room for other thoughts any longer. Fire. The river was on fire. The air was choking with smoke and black powder. He could feel old pains flaring in his arm and neck. The burning hot door. The desperation. His little sisters...

"Fireworks. You didn't tell me there'd be fireworks."

"You're hurting me, Tamino." Carlo's face was waxen.

It was too hot. He couldn't breathe. Smoke in his throat. Hot bodies pressing against him. The pulse in his ears throbbing, throbbing.

"I can't stand this."

He grabbed a fistful of Carlo's cloak and ran. He didn't care where he was going. He just had to get off the bridge. Downriver. Flee the fire.

"Ow!"

"Mind where you're going, young scoundrel!"

Tammo pushed and shoved to get the revellers out of his way. Feathers tickled his ears and tasted wet in his mouth. Someone poked him in the ribs with a cane. Another person brought a folded fan down on the brim of his hat. Half his field of vision disappeared.

Ooh!

Another explosion. Tammo struggled toward the flight of stairs. Carlo blundered behind him, gasping and sniffling. Everyone was surging toward the riverbank, waving fans and handkerchiefs, throwing roses.

"Get out of my way!"

Tammo snarled, his voice a throaty roar. Several people

stepped back, muttering. A beak-masked man retorted, "Do you know who I am?"

"Don't care!" he yelled over his shoulder.

He yanked Carlo through the indignant crowd. Where had so many extra people suddenly come from? He had to run. Run hard and fast. The river was burning. A thousand fireballs plummeted toward the water. He tripped over his feet and ran into a couple in matching blue and silver outfits. The impact knocked all the breath from his chest.

"Tamino, please. Please stop."

Tammo paused and looked back. Carlo was swaying, his eyelids heavy. His voice was cracked and high. He sniffled into his handkerchief and blew his nose. Tammo's pulse pounded in his eardrums. His neck sweated. Everything inside him was saying *run*. He had to try and make himself remember why he was here. Why he needed to stick by Carlo.

"You young imp! Apologise to the lady now!" said the man in the silver disguise.

"That's the one." The beak-mask was saying over the heads of the crowds. "Dressed as a choirboy in a golden mask. Ran straight into me."

"Apologise now, or by God, I'll make you smart for it!"

There was a gap in the crowd. If he was quick, Tammo could dodge through it and be away. But it would mean leaving Carlo behind. The eunuch would never keep up in his present state. And then why would become of him?

"Did you hear me, rogue?"

The man in blue and silver reached for his sword. A number of people shrank back and gasped.

"Don't, Garibaldo! He's just a boy." The blue-and-silver woman reached for her paramour's arm. The man shrugged her off.

"He needs to be taught a lesson."

"Right over there," the beak-masked man was saying. "Hoi, ferryman! How far to the nearest barracks?"

"Tamino...?" Carlo clutched at his arm.

"What on Angelio's good earth is going on here?"

The crowd fell silent. A nobleman in a golden coat and a huge golden headdress was being handed out of a barge by a servant in maroon livery. He stepped onto the walkway with an air of calm authority. From inside the barge's heavily draped awning, a female face could be seen peeping from behind a half-moon mask.

"Well, then?" He stared at the man in blue and silver. "You know His Grace has forbidden duelling?"

"I was merely schooling a brat in manners, your lordship." The man hastily replaced the sword. "A tap with the flat of the blade was all I intended."

"And what kind of schooling does this brat require?"

The nobleman took Tammo by the collar—firmly but not roughly—and turned him so they could look one another in the eye. A queasy sensation ran through Tammo's body. That face. Those intelligent eyes. He'd seen them before. He glanced across to the barge again. Its figurehead was a golden pheasant.

"Count Pageno. Forgive me..." he mumbled.

The Count's eyes narrowed. "Have we met before, young citizen? I don't recall your face."

"Who is it, Papa?" said a voice from the barge. An all

too familiar voice that turned Tammo's bowels to water. "Is it someone we know?"

Carlo suddenly sneezed.

"Long life to you," said Tammo.

"Bless you, Carlo!" Celestina pulled back the curtains of the canopy. "It is you, Carlo, isn't it? How dreadfully ill you look!"

Count Pageno released Tammo in an instant. In two strides, he was towering over Carlo. "Carlo Bianci? What are you doing here, boy? Where are your maestri?"

"Forgive me."

Carlo's voice was a rattling squeak. His eyes were glazed and watery. In a heartbeat, the heat evaporated from Tammo's flesh and he became cold sober. Carlo had been caught out by his patron on the streets of Angelio. This could have the direst consequences. And Carlo's usual wit and warmth could be of no aid to him tonight. For the first time, Tammo allowed himself to look at Carlo properly. Celestina was right. He really was ill.

"It's my fault," he heard himself say. He got down on his knees in front of Count Pageno, face flushed with shame. "I tempted him to leave his studies and come to Carnival. He wouldn't have come if not for me."

"Carlo?" There was anger in the Count's voice. And possibly hurt as well. "Did we not have an agreement? Have I not given you every advantage?"

Carlo nodded feebly.

"I treated you like a son." The Count's voice shook.

"He won't do it again," Tammo promised.

"Have I made a mistake in linking my name with yours?" the Count said.

Carlo sneezed again. Harder this time. Count Pageno sighed.

"Vittori, engage a chair to take Master Bianci home before he catches his death of cold. And take this other scoundrel with you." A well-dressed manservant appeared silently at Count Pageno's side and bowed. "You may inform the rector that I found the pair of them truanting at Carnival. I will speak to him personally in the morning."

He gestured to one of the footmen, who brought a shawl from the barge and placed it unceremoniously on Carlo's shoulders. Celestina leaned out from the awning, concern on her face.

"Please don't be angry with Carlo, Papa. Only see how unwell he is." Tammo could hardly bear to see her looking so stricken.

"Get back under the awning, Celestina, before you catch a cold too." The count's tone was firm. He turned suddenly to his daughter. "I trust this has nothing to do with you, because if I discover it has..."

"No, Papa." Celestina shuffled back under the canopy. In the moment before she drew the curtain, she fixed her gaze on Tammo. There were tears in her eyes.

Tammo was forced to trot all the way home with Vittori's hand on his shoulder, trying to keep pace with the manservant's long strides, and with the quick march of the chairmen, who were eager to move on to a new fare. The link boy, carrying a torch alongside, kept wandering ahead in the fog, only to be called back, "before we all break our necks". The sounds of Carnival no longer seemed inviting. Strains of music sounded like drunken lurching. Screams and laughter became ghastly and chilling. Carlo kept sneezing inside the sedan chair. Tammo could hear him blowing his nose and sighing. If only he could get just one word alone with his friend! But Vittori's hand was unyielding on his shoulder, and the walls of the conservatorio were looming.

The porter was standing at the gate, lantern in hand. His eyes opened wide when he saw Carlo leaning on Vittori's arm.

"Master Bianci, where have you been? The whole school has been out looking for you. Rubin is beside himself."

"Count Pageno found these two down by the riverside." Vittori's voice was absolutely without emotion. "He'll be speaking with the rector about it tomorrow."

"Count Pageno?" The porter swallowed. He held up his lantern and peered more closely at Tammo and Carlo. "Here, weren't you two together in my lodge the other day? Have you been plotting on my watch? When I tell the rector..."

"If you don't mind, my good man." Vittori stuck out his chin. "This young fellow needs to be in the sanatorium. He has a fever." He gave a nod toward Carlo, who was shivering hard, his eyes unfocused. "You may do as you wish with this one." He pushed Tammo toward the Porter.

"I'll call a boy to show you the way." The porter made

a half-bow to Vittori. "And you, my lad…" He took Tammo by the ear. "You will go to the rector's lobby and stay there until he is ready to deal with you. I believe he went to bed half an hour ago, so you could be waiting some time."

"Carlo!" Tammo yelled over his shoulder. "Carlo, I'm sorry! It wasn't meant to be like this."

But the porter pinched harder on Tammo's ear and dragged him across the wet cobbles.

13. Consequences.

A bell rang. Carlo tried to swallow. It felt like there was something sharp in his throat.

"*Laudate pueri Dominum.*"

His lips were moving but only the most strangled squeak came out. His eyelids, his whole body, felt heavy. He tried to get out of bed and fell to the floor. The floorboards jarred his knees and hurt him.

"*Laudate pueri.*"

No one else was singing. He tried to force his eyelids open. He wasn't in the dormitory. He was in a room with whitewashed walls and several empty beds. A fire was roaring in the grate close by. A pale curtain hung across the middle of the room. Carlo shivered. He was so cold, so hot, so he-didn't-know-what. He started sneezing.

"Carlo, my boy, what are you doing down there?"

A face with small copper spectacles on the end of its nose looked round the curtain. Signor Cavalli, the school physician.

"Do you need help using the close-stool?"

Carlo blinked. "What hour is it? Have I missed chapel?"

How much it hurt his throat just to say those words!

And his voice! A cricket could have produced a stronger sound. Of all things, Carlo's voice must not be weak.

Signor Cavalli came and placed a kindly hand on Carlo's shoulder.

"No chapel for you today. Just plenty of warmth and rest. Back into bed now."

Carlo couldn't manage to think straight. If he wasn't in the dormitory, where was he? What was the last thing that happened last night?

"But Maestro Sarastro comes today. I must rehearse my recitative to him."

He clutched at his chemise. It was damp with sweat. Signor Cavalli placed a hand on Carlo's forehead.

"Your fever is still up. Use the stool and get back into bed. I will bring you another evacuant."

A nameless panic rose in Carlo's breast. "No. I need to rehearse. It's only two weeks until the opera."

Signor Cavalli crouched by Carlo and took him gently by both shoulders. "Carlo, you have a severe cold. You're fortunate not to be much worse, given the condition you came home in last night. It is imperative that you keep warm and have complete bed rest." He shook his head. "I don't think there'll be any opera."

He kept dozing off. He would wake with a runny nose and a desperate thirst. The curtain would twitch; Signor Cavalli would appear like a ghost at his side, plying him with hot barley water, or warm milk with spoonfuls of honey. Or else he would force Carlo to drink something that made him retch up his guts into the chamber pan.

"It will bring down the fever," he assured Carlo, when the burning in his throat brought tears to Carlo's eyes. "And it is much gentler than blistering, I assure you. I would not use such harsh treatment on a eunuch. Gentle cures for the delicate in constitution. Sleep now, Carlo. You have done well."

The physician retreated behind the curtain and left him alone again. Carlo was certain he could hear moaning from the other side. Somewhere close, some boy was in dire pain. Gradually, the moaning faded and merged with the sound of Carlo's own sniffles, and he slept again.

At first, he thought the tapping on the window was something from his own dreams. The bell of the fish-armoured acrobat, clanging in his cage, as he capered ever higher in the torchlight. But even after Carlo sat up and sneezed himself into a state of relative wakefulness, the sound continued. *Tap, tap, tap* on the window behind Carlo's head. He turned to look over his shoulder, his eyes bleary.

"Carlo. Let me in. Quickly."

Tammo's angular face stared through the mullions. He pointed at the window latch with an urgent finger.

"Hurry up before they see me."

It was impossible for Carlo to hurry with his head so light and waves of fever running up his back, but he unfastened the latch as best he could. The shutters swung open. Cold air chilled his neck. Gooseflesh stood up. He shuffled back on the bed as Tammo wriggled through the window and tumbled onto the pillows.

"Your shoes…" Carlo said, as dirty water dripped onto the sheets.

Tammo scowled and rolled off the bed, remarkably quietly. He crept to the curtain and peeped round.

"No one there," he said at his normal volume. "Only one of the seniors with his face bandaged up. He won't be telling on us."

Carlo opened his mouth to speak and gave a violent sneeze.

"Long life to you," said Tammo. He leaned past Carlo and closed the shutters again. Now that Carlo looked at him, Tammo had his own share of shadows beneath the eyes and weary pallor. His cropped hair stood out towards every point of the compass. His twin had not slept well.

"Are you all right, Carlo?" Tammo said.

Carlo blew his nose yet again. He watched Tammo's gaze follow his hands to hover over the golden pheasant embroidered on the corner of the handkerchief. It was the one Celestina had given him, the night he stood vigil for Orlando. Celestina! What must she be feeling now? How happy she had been when he'd promised to come to the Bridge of Glories, and how sad she had been when the Count ordered her into the barge last night. Carlo felt a deep ache in his belly. He had been wrong to indulge Celestina's whims, saying he would see her at *Carnevale*, offering to wave from the bridge. He was the elder; he ought to have known better. That was what a maestro would say.

That was what her father would say, and he would be right. Dear, brave, lonely Celestina! She had only wanted a friend to be kind to her, like a brother. Was she being punished for Carlo's sake this morning? Carlo didn't think he could bear to think of her facing the Countess's chastisement. He drew his knees toward his chest.

"You don't look well." Tammo scratched his neck.

Carlo sighed. "I'm not well, Tamino dear. I have such a cold. And Signor Cavalli says I may not rehearse *Hercules*..."

He hadn't been crying a moment before. But the sound of Tamino's voice, the sight of his face in this room of sickness was suddenly too much for Carlo to bear. Tears began to well in his eyes.

"Hey, stop that." Tammo frowned.

"I can't help it." Carlo gave an enormous sniffle. "It's all going wrong, Tamino."

Tammo sighed from deep in his chest. "I know."

He sat on the end of the bed and passed Carlo a clean handkerchief.

"I just spent all night on the bench in Rector Bartolomeo's lobby. By the time his man came through with that chocolate pot, my neck was so stiff I thought I would never move it again."

"Did he punish you?" Carlo said through the handkerchief.

Tammo shrugged. "Never got the chance. What do you think I'm doing here? I ran off, didn't I?"

Carlo blew his nose. "But when they find you, Tamino...?"

"To hell with them," Tammo muttered.

Carol wanted to protest. His twin must not give in like that. He must stay on the straight path, keep to his flute and his bird-charming. It was Carlo's fault he was in trouble now. If he hadn't asked to see Carnival, none of this would have happened. It was Carlo who had let the Archangel down. He wanted to say it aloud, but he was just too weary. Too ill. His eyes began to close.

"Cavalli? Cavalli, are you there, man?" A voice on the other side of the curtain. "It's Aprile."

"The vice-rector!" Tammo stiffened. Carlo's eyes opened with a start.

"I'm not here," said Tammo, sliding under the bed. "You never saw me."

"Cavalli?" The vice-rector called again.

"What do you want, Aprile? I'm up to my elbows in blood here."

"I... Oh. Um. I see." There was a tone of discomfort to the vice-rector's voice. "The rector hasn't had your report on Carlo Bianci yet."

A chill went down Carlo's back that had nothing to do with the window.

"Sweet Michael above!" the physician swore. "Can this not wait? I've just had a boy's tooth out. And they're telling me the lice have broken out in the infant's dorm again. You'd think this weather would have killed them off."

"Yes, well. You do know that the rector was summoned to attend Count Pageno's pleasure at sunrise this morning?"

"Good God! Whatever for?"

"Because of this hullabaloo that went on last night with

Tammo Capell and Carlo Bianci. What do you judge his ailment to be?"

There was a sound of the physician rinsing his hands.

"Violent cold in the head. Slight fever, but he's not in any real danger."

"But his voice." Vice-rector Aprile became urgent. "Is there likely to be lasting damage to the voice?"

There was a pause which, to Carlo, seemed eternal.

"Not if he rests it and takes the treatments I prescribe."

"Rests for how long?"

"A fortnight at the very least."

The vice-rector gave a cry of dismay.

"The boy's exhausted, Aprile," said Signor Cavalli. "I've never seen him so weak. Send him back to work too soon and he'll have much worse than a cold in the head."

"But the rector has just engaged him at the Teatro," said Vice-rector Aprile. "Very much against his better judgement, might I add? Count Pageno expects the boy in the theatre, and at his chapel every week without fail. And he's not at all pleased by last night's incident. We could lose everything, Cavalli. Money and reputation both. Bianci is our finest student."

"You'll lose a lot more than that if the boy doesn't rest," said Signor Cavalli. "No, Aprile. I won't hear any more. That's my final word."

For a moment, Carlo thought the conversation had ended. But, as the door creaked open, the physician spoke again.

"What's become of the other boy? Capell?"

Vice-rector Aprile gave a heavy sigh. "He'll have to go."

Carlo clutched at the bed covers.

"I thought he was a charity boy," said Signor Cavalli. "The rector can't turn him out just because he wants to. It's against the constitution."

"We're looking at sending him to a sister school in Fiorenta. Aquila spoke against it, of course. The bird business, and so on. He has a soft spot for the brat. Sweet Michael knows why! But Carlo Bianci is an investment in the future. The revenue he can generate for this place is far beyond the value of a few songbirds. We can't have him interfered with by a street brat. Did you know anything about this, Cavalli? No one seems to have had the slightest inkling of this liaison until today. Of course, the boy's gone missing again. Perhaps he's saved us all the trouble."

The physician made an impatient sound in the back of his throat. "Do any of you see these boys as more than ducats and lira in a balance book?" He sighed. "If you'll excuse me, Aprile, I have a dormitory to de-louse. God save you."

Carlo waited for several minutes after the door had slammed shut before he dared move. Then he looked down the side of the bed to see Tammo sliding out on his back.

"Did you hear that?" Carlo said.

"Most of it." Tammo stood up and patted dust out of his cassock. "You kept blowing your nose in the important bits."

Carlo paused with the handkerchief halfway to his face.

"They want to send you away, Tamino." Waves of fever and misery washed over him. "We won't see each other again. We won't..."

He was really crying now, weeping the tears so easily shed by the sick. He couldn't do anything to make them stop. In bed for two weeks. No opera. Count Pageno angry with him. And now they wanted to separate him from his beloved twin. They couldn't do this. Tamino was his life, his soul.

"Carlo." Tammo bit his lip and scratched his neck alternately. "Carlo, you're going to make yourself worse." He sat on the extreme edge of the bed and reached out a nervous hand.

"They can't take you away, Tamino," Carlo sobbed.

"Come on now, Carlo." Tammo pulled Carlo into an awkward embrace. "It's going to be all right. Damn this," he added under his breath.

Carlo clung to his twin's wiry body, desperate, bereft. He could feel the sparseness of Tammo's shoulder blades, the warmth of his blood. All he wanted was to be with Tammo. All he wanted was the comfort of his friend's presence.

"They won't send me away," said Tammo gruffly, "because I'm going myself."

"What?" Carlo hiccupped and sniffled.

"I'm getting out of this place. They can't split us up, Carlo. Send me to Fiorenta? Like hell! I'll run away. Live in the woods. I'm not leaving Angelio, Carlo."

"But...but how will we see each other?"

"We'll find a way." Tammo sat back to let Carlo clean up his face. "They can't keep us apart. The Archangel put us together."

"But that's just it." Carlo began crying again. "It's all

ruined now. Celestina. The flute. Oh, Tammo, the flute! You can't go and leave behind the dark flute and your lessons and the bird-charming business. You'll have nothing. Everything I prayed for will be gone." He gave a defeated sigh. "I think the Archangel's angry with us. With me."

"No, Carlo, not with you." Tammo was firm.

"Yes, with me. All I was thinking was how much I wanted to see Carnival. I didn't think about getting you into trouble. Or Celestina. The Archangel said our gifts should be used for friendship, but now I've spoiled everything."

Panic racked his body. He sneezed. Sneezed. Sneezed again.

"Long life to you." Tammo passed another clean handkerchief. "Carlo, you have to calm down. It's not your fault. It's mine. And I'm going to make it up to you, I swear. But right now I have to get out of the Conservatorio. They mustn't catch me."

"But the flute?"

A look of pain came over Tammo's face. "I won't be a thief. I'll not have them say that of me. I'll take nothing."

Nothing. The very word sounded bleak. Carlo pressed the handkerchief to his lips, trying to prevent more tears. Tammo was planning to walk away from the conservatorio in the exact same state he had arrived in, as an orphan boy with nothing and no one in the world. Carlo would not allow it.

"Take this."

Carlo put down the handkerchief and started working the carnival ring off his finger. His hands were sweating; the ring was tight and left a pink circle in the place where it had been. He placed it in the palm of his hand. His greatest treasure. A little part of his own soul. What better gift to give Tamino? Let it never be said that he left the Conservatorio Archangeli with nothing.

Tammo shrank back. "I can't take this, Carlo."

Carlo placed the ring in Tammo's hand and closed both his hands around it.

"You must. You must take it and wear it for my sake. And you must swear that we'll always be twins to the end of our days. That our souls will be joined, even when we're apart. Swear it, Tamino."

"I swear," said Tammo, vaguely. He screwed up his face in a scowl. "But, Carlo, that's Count Pageno's ring. If I take that, I'll be arrested."

Carlo set his features.

"It's my ring. And I'm giving it to my twin. You can wear it secretly, somewhere no one will ever see. Only we two will know."

Tammo shrugged.

"Very well, Carlo. If you wish it."

Tammo began taking off the shoe and stocking from his right foot. He slipped the ring onto his toe. It twinkled mischievously between chipped toenails.

Carlo wiped his nose again, clinging to the handkerchief like a comforter. He must be brave. There were precious few moments to spare. He must say something else before his twin left for good.

"Tammo, you must do me another favour. You must speak with Celestina. She mustn't think we have abandoned her. You have to find her, Tamino. Tell her I'm sorry I can't come to see her. Tell her I'm sorry her father was angry. That it's not her fault. That she must be brave until I can see her again."

Tammo swallowed hard and flushed red.

"Speak to Celestina?" He stumbled over her name. "I'd have to break into..." Tammo shook his head furiously. "You can't ask me to do that. Count Pageno will have me hanged. I'll be..."

Carlo crushed the handkerchief in his hand. He began to shiver.

"No, you must, Tamino. You must." Curse this fever! He couldn't say what he wanted to say. He gripped Tammo's wrist. His friend's skin was like ice. "You must go and speak with her. She cannot be left alone." His voice cracked. His nose was running dreadfully.

"All right. All right. Calm down, Carlo, I'll do it." Tammo blew out a breath and ran a hand through his unruly hair. "I'll do it, Carlo. I'll speak to Celestina. Don't you worry about her. You just get well again, right? And I will find a way to keep in touch with you. On Michael's sword, I swear."

Tammo pulled up his stocking and buckled up his shoe. He gave a nervous glance towards the curtain. "Carlo, I have to go. Someone could come in here any minute."

Carlo took a deep breath.

"Kiss me, Tamino."

Tammo grimaced.

"What? You're full of cold."

"Please." The tears flowed faster. He wanted to keep

Tamino forever. He couldn't bear the loneliness that would fall when the window closed. Tammo sighed.

"Oh, very well. But wipe your nose first."

Carlo did as he was told. He looked up at his twin, fixing the beloved face in his memory, praying that this would not be the last time he looked on it. Tammo placed his hands on Carlo's shoulders and kissed him smartly on both cheeks, like an uncle at a wedding. Disappointment battled in Carlo's breast with bliss at the touch of his twin's lips and overwhelming sadness at his departure.

Tammo squared his shoulders.

"I've really got to go now, Carlo. Open the shutters. And keep your chin up, right?"

When Signor Cavalli came back to give Carlo his next dose, he found the young eunuch sobbing inconsolably.

"Oh dear, Carlo! You're not yourself at all, are you?" He put an arm round Carlo's shoulder. "There, there, my fine fellow. You'll be well again by-and-by."

Carlo was not ashamed in the least to weep at length on the physician's breast.

14. Angel's Wood

Tammo hung on by his fingers and looked back at the conservatorio one last time. The branches of the lime—bare at a distance—had put forth tight buds of leaves, only waiting for the spring sunshine to return and make them open. Between them, mist swirled and revealed patchy views of the dormitory building, the rector's house, the roofs of the maestri's houses across the courtyard. To the Pit with all of them! Tammo scowled and grunted. Send him to Fiorenta, would they? Tear him away from Carlo? He wouldn't give them the satisfaction! And if they missed the revenue from his birding business, let that be their problem! Tammo was not going to concern himself with the doings of the conservatorio ever again.

He had already torn off his cloak and cassock and bundled them at the foot of the lime tree. He ought to have left them with Carlo, he realised too late. The cassock would never fit a boy of Carlo's size, but the cloak might afford his friend a little extra warmth and keep him from catching cold again in the future. Tammo didn't want to be seen in it. If he were to get away from the conservatorio unseen, he didn't need clothes that marked him out so obviously as a music student. The breeches and yellow stockings were bad enough. Tammo tried rubbing a little mud and moss on them to mute the colour. He shivered in his shirt sleeves. It was a miserable day. Carlo's shawls—abandoned the night before—still hung over the branches. Tammo would have disguised himself in one of those, but the mist had soaked them through, making them useless to wear.

"I'll just have to run," he said to Coronis.

The crow looked down from a higher bough, a look of knowing superiority in her eye. Higher up, the sparrows and finches flapped and twittered. His birds. Something balled tight in Tammo's stomach. The dark flute was calling to him from Maestro Aquila's parlour. Yearning after him. Could he run now and get it? He could sneak in by a window, slip it into the pouch at his hip... Tammo's arms shook with the effort of holding on. No. He wouldn't let them call him thief. It was like parting from his own limb, but he had to let it go. Let it all go. Holding a final picture of the rooftops in his mind's eye, he dropped.

There was a harsh caw and Coronis dropped to his shoulder like a scrap of mourning crêpe. Tammo flailed his arms.

"Get lost!" He croaked back. "I can't keep you any more."

Coronis made a lazy circle to land on the other shoulder.

"I said, leave!" Tammo hissed.

How could he hope to ghost through the city without remark when there was a full-grown crow riding on his shoulder? *There's that charity boy,* everyone would say. *He's at the market along with that crow every week.* He'd be back before the maestri within minutes.

"Shoo!" Tammo wriggled his shoulders. Coronis merely stuck in her talons deeper. Tammo felt them as four pins piercing the cloth of his shirt, seeking out his shoulder blades. Coronis cawed in triumph.

"Fine," he said. "Hand me over to the militia, why don't you?"

Yet he couldn't deny a tiny thread of relief as he set off through the back streets with Coronis swaying and flapping by his ear. At least one friendly face would stay close to him, wherever he was going. Though the crow drove him to insanity, he would have missed her.

He set off running the way he had come with Carlo. The discarded favours of last night's feast now lay strewn about the street. Broken clam shells crunched underfoot, along with torn ribbons, scraps of handbills, and a pair of lark's wings without its body. Tammo kicked it out of the way with venom. Why couldn't he just have stuck to the plan? It was all the fault of those pox-ridden fireworks.

He ran hard, slipping here and there on wet cobblestones or on the refuse the horses had left behind. Coronis cawed in protest. Not many people were out on the street this morning. Most were kept indoors, either by the dismal weather or by the after-effects of the feast. Those citizens Tammo saw outdoors turned up their collars and hurried about their own errands, with only a passing glance at him. Even the Sancti Michaelis and the ducal palace looked dull and forlorn in the greyness. Tammo cringed lest the chairmen from last night came round the corner and pointed him out, but he didn't see them anywhere. The only chairmen he saw at their stands were bedraggled and sadly lacking in custom.

The hill out of town had never seemed so steep before. Every step was an effort, and Tammo heard himself panting for breath. He yawned cavernously, rubbing his sore eyes. He hadn't really slept last night either, balanced on that bench, wondering every minute what the rector was going to do to him. In the end, he hadn't been able to take the nervous tension. The moment the servants had opened up the house for the morning, he had fled and hid until he could find Carlo. That had worked fine while his blood had still been pumping, but now it was more like treacle in his veins. He had to pull himself up sharply to avoid bumping into the soldier who stood guard at the city gate. Tammo managed a respectful tug of the forelock before stumbling onward, and the guard looked away again. Why did the top of the hill seem so far away? He'd practically run up this path with Pietro. Tammo felt his knees sag. Thoughts of his bird-charming expeditions only made him more listless than ever. His hand went to the empty sheath at his hip. No flute. No magic. Tammo felt a great pain in his chest. Was everything being torn away from him? He had said farewell to Carlo. He had been forced to walk away from Celestina. And the dark flute—that wondrous instrument that seemed another part of his own being—was now beyond his reach forever.

The ruin by the blacksmith's forge looked like

something from an old revenge tragedy in the swirling fog. Tammo could smell the scent of the charcoal fire and hear ringing blows to the anvil. He slunk behind the trees, tripping on roots and potholes. He would take shelter under the crumbling archway, just for the time being. The blacksmith was busy; he wouldn't notice. Tammo scowled at Coronis, willing her not to caw as he crawled onto a pile of ancient bricks. He wrapped his arms around his knees and shivered. His stomach ached with hunger. He didn't feel like looking for traps any more. He wanted to be with Carlo. He wanted to be sitting together in the lime tree, friendly and cosy like it had been in the autumn. He wanted Carlo to tickle his nose with leaves, and impersonate strolling trumpeters, and call him "dear Tamino". Who else was ever going to call him that? Not a poxy crow, that was for sure.

Tammo scrubbed his eyes; they were watering. It wasn't tears. Men of the world didn't cry. Tears were for girls and babies. And eunuchs. He gave a sniff, making an unsavoury sound in his throat. Carlo had cried so hard this morning. And Celestina too. Everyone was crying around him, and all he had for comfort was a crow. Black. Like his mood.

"You won't find any treasure there, lad," someone said. "Anything worth thieving in these parts went out with the ruff and codpiece."

Tammo started and found himself staring into the grizzled face of the blacksmith. How had an old man with such an obvious limp managed to sneak up on him like that?

Tammo wiped his nose on his sleeve.

"I'm not a thief. I'm just resting."

"Oh. On your way to visit an aunt in the country, are you?"

"Might be." Tammo thrust back his shoulders.

The blacksmith gave what Tammo supposed to be a laugh. "Three centesimi says you're not."

"I don't have any money," said Tammo.

"Aye, and you think I didn't know that?" The blacksmith scratched in his tangled beard. "I'll tell you three things about you: you're ravenous as a wolf, you're fit to drop to sleep where you stand, and you haven't a clue where to go next."

Tammo looked down and said nothing. The blacksmith offered him a calloused hand.

"Get up off that old pile. I've some salt biscuits, and soup on my stove. Do you want some or don't you?"

Tammo moved a bit of rubble about with his toe. He didn't like the way the blacksmith seemed to know so much about him. And he didn't want to take charity either. But he was just too hungry to obey anything other than his stomach. Soup would give him the strength to go on.

"Thank you, citizen." Tammo ignored the helping hand and stumbled to his feet.

The blacksmith grunted and began limping toward the hovel. "Citizen, indeed! The name's Grimaldi, and it's the only one I answer to."

"Tammo," Tammo mumbled.

"I already know who you are," said Grimaldi. "You're the bird boy who isn't afraid of anything. Sadly lacking in birds at present, bar that ill-omened thing. Get indoors and get some food inside you before you collapse."

Tammo had only intended to stay in the blacksmith's hut for as long as it took to swallow some hot soup and be able to feel his toes again. He wanted to be on the road before it got dark, and he didn't want Grimaldi asking him any more awkward questions. But he hadn't counted on how his body would react to sitting in a smoky hovel before an open hearth with a belly full of soup. It reacted in the most natural way in the world. Tammo's eyes started to close. He yawned and yawned until tears came. A detached part of him was still itching to be gone, but the rest was contentedly curling up, ready to nap like a pampered cat.

"Be more comfortable in bed than on a stool, lad," Grimaldi said.

The old man had watched Tammo wolf down the soup in silence, getting up now and again to ladle another portion into Tammo's bowl or to check on the state of the forge. Tammo glanced suspiciously out of the corner of his eye, as Grimaldi heaved his bones from an ancient settle that looked as though it were made from pieces of every tree under the sun, and limped over to a straw-stuffed bed in an alcove between the hearth and the hut's only stone wall. Wooden doors enclosed the bed in a type of cupboard; it looked warm and cosy. Grimaldi opened a drawer and began to shake out a number of blankets that could have been knitted by Tammo's great-grandmother.

"Here. Get your head down. I'm not using it. Got work to do."

"I'm fine. I don't need to sleep," growled Tammo, immediately belying himself with an enormous yawn.

"Oh, I see. You'll sleep when you reach your aunt's, I expect." Grimaldi limped out of the open door and into the drizzle. "Well, God save you. Don't forget to take your shoes off."

By the time Grimaldi came back, Tammo was in bed, snoring furiously.

When he woke up, everything was dark except for the glow of embers in the hearth, lighting up the underside of a caldron. The old man was asleep on the settle. A pang of guilt tugged at Tammo's guts at the thought of stealing Grimaldi's bed, but there was nothing he could do now without disturbing the old man's rest. The only thing to do was to go back to sleep and wait out the night. Tomorrow he would take Coronis, set out into Angel's Wood, and start a new life.

Except that Grimaldi had other ideas.

"You don't think I'd offer you bed and board for free, do you?" he said when Tammo tried to make an early exit. "This isn't a priory."

"I told you. I don't have any money, citizen," Tammo mumbled, trying to scowl at Coronis as if she could somehow be blamed.

"And I told you to call me Grimaldi," said the blacksmith. "I don't expect payment in coin. I expect your aunt will furnish you with that when you see her."

Tammo was getting heartily sick of his imaginary aunt now. He wished he had never agreed to her existence.

"There's other kinds of payment more useful to me. Ever worked a forge, boy?" Grimaldi's silver eyes narrowed.

Tammo's neck began to throb. He balled his hands into fists. "I don't do that anymore. I'm a bird charmer."

He hoped Grimaldi would leave it at that. He didn't.

"Not any more, eh? Well, that's promising at least. You're not completely green. You can work the bellows."

Tammo bit his lip hard. "I don't. Work. Forges."

Grimaldi's face wrinkled under his hair and beard in what might have been a smile. "You afraid, boy?"

Tammo squared his shoulders. His voice lowered to a menacing growl. "I'm not afraid of anything."

"On the bellows then, Tammo," Grimaldi said. "I've some railings to make before nightfall."

The job took all day. By the time it was done, Tammo was grimy with soot, and vaporous in every nerve of his body. His blood felt like water. How had he faced that forge, that burning heap of memories, for an entire day? Even now, the flames flickered in his inner eye. He would have crumbled to the ground in a heap, had it not been for the old man constantly watching. Tammo spat and wiped himself down with a rag, exchanging glances with Coronis. The crow had spent the day flying in and out of the trees, and was now tearing at the remains of something small and furry. Tammo swallowed and spat again. His throat felt like it was full of charcoal.

"Tomorrow we're getting out of here," he told Coronis. "Away from that blasted furnace. We can look after ourselves, can't we?" He nodded at the furry whatever-it-was. Absently, his hand went to his coat, feeling for the precious lock of hair at his breast. He closed his hand round it. "And we still have things to do."

Coronis gave him a look of corvid hauteur and went back to eating her carrion.

The next morning, Tammo woke up sneezing and realised he'd caught Carlo's cold.

He was nothing like as ill as Carlo had been. But he soon had a harsh cough that Grimaldi claimed shook the rafters, and by the third day had lost his voice completely. Outside, the rain drizzled under a miserable sky. It didn't seem like a good time to be taking up a new life as a trapper. Tammo shivered by the hearth, dreaming of a cosy life with Carlo in Angelio. It embarrassed him to admit it, even to himself, but he had no experience of life outside the city. This hut—this little area around the forge—was as far as he had ever come, even with Pietro. And, without his flute, he was occupationally unarmed. He had no way of earning his bread. Coronis seemed to do all right for food in the woods, but Tammo was starting to have doubts about his ability to do likewise. Grimaldi's soup and biscuit was hardly a banquet—it was mostly dried peas and lentils—but at least it was consistent. He was going to miss it when he moved on. The old man had been kind enough to nurse him in his sickness, letting him continue to sleep in the alcove bed, with the cupboard doors shut to keep in the warmth. He'd even loaned Tammo a handkerchief, though it was going to holes at the seams. He didn't talk too much. Tammo liked that. He owed the old blacksmith at least as many days' work as he'd been ill, even if the mere sight of a forge made him shudder. He thought he could bear it slightly better than he had done a few days ago. It was only work. No one had died. Not out here.

"The market gardener's just been through with his wares," said Grimaldi, hobbling in. "I shod his horse while he was here, so he's let me have one or two bits." He put a string bag of clementines and a yellow pepper on the table. "Thought it might do you some good."

He eased himself onto the settle and looked at Tammo's pale face. "Cold no better, eh? You'd better stay indoors and get the soup on. I've got your bird to keep me company, haven't I? Clever young thing. More sense than you."

"I'll make it up to you, Grimaldi, I promise," Tammo rasped. "As soon as I'm well, I'll pay you back in work again."

"Never said you wouldn't, lad." Grimaldi shook his head. "We'd better see about finding you somewhere of your own to sleep. You don't want to share with an old man who can't hold his water." He stood up and patted the settle. "A few cushions on here ought to do for a lad your age. The peddler woman comes through tomorrow. She might have something cheap."

"What for?" Tammo coughed and scowled. "I'll only be here until—"

"Until you go to your aunt's. I know, lad." Grimaldi stroked his beard.

Five days later, he was still there.

He'd put in three days' work in the forge, to pay Grimaldi for his three days of sickness, although he still had a lingering cough and an even more rasping voice than usual. He helped lift the railings they had made onto the heavy cart that came to collect them. He gathered brushwood, and split logs for the fire. He acted as Grimaldi's striker on a piece of heavy work for one of the churches, swinging the sledgehammer where Grimaldi dictated and watching it shape the red-hot iron. If the heat and smell of a forge made him shudder, he didn't let the blacksmith see. All he had to do was get through these three days and then leave. Back to freedom and Celestina's message and...well, whatever it was he was going to do after these three days.

The fourth day arrived, grim and overcast.

"Are you going today, then, lad?" Grimaldi asked, after Tammo had served them both porridge.

Tammo looked into his bowl and slopped watery barley porridge around.

"Can't stand the place myself," Grimaldi said. "The big city. Too many people. Noises. Smells. Too many memories."

He gave Tammo a calculating glance.

"I'm not running away from memories," Tammo

snapped. "I'm running away from..." He blushed and dropped his spoon into the bowl with a clatter.

Grimaldi made *mmm* sounds and nodded. "Aye, lad, you think I didn't know that? Question is: where are you running to?"

He slopped more porridge into his mouth. Tammo couldn't help noticing how much of it stuck in his beard. The old man wiped it with a sleeve.

"Lot of thieves and blackguards in those woods. Wild boar. Keepers with muskets. But you'll know that, of course. Probably uncles of yours."

Tammo slammed the bowl down on the earthen floor, spilling out porridge.

"I don't have an aunt in the country! All right? I don't know where I'm going. I just..." He floundered for the right words and failed to find them. "I have friends waiting for me in Angelio. There are things I need to take care of and...it's private." He kicked the bowl. "I just need somewhere to stay."

Grimaldi carried on eating, occasionally glancing up. Coronis strutted in from the doorway and began pecking at the spilled porridge. Tammo frowned and picked up the bowl again. Coronis cawed and nipped his finger.

Grimaldi stroked his beard.

"Nothing wrong with private, lad. I'd be an old fool to say otherwise. But old fools and young fools both need food and shelter, don't they?"

He reached out his gnarled fingers to Coronis. The crow hopped over to him and he tickled her on the back of the neck. *Little traitor*, Tammo thought.

"Now," said Grimaldi. "As I say, I haven't been down that hill in years and I don't intend to. But if someone with younger legs and friends in the city were to run my errands down there for me, that would save me from wasting my coin on messengers, wouldn't it? And if that someone had young arms and a young back for chopping firewood or swinging a hammer, well, that might cover his bed and board while he did it. Wouldn't you say?"

Tammo grimaced and chewed his lip.

"I'm not signing any indentures," he growled.

"Who spoke of indentures?" Grimaldi raised his bushy eyebrows. "No, this would just be a temporary arrangement, while the young lad got himself back on his feet."

"Young man," Tammo corrected.

Grimaldi shook his head.

"We'll see, lad. We'll see. Now, I need to collect my dues from the Guild of Tailors. You know where their guild house is, boy?"

"Yes." Tammo's voice wavered. "But..."

What if someone from the Conservatorio saw him? Wouldn't they drag him back to the Rector and ship him off to Fiorenta? Knocking on the door of the Tailors' Guild wasn't exactly hiding.

"You afraid, boy?" Grimaldi said.

Tammo wolfed down the rest of the porridge.

"No. Of course not."

"Good. Because I doubt those maestri and what-not you used to hang around with can even remember your name now. The city has no time for failures, believe me. Now, you get off to that guild house and collect my money.

And make sure they give you a tip. Stingy old misers, the lot of them!"

Two years later, he was still there.

Part III

15. Teatro di Palazzo

"You graduate this year, Carlo. You must allow us to find you a new patron."

Rector Bartolomeo put down his chocolate bowl. His waistcoat was now tighter than ever, buttons fashionably undone to show off his ample girth. His servant boy poured more chocolate, expressionless.

Carlo twisted his fingers together.

"Please, rector. Count Pageno has not released me from his service. I hear from Cel—from Noblesse Celestina sometimes. She assures me he will take me back into his household, and very soon."

"Such assurances will not put food on the table, Carlo." The rector folded his hands over his belly. "You're a sensible boy in all other respects. Surely you see it is time to let this go. I hear the bishop of Vulcanetta is looking for singers."

Carlo sighed. Vulcanetta! Might as well go to the desert and have done with it. Angelio was the centre of music. Without an Angelian patron, he would never rise to the heights of a true sopranist. Without Count Pageno as his patron, he would never see Celestina again. He would have lost the friend gifted to him by the Archangel Michael, and Tammo's sacrifice would have been in vain. Their oath of twinship would mean nothing.

He had passed the lime tree only this morning. It looked forlorn, despite the appearance of the first leaves of the year. Carlo didn't like to go near it any more. Occasionally, black wings would appear at the window of the dorm, a sign from Coronis that her master was close by. Then Carlo would hurry to a gap in the fence—he was much too tall and ungainly to climb trees any more—and Tammo and he would exchange furtive whispers. It wasn't enough. Sometimes, the only thing sustaining Carlo was the knowledge that he would soon leave the Cage of Nightingales and be out in the world, free to meet his twin whenever he chose. He could not do that from Vulcanetta.

"Please, rector," he said again. "At least let me wait until after *Perseus*. If he doesn't send for me then..."

It was a conversation oft-repeated. Had it not been for Celestina's communications via Tammo, Carlo would have had no ammunition for his side of the argument. Count Pageno had not sent for Carlo again since that fateful night at Carnival. There had been no early mornings in the chapel, no coffee and cream in the music room. But neither had there been a formal dismissal. Carlo was a soul in limbo, waiting for redemption or damnation. And he was running out of time for either.

The last time he had met with Celestina had been a snatched moment at the gate of the convent, Michaelis Curationum. Carlo had been singing in the chapel as usual, and Celestina was paying a charitable visit to the orphan girls in the nuns' care. A silent plea to their chaperones allowed them the briefest of conversations. Pompey and Caesar had set down the sedan chair in which Celestina was carried, and retreated a mere two steps. It was not ideal. But it was all they had.

"And is it certain you will make your début in *Perseus*?" Celestina said. "The rector has withdrawn his permission so many times, I wonder he means you to have a career at all."

"He's just being cautious." Carlo was not keen to discuss Rector Bartolomeo's motives in hearing of his manservant, even if Rubin's cough obscured most conversation. "But he can't back down this time. Carnival will be over soon, and I must be seen before graduation. It would be suicide otherwise."

"Then I will make sure Papa is there to hear you." Celestina clasped his hand between both of hers. "He is softening toward you; I know he is. After he heard you sing in *Judith*, I said to him, 'Papa, cannot Carlo sing for us at home again?' And he said, 'Perhaps, my angel. We shall see.' Now, isn't that promising?"

"Noblesse, we must leave now, before someone sees us." Teresa, Celestina's governess, was in her usual flap.

"He didn't come to the school opera at Christmas." Carlo was more cautious.

"Oh, you know how busy he and Mama always are over the Twelfth Night banquet." Celestina waved Carlo's caution away. "Yes, Teresa, I'm coming. Michael's buskins, Angel-boy, you'd think we were plotting the Duke's downfall! Yes, I'm coming now. Up, Pompey!"

It was not much of a reassurance, but Carlo clung to it, nonetheless.

"After *Perseus*, rector. Please?" He lowered his pretty eyelashes.

Rector Bartolomeo heaved a button-bursting sigh.

"Very well. After *Perseus*. But that is your final chance."

"Have you seen who else is in *Perseus*? Only Giovanni and Giuseppe!"

Luca waved a newssheet in Antonio's face before galloping from bed to bed, his schoolfellow chasing after him to get a look. The wide-eyed boys of four years ago were now lively striplings of twelve and fourteen, bursting with all the conflicting humours only a eunuch could know.

"Get down before we have the maestri on us!"

Matteo, a boy a little younger than Carlo, was now the dorm's prefect. Carlo was far too busy for such duties. He may have lost his weekly appointment at the Pageno mansion, but he was still the school's greatest export. Weddings. Funerals. Saints' days. Charitable concerts. Anything that could add to the fame and the coffers of the Conservatorio Michelangeli.

Matteo took the newssheet from Luca's hand and passed it to Carlo. Sure enough, the Teatro di Palazzo announced the homecoming of the young castrati Parnasso and Olympio (otherwise known as Giovanni and Giuseppe) who would be performing in the opera of *Perseus* as the Three Muses, alongside the Nightingale of the Conservatorio, who was to make his operatic début.

"Only imagine the larks!" Luca flopped on his mattress and sighed. "Do you remember the time Giuseppe smuggled the laundry maid into the dorm in a hat and cassock?"

"And Giovanni insisted on wearing her frock!" Antonio chortled.

"All right. Leave it," Matteo said. "Give Nightingale a few minutes' peace to rehearse."

He would rehearse in a few minutes, Carlo thought as the others left the room. But first he sank to his knees before the prie-dieu. The candles were cold and smelled of burnt tallow. The Psalter was open at Psalm 6:

Miserere mei, Dominie, quoniam infimus sum. Have mercy on me, Lord, for I am weak.

Carlo crossed himself with holy water and recited the familiar prayer. "Mighty Saint Michael, guard us and grant us justice."

On the right-hand side of the triptych, the Archangel swung his sword at the dragon, his hair in tight curls like watch springs. Carlo's lips trembled as he kissed the painting's hand. What would Michael say, were he to appear in this room now? Those angelic eyes, with their myriad spirals of light and colour, were burned in Carlo's memory forever. The tenderness and might of Angelio's protector. Carlo had always imagined the Archangel smiling down on him, ready to bless. Not waiting to smite sinners on a whim. Surely Carlo and Tammo had been punished enough now for their selfishness at Carnival?

Surely their gifts would now be restored.

The performers' corridor was bustling with backstage staff and the servants of lead singers, all trying to make their way in one direction or another, while squeezing between trunks, racks of costumes and engravings of illustrious performers.

"I'll be all right, Rubin," Carlo told his chaperone. "You get back to the conservatorio."

Rubin hacked up phlegm and nodded. Carlo set his face in the direction of the stage.

As he tiptoed between one obstacle and the next, the door to a tiring room swung open and Carlo caught a glimpse of a female singer reclining on a sopha, less than fully dressed. Leaning over her was a man who bore a strong resemblance to the Cavalier Marchesi. The next moment, the door slammed shut as a seamstress hurried past Carlo, her mouth full of pins and her arms full of ostrich feathers. She only narrowly avoided crashing into a manservant who was trying to juggle two bottles of wine and a corset.

"Have you got the other half of that chariot?" someone yelled from deeper inside the theatre.

"Move!" A boy ran past with a peacock in a cage, almost knocking Carlo down.

Carlo smoothed down his neck bands against his pinchbeck buttons and took a few deep breaths. He mustn't let himself be intimidated. He was here. At last, he was here.

He had begged and begged over the last two years for Rector Bartolomeo to let him make his operatic debut.

"I won't let you down again this time, I promise," he had said.

But the rector was not to be persuaded. Maestro Sarastro had allowed Carlo too much freedom in the past, and look where that had got them! The school's chief pupil would not be exposed to the moral quagmire of the Teatro di Palazzo while under-age, whatever Maestro Sarastro had to say about it. (And the maestro had a great deal to say, most of it profane). Carlo had had to watch both Giuseppe and Giovanni pass him on their way to glory, while he spent lonely nights by the prie-dieu, thinking of Tammo.

When he was seventeen, the rector permitted Carlo to sing the part of Judith in a Lenten oratorio. The crowd had gone wild. Grudgingly, the rector allowed him the role of Mary Magdalene at Easter, and the response was even greater. Angelio loved Carlo. The rector had no choice but to promise him a real operatic debut when he turned eighteen.

He made his way up a short flight of stairs, through wings inhabited by cardboard trees and turrets, precariously dangling ropes, and ballet dancers in frantic rehearsal, and finally blinking with wonder onto the stage of the Teatro di Palazzo.

Carlo felt the breath leave his body. The space was vast. As he gazed up, workmen perched high in the rafters lowered a canvas painted to look like a sumptuous garden, complete with fountains, mazes and olive groves. Further back, a ramp sloped downward to where a groom was leading a white horse with a pair of golden wings strapped to its back. Standing to attention stage left, pikes in hand, was a contingent of the Duke's personal guard, their gold-and-white uniforms spotless.

"They are to engage in real battle in the third act. How utterly thrilling." a voice whispered in Carlo's ear. He turned to see an alabaster cheek and a long ringlet.

"Giovanni!" The two eunuchs embraced. Carlo had not seen his former classmate since Giovanni's graduation two year before. "Signor Parnasso" had been busy establishing his career in the cathedrals and theatres of the Vatican States. Giuseppe had been in Lysfleur.

"And there he is now, by Maestro Sarastro." Giovanni pointed a perfectly manicured finger.

The maestro was in the pit, gesticulating furiously over a harpsichord at an orchestra of strings, oboes and flutes. Behind him, the whole expanse of the auditorium opened out, layer upon layer of balconies supported by marble statues. Boxes gilded and adorned with stuccoes, mirrors and candelabra. The ceiling painted with flights of angels amidst the clouds. And, most splendid of all, the ducal box, surmounted with a crown and fountain, supported by seraphim, and decorated in the height of comfort and fashion. A thrill of destiny shivered through Carlo's breast. The Teatro di Palazzo! This was his home, the place where he belonged. At last, he was on its very stage!

"Ah! I see the young nightingale has arrived," said a nasal voice.

Carlo looked down to see a lean man in good clothes with a slightly bent nose looking over a leather-bound folio together with another man dressed in claret.

"Very good, Signor Contarini," said the claret man. Carlo thought his accent sounded foreign. "Perhaps, then, we can commence with Act Three? Maestro Sarastro, are you ready?"

The maestro looked up from his harpsichord with a

look of suppressed frustration that Carlo knew only too well.

"As ready as any man might be with this gaggle of lackwits for musicians. But go ahead, Herr Wilhelm. God forbid that my music should stand in the way of a performing horse."

A whiff of expensive scent tickled Carlo's nostrils as Morestelli strode onto stage. The famous man's embroidered coat-tails swung dramatically. Carlo's heart and lungs fought a battle for space in his chest. Morestelli!

"Are we doing Act Three or not, Herr Wilhelm?" His celebrated lung power ensured his soprano voice carried across the general hubbub. "Only I do think someone ought to inform La Floretta. She chooses the most inconvenient times to receive her admirers."

"Merciful Michael help us." Signor Contarini put his hand to his forehead in a manner that suggested a headache. "Send one of the dancers. A young one with good calves. That generally persuades her."

Behind Carlo, Giovanni suppressed a giggle.

"Signor..." Carlo heard himself say. Morestelli was standing so close to him now. Surely the great man would acknowledge his presence by some token: a bow or even a nod of the head. At Count Pageno's mansion, the primo castrato had gone so far as to toast Carlo's future in muscat and call him a "divine child".

"Signor..." Carlo tried again.

The leading singer glanced to his side as if he had heard a bee buzzing, passed his eyes over Carlo, and strode across the stage to speak with one of the ballerinas.

"Ouch! I think someone's been cut," said Giuseppe, coming to join him.

"It's no matter." Carlo smiled.

It was a lie. The pain was like that of a real knife. Morestelli knew Carlo had been dropped, and no matter that it was two years ago. Without Count Pageno's favour, Carlo would be an outcast in Angelio's musical sphere. He must win it back. He would. It was his destiny.

The rehearsal for Act Three of *Perseus* went smoothly, with only two tantrums from La Floretta, three outbursts from Maestro Sarastro, and one almost-disaster during a triumphal march, when the pikes of the mounted cavalry came within an inch of dislodging the gods Jove and Minerva from their celestial vantage point seven feet above the stage.

Carlo found the plot a little hard to follow, since it bore scant relation to the legend of Perseus he had learned in school, and contained some arias that had nothing to do with the story at all. There was a great deal of unrequited love and mistaken identity in it; at least two characters were in disguise as the opposite gender. But Carlo could tell that it was going to be splendid. The music was heavenly. The ballets were divine. And for the last opera of the season, the Teatro had spared no expense. There was stage machinery, processions and a veritable menagerie of birds and beasts. In fact, the main problem he and his friends would have, as far as Carlo could see, was actually getting to the stage, what with all the soldiers, horses, dancers, chorus members and stagehands they had to fight their way through to get there.

The grand climax was to be during Perseus's wedding feast, with the Three Muses descending on a cloud as they sang. While they awaited this gravity-defying moment, the three were shepherded into a backstage room where several seamstresses measured and pinned them for their Muse costumes. These, it seemed, were to be cut from a cloth covered all over with glass beads, so that they might shimmer in the candlelight.

"And we'll be working all night to get these done," one of the seamstresses said. "So no spoiling them."

"We shall treasure your fair handiwork as a gift from Minerva herself," Carlo assured them. The one who had spoken blushed prettily.

"Go to, you coxcomb!" she said, pinching Carlo's cheek.

At least someone still appreciated his presence, he thought.

"Be careful on that ascending platform," another seamstress added. "In *Emperor of Mingguo*, one of the demigods got stuck between heaven and earth for three arias."

"I can do that for you, Signorina," said Giuseppe with a wink. The seamstresses burst out laughing. Giuseppe's face fell.

In the end, the descent on the platform turned out wobbly but disaster-free. The Three Muses were pronounced, "charming," by Signor Contarini and dismissed for the day. No one mentioned Carlo by name or introduced him to anyone.

I have become invisible, he thought.

It was not a pleasant notion. By the end of the rehearsal, Carlo's store of energy had quite run out. It was a long way back to the Conservatorio, all along the side of the River Almira from the Bridge of Glories, through the naval docks, as far as St. Uriel's bridge. By the time he reached the porter's lodge, Carlo had no idea from where he would find the strength for harpsichord practice.

"Now, Nightingale," Giovanni was saying. "We really must celebrate your debut upon the stage of the Teatro. We must not let it go unsung."

"Certainly not," said Giovanni, between pinches of snuff. "You must join us for billiards after the performance."

"Oh no, I couldn't." Carlo shook his head. "The rector..."

And never mind the rector. The exhaustion!

"Tush and nonsense!" Giovanni gave a flick of his lace cuff. "We both celebrated on our opening nights, didn't we, Giovanni?"

"I say, look! A crow. On the chapel roof," said Giovanni.

Carlo's throat tightened. A message from Tamino!

"Pray, never mind the wildlife," said Giovanni. "Don't you think our Nightingale would be an absolute natural at billiards. Carlo, you simply must come."

"I'll think about it."

Carlo's mind was no longer on anything but the crow. She strutted to the apex of the chapel roof and cocked her head. Waiting.

"Coronis?"

The crow cawed and took off from the chapel roof to land at the edge of the courtyard.

Giovanni put a lorgnette to his eye.

"Isn't that your society friend, Nightingale? I do hope he doesn't cut you too. Imagine the humiliation, la!"

"Come off it, Giovanni," said Giuseppe. "Let Nightingale be."

"Oh dear! Still sore about that seamstress? Never mind. I hear there are some simply delightful sheep in Act Two." Giovanni tittered.

"After you, signor." Giuseppe made a mock bow.

The two other eunuchs walked away, deep in discussion about the charms of ballerinas.

Carlo looked back at the crow. Was that something tied about its neck? A piece of bark or something?

"Coronis! Here, girl!" He held out his hand. "Come to me, darling of Apollo."

The crow hopped and strutted in Carlo's direction. He reached out a hand to pat the bird's glossy feathers. She lifted her beak and made a clacking noise. Yes, there was something about her neck. A leather thong. And fastened to it, a rolled-up sheet of birch bark and a tiny leather bag. Carefully, Carlo untied the knot and unrolled the bark. His heart jerked. A message in Tammo's hand, scratched on the bark in charcoal:

C. Box 43. Perseus.

T.

Carlo pressed the bark to his lips and kissed it. *Bravo, Tamino!* All was not yet lost. Celestina would be in the

Pageno box on opening night, which meant that the Count would surely be there too. And when he heard Carlo sing...

He ran the back of his little finger over Coronis' head.

"All shall be well again," he sighed. "There'll be no Vulcanetta for me."

16. Messenger of the Gods

It had been a good day. After chopping Grimaldi's firewood at first light, Tammo had followed Coronis into the wood, and together they had come across the carcass of a rabbit, abandoned by a fox in mid-hunt. Tammo had managed to keep Coronis from eating the best bits until he had taken it back to Grimaldi. The old blacksmith seemed pleased with his find, although Tammo strongly suspected he would be the one skinning it and doing the other unpleasant bits.

"I couldn't have done it without Coronis," Tammo said. "She knows where to go. Perhaps we'll find you a pheasant tomorrow."

"And have the Duke's keepers knocking at my door?" said Grimaldi. "You be careful what you find in those woods, lad."

But he was smiling as he took the rabbit by its neck and went to hang it at the hovel door. Tammo wrinkled a half-smile in return. He had grown to love the old blacksmith, although he would have died before admitting it. He had a decent life here, as lives went. Although it wasn't the life he'd hoped for.

This morning, the act of walking the familiar paths by the forge reminded him too strongly of the dark flute. Of the hours he had spent in these very trees, the breath of the forest his own breath, the summons of the flute bringing birds to circle around him in a magical ballet, their hearts and his heart and Carlo's scarcely distinguishable one from the other.

"Now all I have is you," he said to Coronis. "You big, black murderer."

He carved himself a flute of sorts from a hollow branch, working on it night after night by firelight in Grimaldi's hut after days spent pumping bellows in the forge.

"Planning on giving us a tune, boy?" Grimaldi said.

Tammo merely hunched his shoulders and concentrated on the tiny shavings as they peeled away.

When it was done, he took it deep into the forest to test the sound. Carlo would have cringed, he thought. The flute was tuneful enough, in its way. But the sound was flat, dull. To compare it with the dark flute would be to compare a peacock with a sparrow.

Nonetheless, he felt compelled to try charming birds with it.

He began by weaving a cage to catch one in. That wasn't so hard. He had managed to make one for Orpheus, hadn't he? He wondered how Orpheus was doing these days, whether Carlo still used him for nightingalising. Tammo blinked and swallowed hard. Best not to go down that pathway. Best not to dwell on former closeness with his sworn twin, now lost forever.

He tried for a simple bell shape, with a hole to let the bird through and a string of bark to fasten it shut. It didn't turn out quite so well as he hoped—more of a lumpy mess than a bell—but it held together.

Next, he built a hide. He chose a sheltered spot, downwind of the river, and wove together dead branches and bits of brushwood, covering it with brown leaves and moss. He laid a trail of fat scrapings from the pan and lay in the hide on his belly. He kept the flute's music to a simple *pip-pip-trill*, the call of a tom-tit or finch.

Soon, a little fluff-ball of a bird came hopping into view, bouncing in the air from branch to branch. Tammo stilled his breath and trilled again. The tom-tit trilled back and came a little nearer to inspect the scraps. One peck, another, and he would have it. But it was a hollow victory. There was no tug in his chest, no yearning in his soul. Whatever the desires of this tiny heart, they were dead to him. This flute would be useful as a lure. He would be able to earn a little here and there with a captured bird. But the gift of the Archangel he had known with the dark flute, that was gone. He had lost it at Carnival.

One thing he had never lost sight of, however, was his commission to Celestina. As soon as he was settled into his new home in Angel's Wood, he had crept back to Angelio and the Pageno mansion. A maple tree around the back was easily climbed, and let out onto the open arch of a belvedere tower. That first autumn afternoon, Tammo had scuffled and slipped across tiles covered in algae to discover a door. Glancing around him, he lifted the latch and put his shoulder to it...

Two female voices screeched in discord. Tammo flinched. He had come into a sewing room, where two maidservants were seated in wicker chairs by the fire, plying their needles on shirts that seemed more lace than actual shirt. The closer of the two eyeballed Tammo furiously and leaped to her feet. She stood all of four feet tall, including her cap.

"Tammo Capell! Do you make a habit of fraying my nerves? What in Michael's bootstraps are you doing here?"

Tammo swallowed hard and stared at the gorgonesque figure of Fenice that was advancing toward him.

"Don't tell!" He held up his hands, palms outward. "I need to speak to Celestina. To the noblesse. Carlo sent me."

Fenice gave an angry snort and shook her needlework until the lace trembled.

"And what about me, lackwit? What happens to my promotion if Signor Platini finds you here?" She waved a hand behind her. "See this? A trial period as seamstress, I've been promised. A nice cosy seat upstairs instead of laundry and steaming coppers in the kitchen. I'm not going to lose my chance for the likes of you."

"Nor I my chance of Countess Pageno giving me permission to wed," said the other girl. She bit off a thread with her teeth. "That'd be both of us scuppered, Fenice."

Tammo cleared his throat. Fenice eyeballed him so hard, Tammo was sure she could have used his face as a torch.

"So, the little songbird sent you, eh? Another little bird told me he's not very well. Or is that just a cipher for the fact that he's in disgrace?"

Any more of this and they could have grilled fish on his forehead, too.

"He's not well. He has a monstrous cold."

That had been true when he had last seen Carlo. No need to go into details about the Carnival, their joint disgrace, nor the fact that Tammo had been ill himself. If he scrunched up his toes, Tammo could feel the carnival ring in his shoe. He could remember Carlo's kiss and the oath he'd made Tammo swear. What was between him and Carlo was private. He wasn't about to discuss him with Fenice or anybody else.

"I have to give a message from him to Noblesse Celestina. In person."

"Oh, do you now?" Fenice cocked her head. "Well, it just so happens I have a soft spot for your singing friend. And the noblessse could do with some good news. Word has it she was weeping over her breakfast this morning."

"Where is she?" Tammo couldn't help himself asking.

Fenice smirked.

"Keen, aren't you? She's usually about her studies at this hour. Not alone. Don't think it's as simple as that, Mercury. But you've got Fenice to help you out now, haven't you? Aren't you going to give me a little kiss to thank me for my troubles?"

Both girls fell about laughing at the obvious horror on Tammo's face. Fenice sidled up and pinched his cheek.

"Try me again in two years' time. I reckon you'll be about ready by then. Hey, Tammo Capell?" She laughed again. "Follow me. And keep quiet."

That was how it began. The secret visits to the mansion

through Fenice's sewing room. That first time, Fenice had led him through a passage to the far side of the musician's rooms, and then on into a schoolroom. Terracotta tiles covered the floor, and the walls had been painted with scenes depicting the four continents. Allegorical figures of literature, mathematics and rhetoric danced across the ceiling. Desks, bookcases, globes and writing materials filled all other space. Apparently, the Count did not share the rector's view that young people learned best with as little distraction as possible.

Tammo blushed to the roots of his hair when Celestina wheeled her house carriage toward him.

"Fenice said you have a message from Carlo." Celestina leaned forward with urgency. "How is he?"

"Not well, I'm afraid," said Tammo. "He was in bed with a cold last time I saw him."

"Oh, poor Carlo!" Celestina clasped her hands to her chest. "Is he very miserable?" And then before Tammo had time to frame an answer: "Oh, but he will be miserable if he cannot sing. I know it. I should have Teresa send him some oranges."

She scowled. To Tammo's eyes, it looked as if a tiny fold had appeared in a pure silk handkerchief.

"But Papa says I mayn't send messages to Carlo. I must stay in my rooms or at my harpsichord and devote myself to accomplishments and prayer."

She struck the lacquered surface of the house carriage with more force than Tammo expected her to possess.

"That is so unfair! Is it not also pious to care for one's friends? What do you say, Tammo Capell?"

"I...er..." Tammo began.

"And is he very poorly?" said Celestina. "Have they bled him? I do so hate to be bled."

"I...don't know." Tammo was finding it increasingly difficult to follow the conversation and exercise control over his humours at the same time. "He blows his nose a great deal and sneezes."

"Oh, poor Carlo!" Celestina said again. "His poor, dear nose!"

A pang of jealousy shot through Carlo's heart. If Carlo could excite Celestina's sympathy with a red, fraying nose, what chance did Tammo have? Unthinking, he rubbed his own nose. It was still a little sore, but Celestina said nothing about that. Better give his attention to the task in hand.

"He asked me to tell you... He wanted me to say that he's sorry he can't come and see you. The physician says he must stay in bed for two weeks. And you mustn't get upset. It's not your fault the Count is angry."

This last piece of information did not have the effect Tammo hoped for. Instead of pouring out relief and gratitude (and some tender reward) on the messenger, Celestina shifted uncomfortably in her chair, her eyes downcast. To Tammo's horror, he saw she was about to cry.

"But Papa is angry with me. And Mama too. Mama says it's not right to have a eunuch for a playmate, and Papa should never have brought him into the house. She says I've been in...decorous." Her lip began to tremble. "What does that mean, Tammo? Is Carlo in trouble? I didn't mean to be bad. I just miss Orlando..."

Sweat stood out on the back of Tammo's neck. What

was he meant to do now? He could see tears beginning to
spill from Celestina's eyes. The crazy part of him wanted to
catch them in a handkerchief and treasure them as pearls.
The rest of him just wanted to run away. Carlo was so much
better at this sort of thing. The eunuch would put a friendly
arm around Celestina's shoulder, tease a smile from her lips,
kiss her fingers without embarrassment. Tammo could no
more do that than fly. If he laid a hand on Celestina, he was
sure it would erupt into flame.

But Carlo was not here now.

"No, no, you've done nothing wrong, noblesse,"
Tammo managed to say. "Anyone can see what a genteel
lady you are."

It wasn't working. She just kept weeping.

"He used to sit at that desk. Right there, every day. We
passed notes when Teresa and his tutor weren't looking.
Once, he put a live frog in the tutor's water jug. How we
laughed!"

It took a few mental contortions for Tammo to realise
she was speaking of her dead brother. He searched in vain
for suitable words and found nothing but the memory of his
sisters. He forced them down. He would not show weakness
before Celestina.

"I just wanted it to be like that with Carlo. To laugh
and have fun and be friends. I love him so dearly, Tammo.
It's so wretched to think of him sick in bed where I can't see
him."

"He'll come when he's well, noblesse," said Tammo,
hoping to Michael it was true.

"And if he doesn't?" Celestina wiped her eyes. "Tammo Capell, you must give him a message from me."

She reached for a purse about her waist and took out a pair of silver scissors. Before Tammo had time to wonder what she was doing, she had snipped off a lock of her honey-brown hair and looped it into a knot.

"Give him this. With my love."

Tammo made another bow to hide his blushes.

"I am always at your service, noblesse. You can rely on me."

It had taken some time to work out how to deliver the message safely. By the time he received it, Carlo could be fit and well, and singing at the Teatro. Tammo truly hoped so. In the meantime, his only confidante was Coronis, who insisted on staying by his side. He may have lost his link with other birds, but Coronis still gave every sign of sharing his feelings. Could it be that Coronis was his last link with Carlo? Carlo's talent had gone into making his miraculous skill with the dark flute, and Coronis was still bound to him by the early force of the flute's summons. Would Coronis fly as his messenger to Carlo if he willed it strongly enough.

He persuaded Grimaldi to let him have a little bit of leather and a needle made from a leftover filament of iron. Sewing was hard work. Tammo found himself swearing and sucking at his bleeding finger more than once. Now was a time when he could have done with Fenice's help. How did girls manage to sew in patterns, for sweet Michael's sake, when even a simple in-and-out was so exhausting? The finished bag was not exactly to Tammo's satisfaction, but it was small enough to go around Coronis's neck and would hold Celestina's hair safely. Tammo felt heat come to his cheeks at the moment of parting with the precious lock. He felt sure Carlo would have kissed it, or something like that, but that just felt embarrassing. Instead, he kicked at tree roots, trying to fight against the emptiness inside.

Willing Coronis to fly to Carlo also took longer than Tammo expected. For one thing, he still had Grimaldi's errands to do, and it turned out customers were more likely to pay willingly when the messenger did not have a large corvid sitting on his shoulder. Coronis was currently banned from coming with Tammo into Angelio. That meant he would have to release her from Angel's Wood, and will her to fly all the way to the conservatorio. Tammo wasn't at all sure Coronis understood this. He would sit her on his wrist and think about Carlo as hard as he could, right down to imagining the chafing on the end of Carlo's nose from all that nose-blowing. Coronis would take off with a terrific flap and Tammo's spirits would rise. But a few minutes later she would come flying back, having clearly been no further than a nearby grove of olive trees.

The day she did finally go, Tammo barely noticed at first. Grimaldi had wanted him to act as striker again, swinging the hammer while the blacksmith held the red-hot metal against the anvil. It was wearying work. Tammo's muscles had never ached in his life as they had done since he came to the woods. Life at the conservatorio hadn't prepared him for lifting anything heavier than a music stand or—more recently—a birdcage. And if he tried to catch his breath, even for a moment, Grimaldi would come out with some comment like, "Is this the sort of stamina young people have nowadays? When I was your age, I could swing a sledgehammer from dawn till dusk without even breaking a sweat."

This irritated Tammo so much that the next thing Grimaldi said was usually something about minding how he went before he had the hammer flying off its handle. At any rate, the exhausting nature of the work kept his mind off bad memories and, as it happened, off Coronis's mission as well. So, it was only when Grimaldi decided to break for some bread and cream cheese that Tammo noticed Coronis on the roof of the forge. The roll of birch bark he had tied about her neck with a message for Carlo was gone. He swore.

"Where is it? Ill-omened bird! What have you done with Carlo's message?"

He chased Coronis around the clearing until the crow decided he was in a better temper and came to him of her own free will. It was only then that Tammo considered Coronis might have delivered his message. He tore the leather bag from Coronis's neck and pulled its drawstrings open.

Something winked at him from the bottom. Tammo put his fingers into the bag and pulled out the button. Its familiar lyre emblem sparkled in the sunlight coming through the trees. The emblem from a conservatorio uniform. From a cassock just like the one he had abandoned under the lime tree.

"Carlo," he whispered, clutching the button tight in the palm of his hand. His friend had got the message. Celestina's mission had been fulfilled.

After that, there was no stopping him. He was Mercury, messenger of the gods. And Coronis was his familiar. Black wings flew back and forth across Angelio, from the lime tree to the maple and back again. Carlo was well. He was singing again. Celestina had learned a new prelude and fugue upon the harpsichord. A poet from Lysfleur had been to visit the mansion. The Pageno family were going to their villa in the countryside for summer. Carlo had been given the lead part in the school opera. Back and forth. Back and forth. Forth and back. Summer and autumn. Winter and spring.

And every season, Celestina grew more beautiful. Her baby softness turning to womanly curves.

"Is she well, dear twin?" Carlo would say to him as they sat, each with their back to the school gate, shooting stars streaking the heavens with silver.

"Very well," Tammo would reply, thankful that the darkness hid his blushes. How could the question be answered with mere words? She was a goddess. A vision. Had he the dark flute once more, he could do her beauty justice in music, but not otherwise.

"When I attain my liberty," Carlo said, "the three of us we be reunited. Friends forever."

Tammo had no words. He clasped his chemise to his heart and looked into the sable sky. Another star fell.

There was nearly a hundred lira in silver and copper secreted in a hole between the bricks by the fireplace. Business had been good recently, both smithing and birding. Tammo counted out the last few centesimi and looked with pride on the little piles of coins.

"Ought to get yourself a new coat and breeches with that lot," Grimaldi said. "You look like a scarecrow, boy."

Tammo considered retorting that the blacksmith looked like a haystack but thought better of it. He had never grown much taller or broader than he had always been, but his old breeches had been let out so many times they were frayed at the edges. And the second-hand coat he had bartered from a tinker was too long in the sleeves and smelled of horse.

"There's a little tailor's by the side of St. Remiel's. Just before you get to the fish market. Do you know it, boy?"

"Aye. I know it." Tammo wondered how Grimaldi knew Angelio so well; he never went there.

"Well, you go there and get yourself measured. Fustian will do. No extras. Tell them Grimaldi sent you."

"There's no need..." Tammo began.

"I'll decide when there's a need, lad," said Grimaldi. "And you can get me some mullet heads while you're out."

"Yes, Grimaldi."

Tammo scuffed his shoes against the ground. Honestly, it was as bad as being back at school sometimes!

"Is that the sound of you setting off?" Grimaldi said from the hearth. "Sooner you go, sooner you get back."

The tailor's shop was not too much of an ordeal. The greasy little tailor smelled of snuff, and poked pins into Tammo's legs at least four times, but he didn't speak except to complain to his assistant, and Tammo could entertain himself by wondering if the man's wig was about to unravel itself any time soon.

Tammo hoped there would still be some mullet heads by the time he got to the fish market. All the best stuff went early in the morning, but he hadn't wanted to stink out the tailor's parlour with a package of fish heads and bits of fin. He slunk between the various barrows and baskets, thinking how odd it was to be a customer here instead of begging for money. He looked toward the place where he used to stand, but it wasn't a conservatorio day and the place was empty. Under the tree by the river, a glockenspiel was churning out tunes from the opera. Further down the footpath, someone had set up a fortune-telling booth. Tammo felt in his pocket for a spare centesimi. He could have his fortune told. Find out if he would ever get the dark flute back. Father Dominic had railed long and hard against that kind of thing, and the Archangel probably wouldn't like it, but Tammo was on his own here. He needed all the help he could get.

"Tammo Capell!" A voice came ringing across the market.

Tammo spun on his heels, his neck-bands choking him. Who would call his name out in the marketplace? Whatever the reason, it couldn't be good.

"Tammo!" said the voice again. "Oi, Mercury! Over here!"

His breath eased out of him as Fenice came hip-walking from the side of the glockenspiel player, a basket on her arm. Tammo scratched the back of his neck and hid the fish behind his back.

"Fenice! What are you doing here?"

He didn't think he'd ever seen her outside the Pageno mansion; she looked wrong in the open air with her face shining and her cap-strings fluttering in the breeze.

"I'm very well, citizen. Thank you for asking." Fenice gave a sarcastic grimace.

"Oh, sorry." Tammo attempted to bow. "How are you, Fenice, this fine...er...day?"

Fenice sighed, as though the sport of tormenting Tammo was too tiring at present.

"As well as can be expected."

There was so something not right about her today, Tammo thought. Not so much swagger. Not enough Amazonian passion.

"Are you...all right?" he managed to say.

"What do you think, lackwit?" The lost fire blazed from Fenice's eyes. "When the world's all wrong." She sniffed. "You may as well know, Tammo Capell, for soon everyone will."

Tammo had the feeling he'd missed an enormous chunk of conversation.

"Know what?" he asked.

Fenice took a breath.

"It's Noblesse Celestina," she said. And burst into sobs.

17. Box Forty-three

He had made it to opening night. Carlo hugged his cloak tightly round his beaded Muse costume, trying to find a fragment of floorboard to call his own. The tiring room was thick with the smell of face powders and perspiration, clamouring with hastily-rehearsed scales, vulgar military jokes, cries of "Where's my boot? I'm on in five minutes", and other such jollities.

"My wing is bent."

Giuseppe held it up, shooting accusing looks at the nearest guardsman. His sudden movement caused both Carlo and Giovanni to receive elbows in the ribs. Giovanni elbowed back and returned to examining his features in a small hand mirror.

"Give me some of your padding, Giuseppe. My bosoms look quite forlorn."

"Fat chance," muttered Giuseppe, with more emphasis than was necessary on the *fat*.

Carlo passed Giovanni a crumpled stocking, before wrapping his arms back around himself. His stomach had begun to hurt, and he could barely remember his lines. The same thought returned to his mind over and over again. Box forty-three. Celestina. The Count. He had made a point of looking, during the general rehearsal, at the crests of noble houses that had been fixed up on the more conspicuous boxes. The golden pheasant was on the third box up, stage left. It was one of a number of boxes that actually overlooked the sides of the stage as it jutted out into the pit. Count Pageno's neighbours, one box beneath, could have reached out and shaken hands with Morestelli as he strode about the stage, had they wished. These were boxes for people who wanted both to see and be seen. And from his vantage point in the third box up, Count Pageno would see a great deal, both onstage and off. No wonder Celestina had said her father was indispensable to the Duke at the opera. With His Grace in the ducal box, Count Pageno in box forty-three and another retainer in a corresponding box on the other side of the stage, the Duke could effectively keep an eye on his entire court and many of his subjects at the same time.

And from the descending platform, Carlo would have a perfect view into the Pagenos' box. He had checked during rehearsal, while singing soaring hymns to Hymen and wobbling gradually lower behind a cardboard cloud. Box forty-three ravished his senses. A rich Turkey carpet had been laid on the floor. An extravagant gilt mirror covered the entire back wall so that, even when deep in conversation, the Count could still see the spectacles taking place on stage. A brocade curtain could be drawn across the side facing the auditorium, should the Count require privacy. Tastefully matched chairs, footstools and buffet tables completed what Carlo imagined was a perfect setting for an evening of comfort and entertainment. What a world Celestina inhabited! He must regain the Count's favour. He must.

For all the tedious waiting, once the call for the

wedding scene had been given, time seemed in precious short supply. Everyone was trying to apply face paint, adjust wigs and warm up their voices with scales. Carlo managed a glimpse of one ear and half his chin in the communal mirror, and even then, he wouldn't have sworn under oath they were truly his. He pouted and flexed his lips, wondering if he looked heroic. He must look his best for Count Pageno. For Celestina. He had to make them believe in him once more.

"Ow! You stepped on my foot," someone said.

"At least you're wearing buskins." Giuseppe was still trying to fix his lopsided wing. "Mine broke during rehearsal, so I've had to draw on sandals with stage paints." He looked down at his criss-crossed legs with a disappointed frown.

"Never mind that." Carlo's heart was pounding. "We're on now. Get in formation, quickly!"

There was a frantic scramble as everyone tried to get into the right order without crushing everyone else. The undignified shuffle to the door reminded Carlo of a flock of sheep. A dancer dressed as a fanciful shepherd leaned amiably in the door frame.

"In the mouth of the wolf!" he said.

"May the wolf choke!" several people behind Carlo replied. A tall man accompanied this by spitting on the floor. For luck, Carlo supposed. He smiled at the dancer, trying not to look as nervous as he felt. The dancer winked and slid out of the way.

And then they were in the wings, weaving their way through stage hands, peacock handlers, servants of the leading singers who stood by with rosehip water and hand mirrors, and several people whose only function was getting in the way. From onstage, Carlo could hear Morestelli pardoning the tenor and welcoming Il Cupide and Figliolo to his wedding. A ladder led up to the rafters and the descending platform. Carlo, Giuseppe and Giovanni climbed, trying hard not to look up each other's skirts. As Carlo stepped onto the rungs, the orchestra launched into the introduction to Perseus and Andromeda's reunion duet. It was time.

Carlo climbed as steadily as he could manage. He would not think about the fall he would have if he slipped. It was like the tree, he told himself. Like climbing the lime tree with Tammo. He could do it. He wasn't going to slip and crack his head on that wooden elephant directly beneath him. Giovanni reached for his hand and steadied him as he reached the top. The platform rocked slightly as everyone shuffled into position. Carlo prayed. *Please don't let Count Pageno have retired to the gaming room.*

A backdrop came down behind them, creaking as men struggled with the pulleys. Onstage, more men hurried to slide cardboard arches into position. At the same moment, two trumpets sounded from the pit. That was their cue. The starting note. The platform began to wobble downwards.

Now from Olympus' golden height, they sang.

Their voices echoed back at them from the ropes and rafters. A tiny sliver of gold and crimson began to emerge below their feet like the dawn breaking in reverse.

Hosts of Hymen come to bless.
Hosts of Hymen,

Hosts of Hymen come to bless, to bless, to bless.
Hosts of Hymen come to bless.

Carlo could see the very top tier of the auditorium. Dim figures in carnival masks leaned over the pit, playbills in hand. Sheets of sonnets came fluttering down. The stage around the performers' feet was littered with papers, roses and lace handkerchiefs.

Borne on lovers' gentle sighs,
To attend each sweet caress.
To attend each sweet,
To attend each sweet, each sweet caress.

The sensation of looking over the theatre made Carlo's stomach flutter like birds were hatching inside him. *Remember your training*, he told himself. *Breathe from the bowel.* They were coming to a level with the highest boxes now. Soon he would see the Pagenos' box. The descending platform was going to pass right by it.

Watered with your joyous tears,
May constancy eternal grow.
Constancy, constancy....

There. There was box. He could see the golden pheasant. Silk and satin shimmered in the candlelight. There were five people inside. One of those tall, silent footmen standing right at the back with a salver in his hand. Not Pompey; the other one. Two gentlemen Carlo didn't know, leaning round the pillar to flirt with the ladies in the next box. Vittori, who had escorted Carlo home on Justice Night. The Count, as silent as his footman, his mouth tight, his eyes dull and unseeing.

That was all. Carlo almost missed his cue for the next

line and had to mouth the first word to avoid making a discord. There was no one else there. Celestina was not there. There was not the slightest sign of her presence. No painted fans, no chocolate creams, no female servant. Nothing that even suggested a female. The party was entirely male and adult. Celestina was not among them.

The aria returned to the start. Carlo was forced to sing about Hosts of Hymen all over again, as the lead singers joined hands for the final song, and peacocks fanned their tails and screeched over La Bellina's soaring soprano.

Where was she? Celestina had gone to the trouble of sending a message via Tammo, telling Carlo to look out for her on opening night, and now she was not here. Why? Had something gone wrong? Had the Countess intervened? By the time the descending platform reached the stage and Carlo came forward to take his bow with the other Muses, the feeling in his stomach was very bad indeed. And it had nothing to do with vertigo.

She was not there the following night either. On the third night, box forty-three was empty. Even the Count had gone. Carlo worried about it all day at school. It was the final, glorious week of the opera season. *Perseus* was to be the grand climax before Lent. Maestro Sarastro had no time to give lessons at the conservatorio, and there was no one else who knew the dealings of the great families well enough for Carlo to ask after Celestina's wellbeing.

There had been no summons from the Pageno mansion. Carlo kept seeing the fixed stare of the Count as he sat dumbly in his box. He would not even look upon his former pupil. It was a forlorn hope, a child's hope. Carlo was no longer a cherub child. He was a trained castrato on the verge of taking flight. He could not cling to a long dream and a promise he had broken.

He had crossed the courtyard to knock on the rector's door when the sound of a flute broke in on his thoughts. For a moment, his heart leapt. The dark flute! Tamino! Then reality took charge once more. Did he still expect to find his twin sitting in the lime tree, fourteen years old again? The dark flute was no longer in Tammo's possession. The flautist was Maestro Aquila.

Carlo looked toward the cream-coloured house with its pear tree and bas-relief of a wreath and lyre above the door. The maestro was sitting at an open window, flute to his lips, staring out across the courtyard. Carlo knew the melody he was playing. It was one of Figliolo's famous pathetic arias, *My Heart Weeps*. As Carlo listened, the notes faltered and the flute slipped to the maestro's lap. Carlo cleared his throat.

"God save you, maestro."

Maestro Aquila started. A sorrowful smile came to his lips. "God save you too, Carlo Bianci."

Carlo didn't know the flute master well. His own studies had been restricted to vocal training and the harpsichord. But he knew how kind the man had been to Tammo. Aquila rubbed his chin and leaned out of the window.

"Could you spare me a few moments, Carlo?"

"Of course." Carlo made a bow.

Maestro Aquila disappeared from the window and appeared moments later at the door.

"Come in." He gestured with his arm.

Carlo stepped around a pile of books that looked as if it was held up by some law outside the realm of natural philosophy. Where to step next, he was not entirely sure? The clutter in this room was a veritable offence to good taste! How could a master of the art musical tolerate such squalor? When he had his own apartment, Carlo decided, it would be a shrine to beauty and order. Nothing ugly or messy would be allowed in it.

Maestro Aquila swept a stool clear of yet another precarious pile, so Carlo could sit, and perched his lean backside on the windowsill. He had picked up the dark flute again, Carlo noticed. His long fingers ran absently over its finger holes, toying with a half-remembered tune. The maestro sighed.

"Why did he do it?" He shook his head and sighed again. "I've never been able to understand his running off like that. He was the most gifted student I ever had. I thought the birding business would turn him around. But perhaps he was just a hopeless case after all."

Carlo sat gingerly on the stool and folded his hands in his lap. "We're talking about Tammo Capell, aren't we?"

The maestro nodded, scratching his chin until Carlo could hear tiny hairs bristling.

"He didn't even come for the flute. That's what I can't understand. You were his friend, they tell me. Were you aware of this ability, this gift he had? I never saw its like. He seemed like a different boy when..." He turned the dark flute over in his hands, fingering its leaf and bird decoration. "When this instrument was at his lips, he did things I never could." The maestro smiled to himself. "Call me an old fool, but I keep playing it in the hope that birds might come to me, as they did to him. They never do."

"It was a gift, maestro." Carlo spoke carefully, unsure how much to reveal. That Tammo still made secret visits to the school, under cover of night? That he lived in Angel's Wood, attempting to charm birds with a flute made from a stick? Not likely! But he would not leave Maestro Aquila with a false notion of Tammo's motives. This might be his last chance before leaving the conservatories for good. Besides, the maestro seemed so unhappy. Carlo could not bear to see a person suffer without offering comfort.

"He was not casting the gift back in your face," he said. "Bird-charming meant the world to him. I believe it still does. But he would not have you call him a thief, maestro. Had he left with the flute in his hand, that is what he would be."

"It would not have been theft had I placed the flute in his hands," said Maestro Aquila.

Carlo considered. "You would have given Tammo the dark flute, maestro? Even though he was running away?"

The maestro shifted in the casement with a half-laugh.

"You have me there, Carlo! Had he gone to Fiorenta as the rector wanted, yes, I would have placed this flute in his hands and bade him learn it well. No one else could ever play it as he did. But had I caught him as a runaway, my only thought would have been to keep him within these walls. I would have held back the flute as a bribe to keep him here."

"He is not in Fiorenta," said Carlo. "And he will not come back within these walls."

"And yet bird charming means the world to him?" The maestro fingered the orioles and linnets carven along the length of the flute.

"Yes," Carlo said. He had never been more certain of anything.

The maestro stood up slowly. "And if he were to, say, pay a passing visit? Do you think that sort of thing might happen, Carlo? Might he call by to give his regards to a former schoolmate.

Carlo kept his face an expressionless mask. "That would be against school rules, maestro."

"Of course, it would. As you say."

Maestro Aquila walked to the wall and hung the dark flute in its special rack, between two lighter instruments.

"It shall remain here for the time being. No other student plays it now. I shall not remove it from its place, I think. Here. On this rack. In this room."

"It looks well there, maestro," Carlo said, politely.

The maestro nodded.

"For the time being. And where does life take you next, Carlo Bianci?"

Aquila's voice was still inside his head as the rector's manservant led him through the small passageway into the study. Rector Bartolomeo's straining waistcoat overlapped the desk as he bent over, examining a ledger through a horn-rimmed magnifying glass.

"Ah, Bianci!" He looked up with a smile that made his eyes partly disappear behind his plump cheeks. "What can I do for you? I trust your time at the opera is not causing you to neglect your prayers. Never forget you are a servant of Saint Michael."

"The thought is daily before me." That was true enough, and more forcefully than the rector could ever suspect. "But I wished to speak of my future. I have been considering your words and…"

He took a deep breath. The next words would change the course of his life for ever.

"You were right, rector. I wish to take the post in Vulcanetta."

18. *Resurgam*

Tammo picked at a scab on the back of his hand until blood started to ooze between his knuckles. He bit his lip and started on another one, nearer the wrist. Where was she? She had promised to meet him under this tree, at first light, and she was nowhere to be seen. And now he had been joined by the glockenspiel player, trying to warm up his machine for the day. If he had to listen to the first two bars of *O, Glorious Majesty* one more time, he was going to go mad.

"Bloody girls!" he said to Coronis. "Where is she? What's happened?"

Coronis gave a haughty caw at Tammo's abuse of her sex, but other than that, Tammo thought she seemed to agree. The crow was as restless as he, flapping from branch to branch of the tree, and flying down to make mock attacks on the glockenspiel player. It was all Tammo could do to prevent her making off with scraps of fish from the costermongers' baskets as they unloaded their wares from the barges. Tammo closed his fist on the flute case that hung at his hip like a scabbard. He wished there was a real weapon inside it. He felt the need to be armed, to be prepared for action.

Fenice's last news had made iron fists close about his

heart. His only way to cope had been to run the entire distance from the fish market to Grimaldi's forge without stopping, take up an axe the instant he got there, and chop firewood until he sank to his knees, his arms shaking uncontrollably.

"What's all this?" Grimaldi had said when he found Tammo hunched over a huge stack of firewood, surrounded by wood chips and sawdust. "Did you bring those mullet heads I asked for?"

"On the table," Tammo grunted.

He hadn't wanted to tell Grimaldi what was burning a hole in his gut. If he didn't speak the words, it would not be true. But Fenice had spoken. There, in the fish market, under a bright sun that should have been ashamed to shine on such tidings.

"Noblesse Celestina is ill," she had said.

Tammo hadn't understood at first. Hadn't wanted to.

"A cold?" he said.

"Not a cold, lackwit!" Fenice had come close to slapping him. "You think I would shed tears over a sniffle? She's ill, I say. Fever. They're afraid that..."

She had turned away. That was when Tammo had got really scared. If Fenice the Amazon could be so shaken by the news, then it must be grave indeed.

"Afraid of what?" He had wanted to shake the truth out of her. "Tell me, Fenice! I have to know."

Fenice's face had contorted with the effort of holding back tears. That was when the iron fists had closed.

"That she has the same illness as Nobile Orlando, lackwit!"

And now all he could do was wait under the tree, hoping Fenice would turn up as she said. She'd promised to bring him news, whether good or bad, at the next fish market. The suspense made him feel like throwing up.

"Where is she?" Tammo said for the hundredth time.

"I'm here," said a voice at his chest. "Try looking down once in a while."

He knew as soon as he looked at her. Her face was taught with lines of worry; her eyes were shadowed with purple bruises. For the first time, he thought he glimpsed something in Fenice other than frightening femininity. He tried to speak but nothing came out. Fenice took several deep breaths. Coronis flew to Tammo's shoulder and stayed there.

"She has the rash." Fenice's voice was blank, without emotion. "The physician bled her this morning, but she hasn't woken since yesterday." Fenice's lips twitched and her voice sank to a husky baritone. "Pray for her, Tammo. That's all you can do."

"No!"

Tammo punched the tree trunk, making his knuckles bleed and birds scatter in terror. Coronis gave a violent caw.

"She's not going to die! I prayed to the Archangel for Carlo to meet her. He promised with his own lips. I heard him and Carlo did too. How could the Prince of Seraphim lie? He can't let her die!"

Fenice took a step back.

"Tammo, what are you talking about?"

Tammo squared his shoulders and put his hand on his flute sheath.

"I'm talking about Noblesse Celestina not dying!"

Without a word, he turned and ran through the market square, scattering children and dogs as he went, sending birds flying up in chirruping clouds.

"Tammo Capell! Where are you going?" Fenice yelled.

But he didn't turn back.

He arrived at the conservatorio walls before he'd even begun to think where he was going. His heart was pounding and a whole flock of birds was trailing in his wake. Carlo. He had to find Carlo and tell him. The consequences could go hang. They had to save Celestina.

He was right opposite the lime tree. Right at the place where he and Carlo had jumped down on that ill-starred night when everything had begun to go bad. The same spot, too, where he had jumped from the wall alone on a miserable morning, thinking he would never return to this place again. It was a high wall, but he didn't care. He stepped back and took a run up to it, feet scrabbling at the bricks, fingernails breaking with the effort of clinging.

And he was up. He crouched for a moment, holding on, panting. There was a flutter in the branches of the lime, and his old finches and starlings came down to perch on his head and shoulders alongside Coronis. He gave a grim smile.

"Nice to see someone thinks of me fondly. Now, where's Carlo?"

A quarter to eight by the clock. The whole school would be in chapel, singing matins. If he went quickly and quietly, he could do this without being seen. He clambered through the branches of the tree and let himself down.

"You stay here," he willed the birds. There was only one bird he needed right now. Coronis was too well-known, too big and obvious, for the task Tammo had in mind. He needed a bird with intelligence, a bird that knew his mind. A bird that loved Carlo.

Tammo ran along the edge of the courtyard, hunched as low as possible. Let every last servant and steward be at prayer right now! Let no one leave the chapel early, for duty or for sickness' sake. Most of all, let the porter not be in his lodge. Everything depended on that.

The low, wooden door was open a crack. Tammo prodded it with a finger and peeped through. Praise be to Michael! Old Pascual was at his prayers with the rest of the school. Tammo tiptoed into the parlour where he and Carlo had hidden from winter's chill. A musical twitter erupted from among the smoke-blackened beams. Tammo's eye found the spot instantly. He reached up to the cage with its wire dome and unlatched the door. Orpheus hopped out to nestle in his palms as if the two had never been parted.

"Come with me, old friend," he whispered to the song thrush's head.

He tucked Orpheus inside his coat and crouch-ran along the perimeter again. When he reached the chapel, he flattened himself against the wall and put his face to the window. The seraphic sound of *Salve Angelus Carminum* floated out to meet him. For a moment, it was all he could do to press his lips together and remind himself to be a man. That was Carlo's voice, soaring above the rest. Tammo cradled Orpheus in one hand and reached under his chemise to draw out a leather thong. Suspended from it was Carlo's carnival ring. He held Orpheus close and placed the ring in his beak.

"Take this to Carlo," he breathed.

Tammo closed his eyes. The dark flute may be lost, but Orpheus was still one with him. He could feel it. Placing his hands inside the open window, he threw Orpheus forward and let go.

The worst part was the wait. Tammo felt he'd been in the tree for hours. Every possibility, every disaster ran through his head. If Orpheus were to cause an uproar in chapel instead of flying to Carlo quietly. If Carlo could find no way of escaping, what then? What could Tammo do next? Flee the conservatorio and seek out Celestina alone? Find some other way to get to Carlo? Tammo watched the chapel door until his eyes ached. The flock of birds he had inadvertently gathered, huddled around him like a cloak. He bit what was left of his fingernails and scowled.

When Carlo eventually came, it was at a run. Tammo couldn't remember ever seeing a eunuch run so fast. His cloak streamed out behind him in the wind. His curls lifted from around his face. He was clutching Orpheus against his chest, panting with exertion.

"Tamino! Dear Tamino!"

He swung himself into the tree and smothered Tammo with embraces. He smelled of aniseed and ecclesiastical incense. Orpheus fluttered between them, before nestling once more in Tammo's coat. Carlo pressed the ring on its thong into Tammo's palm.

"I knew you would come. When I told the rector of my decision, I knew. I could not leave without this last farewell. And we will always be together in our hearts. Dear Tamino!"

He made as if to kiss Tammo again. Tammo held him at arm's length, surprised by how easily he could now keep his friend at bay. Years of chopping wood and pumping bellows had given him a man's strength.

"What are you talking about, Carlo? I'm not here to say goodbye. I've come—"

"Oh, but you have, dear twin, whether you know it or not. The time has come for us to part, but I will return to Angelio one day, I swear. I have accepted a post in Vulcanetta—"

"Vulcanetta, my arse!" Tammo squared his shoulders. "Now you listen to me, Carlo. I've come here about Celestina."

That shut him up. The wide-eyed shock on Carlo's face almost made Tammo's resolve fail. He cleared his throat.

"Carlo, I saw Fenice in the marketplace..."

He swallowed. Swallowed again.

"Celestina is gravely ill." There, he'd said it. "She has the rash like her brother, and she won't come out of her fever. Carlo, are you all right?"

The eunuch had gone death-pale. His limpid eyes stood out unnaturally large in his face. His lips were bloodless.

"Carlo, don't faint on me."

Tammo slapped his friend a couple of times on the cheek. Not hard. Hitting a eunuch was like hitting a girl; he hadn't forgotten. Just enough to raise a little colour and bring Carlo's eyes back into focus.

"Are you still with me, Carlo?"

Carlo nodded slowly. Tammo waited for him to catch his breath again.

"Carlo, we have to do something. We can't let her die."

Carlo took hold of Tammo's wrist. His grip was weak, but Tammo could feel the fingers tightening as he spoke:

"You are right, Tamino. We must ask the Archangel."

The chapel was empty. Everyone had gone to breakfast. From the refectory, a sharp-eyed person might spot two boys going in through the chapel doors, but Tammo had other plans for getting inside. He needed to push Carlo on his fleshy backside, in order to squeeze him through the gap in the window, but he went through in the end. Inside, all was silent. Father Dominic and the two infants acting as altar servers that morning had been the last to leave. Smoke was still rising from extinguished candles. The scent brought a tightness to Tammo's throat. A memory of all those mornings and evenings as a charity boy. A past that could never return.

Both friends turned to look in the direction of the portrait at the left-hand side of the altar. Tammo felt his stomach go queasy. The last time they had seen Michael, Tammo had been so convinced of the right path, so confident in his ability to keep Carlo safe. Look where that had got them! He didn't know if he could approach the city's patron with another petition. The memory of those burning eyes, alight with knowledge and love, turned him to a quivering reed. He had sinned. It was as simple as that. Tammo wasn't worthy to face the Prince of Seraphim. How could he ask another favour when he had messed up the first one already?

"We must confess." Carlo's voice grew a little stronger. "It's Ash Wednesday tomorrow: the first day of Shrovetide. What better time? We should kneel before the Archangel and re-dedicate ourselves to his service. You and I together. It was for the sake of friendship that the Archangel granted our prayers. Let us kneel together in friendship once more. Surely then he will hear us. For sweet Celestina's sake..."

Carlo's voice trembled and his grip on Tammo's wrist tightened.

"Very well," Tammo said. He couldn't let Carlo go to pieces now. "We'll do as you say. We'll pray before the portrait."

Their footsteps echoed in the hushed chapel as they made their way over to the portrait of St Michael. Together they knelt, crossed themselves and kissed the Archangel's hand. The golden-haired image beamed down at them. Tammo was relieved it looked nothing like Michael did in real life. He didn't think he could have done this otherwise.

"Let's begin with *Miserere Mei*." Carlo clasped his hands before him in prayer.

"Very well," Tammo said again.

Carlo began, in his beautiful voice, to sing the words of the Psalm of repentance. Tammo croaked along as quietly as possible. If beauty of voice was a guarantee of angelic favour, then only Carlo was going to be heard.

Carlo gave him a nervous smile as they finally reached *amen*.

"Shall I speak for both of us?"

"Please."

Tammo pressed his hands together and screwed his eyes up tight. Suddenly, he felt five years old again, praying at his mother's knee. He tried to ignore the smell of fresh bread and olive oil that leapt to his memory, but that only made it grow stronger.

"Merciful St. Michael," Carlo began. "We, your unworthy servants, Carlo Bianci and Tammo Capell, humbly ask your pardon for our misbehaviour on the night of your most sacred justice. Forgive our selfish use of your gifts and our neglect of one another. And, beloved St. Michael, we dedicate ourselves to your service from this day forth. As we have sworn to each other to be twins for life, so we swear before you this day. And we beseech you: come to the aid of your child, Noblesse Celestina Pageno. Deliver her from evil and bring healing on your wings, we pray."

Carlo's voice was trembling too hard for Tammo to hear the words. Tammo cleared his throat and finished the prayer for him.

"*In nomine Patris, et Filii, et Spiritus Sancti. Amen.*"

He reached for Carlo's hand and took hold of it. Then he looked about the empty chapel. It was silent but for the sound of their breathing. The scent of extinguished candles filled the air.

"So, what happens now?" he said.

19. Night Flight

Silence. The chapel was thick with it. That special kind of silence Carlo had only ever known in places of worship, where centuries of prayer still lingered as a hushed breath. Stars twinkled on the painted ceiling, silver against deep blue. A shaft of changing sunlight made the gold of the Archangel's hair glitter, then fade to dark saffron as shadows fell.

Carlo knew what they had to do. He turned and looked at Tammo.

"We must go to the Pageno mansion," he said. "Tonight."

"How...?" Tammo began. Carlo held up a hand to silence him.

"You must play your flute to her. And I must sing. The two of us together as one, don't you see? We will be in harmony together, harmony of souls. Just like in the beginning of Angelio. The seraphim host stood as one, and their music drove out the wicked Count. Harmony is angelic power, Tamino. And that's what our friendship is, our vow as twins. Angelic harmony. We can drive out the sickness."

"Angelic harmony?" Tammo wrinkled his face. "Come

on, Carlo. I hardly think that's us. Well, I hardly think it's me, at any rate."

If only his twin could see himself in the midst of his birds, thought Carlo. He would think differently then.

"You underestimate yourself, Tamino dear." Carlo reached out a finger. "I find you quite seraphic. In the right mood, of course. And the correct candlelight."

He grew serious again.

"I know this is right, Tamino. I know this is what the Archangel would have us do. Let us not disappoint him again."

"But I don't..." Tammo looked down. "I don't have the dark flute."

He unclasped the flute case and pulled out the makeshift flute.

"All I have is this feeble thing. It can't even charm a sparrow, never mind drive out sickness."

Carlo smiled, weakly.

"Perhaps that's as it's meant to be. Me without favour; you without your flute. Dependent on Michael to weigh all in the balance."

"Perhaps."

Tammo looked down. He was silent for so long, Carlo wondered if he would ever speak again. He held out his hands.

"I have to go, Tamino. I must return Orpheus to his cage. Meet me tonight, at the stage door to the Teatro, after the performance. Bring a lantern."

Tammo took a hasty breath and let it out. He stood up,

making Coronis caw and wheel about the nave. Carlo had seen that defiant stance before.

"No, Carlo, you can't. The night air... And what will the maestri say when they find you've gone missing again?"

Carlo took Orpheus in his arms and began walking away.

"Find that I've gone missing? At the climax of *Carnevale*, with the whole city at play?" His eyes twinkled. "Trust me, Tamino. Stage door. Bring a lantern. Now, go before someone sees you."

The Night of Magnificence was every bit as splendid—and as chaotic—as Carlo expected. As the descending platform lowered and hosts of Hymen came to bless for the last time, Carlo's view of the auditorium resembled a jeweller's workshop. Silver and golden faces shone back at him from the boxes. Head-dresses like glorious sunbursts, gauze wings and garlands of roses, dazzled his sight. Fans fluttered; sonnets cascaded from the balconies. In the pit, one-night paramours had already begun to embrace. The cheering and shouts of *bravo* were so loud, Carlo could scarcely hear the orchestra.

Morestelli and La Bellina were forced to repeat their final duet four times. By the time they were done, Pegasus had grown decidedly skittish and almost kicked his groom, and the peacocks had fouled several parts of the stage. Carlo heard La Floretta complaining loudly about the effect on her shoes as the curtain fell and everyone fought their way back to the tiring rooms. The performer's corridor was even more crowded than usual. Several patrons and well-wishes had hurried backstage to attend on their favourite performer the moment the last aria began. There were so many mysteriously masked and disguised people, it was tricky to tell which the performers were, and which the patrons. Someone in a plague doctor disguise jostled past Carlo, holding in their hand a necklace with an enormous sapphire hanging from a pale blue bow. He had no idea who it was for.

"Are you coming to the billiard hall, Nightingale?" Giuseppe said in Carlo's ear. They were struggling to remove their wings without taking each other's eyes out. In a corner of the tiring room, Giovanni surreptitiously pocketed a pot of rouge.

Carlo slipped his beaded tunic to the floor.

"I have a little matter to attend to. Perhaps I shall join you later."

A chorus of hoots erupted.

"I hope you can still walk straight by then." Giuseppe gave a leer.

Giovanni pouted, prettily. "Don't mind him, Nightingale. He's disappointed because the fair Belinda won't look on him."

"Whoever she is, she's far too old for you," said Giuseppe. "Stick to your bird-charmers."

Carlo fluttered his eyelids.

"Perhaps I intend to."

"Oh, Lord!" Giuseppe threw up his hands, accidentally catching a dancer across the jaw. "Not the peacock boy. He has more smallpox scars than face. You may as well go gallant with one of the peacocks!"

Carlo suppressed the cold chill such comments gave him and carried on dressing.

"You have a filthy mind, Giuseppe. Perhaps I only wish to offer some words of admiration to our fellow performers."

He wrapped his shawl about him with what he hoped was nonchalant elegance.

"Until later."

Much later, Carlo thought, as he made his way through the overcrowded passageway to the stage door. There were some distinctly unchaste noises coming from behind some of the sopranist's doors now. Carlo cringed. Tamino had better have brought the lantern. He didn't want to be approached by someone telling him he was a sweet boy on a night like this. He needed to keep a steady nerve for Celestina's sake.

He heard Coronis's caw before he saw Tammo. His friend was waiting in an archway under the portico, chewing aggressively at his fingernails. He was wearing a new fustian suit and a cocked hat that looked as though it had survived the last two wars. A little spot of warmth kindled in Carlo's breast. If only he wouldn't stand as though his body belonged to someone else, Tamino could look quite handsome in that outfit. It certainly suited him better than a conservatorio cassock. He raised a hand as Tammo caught his eye. Tammo lifted a rustic storm lantern in greeting. Good. That was a start. Carlo strode over to his twin, using a walk he had copied from Morestelli's Perseus.

"I'm a leading sopranist; you're my servant," he said in

an undertone. "Follow my lead. We're going to the front portico."

Tammo opened his eyes wide but said nothing. Carlo strode on and hoped he would follow. Preferably with the lantern.

He needn't have worried. The waterfront tonight was as well-lit as it had been during the firework display. The porticos at the grand entrance to the Teatro were lit with torches, as were the moorings of the ferrymen, all twitchily awaiting their first fares. The archways and the cobbles in front of them were crowded with coachmen, grooms, valets and chairmen, sipping brandy against the cold and exchanging gossip. Lanterns burned on the sides of carriages. Horses snorted and stamped as grooms removed their nose bags in readiness for departure. Link boys yawned and shifted their torches from hand to hand. Across the water, there was an occasional flash as tumblers or excited citizens let off squibs. Tammo stiffened.

"Hail me a chair to the Pagenos'," muttered Carlo. "And be convincing."

He held his breath as Tammo walked, stiff-legged, out from under the portico. Acting was not Tamino's strong suit.

"Hoi, chairman!" *Hold your head up*, Carlo thought. *Look him in the eye.* "My...er...master needs a chair to Count Pageno's mansion. Urgently."

The chairman stopped picking his nose and smirked at his companion.

"It's double fare at this time on Shrovetide Eve. I hope your master knows that."

Tammo looked back at Carlo, panic on his face. The chairmen sniggered. Time to put his rehearsal into practise, Carlo thought. He puffed out his chest and swaggered over to the chairmen.

"And there will be a bonus for you both for a swift conveyance." He tossed his curls. "Excuse my servant. He's new."

Coronis flapped her wings and gave a loud caw.

"Here, what's that thing doing here?" The chairman made a sign against evil.

"Why, dear Coronis was a gift to me from the Count himself." Carlo settled himself into the chair and held out his wrist. "Come along, sweetheart."

Carlo hoped to Michael that Coronis stayed on his wrist. The idea of being trapped in a sedan chair with a large crow desperate to get back to Tammo did not appeal.

"It'll be extra for the bird," the chairman said.

"Then I expect to find my coin has been used to convey her in comfort and safety," Carlo retorted. There went his allowance, he thought. Thank goodness there was nothing to spend it on in Lent.

"There won't be much comfort for you at the Count's, from what I hear. Received a funeral invitation, did you?"

Terror gripped Carlo's heart. Were they too late already? He swallowed the emotion down as best he could and tried to keep his voice steady.

"I'd thank you to consider how to address your betters, sirrah! Now, walk on. My servant will walk alongside you to ensure you take the quickest route."

The chair door closed, shutting him in the dark with

Coronis. His stomach lurched as the chair was lifted and began to jog along. His breath came in gasps. So far, the plan was holding. Only let them have come in time! Merciful heaven, please!

The chair stopped just at the point Carlo was convinced he was going to vomit. He stepped onto the beautifully solid ground with as much lordliness as he could muster.

"Tammo! Pay the men their dues."

He held out his purse at arm's length, as though the vulgarity of money disgusted him.

The chairman gave a nod toward the unlit façade of the mansion. The burnt umber walls were silent and unwelcoming.

"Private meeting, is it?"

Carlo ignored him.

"Count Pageno has come to a sorry pass, consoling himself with cripple boys," he whispered to his companion as they turned the chair about to face townward. His tone was calculated just loud enough for Carlo to hear. "Do you think it's true, that he's losing his reason?"

"Don't listen to them," Tammo said when the chair was finally out of earshot. The familiar scowl brought Carlo a measure of comfort. Chairmen's gossip was not to be trusted. "Whew! You're a rare one, Carlo. New servant, indeed!" He shook his head. "Come on. I'll show you how to get in."

The wall at the back of the mansion was higher than Tammo had made it out to be. Carlo swallowed hard as his twin lifted the lantern and pointed out which branch of maple tree they would need to use first, which next.

"It will bear my weight, won't it, Tamino dear?" he said. "Yes."

Tammo didn't even look round to grunt out his reply. Fear. They were both feeling it. Not for the climb, but for Celestina. What state was she in now? Had her parents begun to give up hope? She was such a strong little person. So determined. *Be brave, my pretty soulmate*, Carlo prayed. *We're coming.*

Carlo climbed first. Tammo reached and hung the lantern at his feet on each branch he had to climb, then scrambled up himself and retrieved it before re-hanging it for Carlo.

"I'm not losing this," he said stoutly. "Grimaldi will kill me."

The maple had begun to flower. Its branches smelt of fine pollen and moss; its new leaves were cool against Carlo's cheeks in the darkness. Such exquisite beauty! And such potential, too. In the hands of a master, a maple could be crafted into a violin, and make music to ravish the soul. It seemed completely out of place in the midst of such terrible urgency. And yet there it was—nature's perfection—innocently unaware of mortal sorrows.

"What do I do when I reach the top?" he said to Tammo.

"Step across into that belvedere. Be careful: it's slippery."

Carlo put out a foot with caution, then the other. He would wait for Tammo to catch up with the lantern before attempting to go further. He tried to look about himself, but there was nothing to be seen in the darkness. Had Celestina been here, in happier times? If he had pleased his patron, would Count Pageno have brought him up here in the summertime, looking out over the winding of the River Almira, while quietly instructing Carlo in the etiquette of polite society? Here in the darkness, there was nothing but slime underfoot, and Tammo's gasps as he hauled himself and the lantern from the maple. Coronis ghosted past at head height and alighted by the doorway, waiting.

"Fenice's sewing room is beyond that door." Tammo jerked his head to indicate. "I'll see if anyone's inside. Wait there."

Tammo crossed the belvedere floor in three silent steps and tried the handle. No light came from the opening. He peered inside.

"There's no one there. Come on. It's musicians' rooms beyond this, so go quietly."

They crept silently through darkened passageways, the light of Tammo's lantern bobbing on the plastered walls. There was no sound from behind the doors of the musicians' bedchambers, and the practice room with its harp and harpsichord was deserted. The candles were unlit, the tables empty.

"Where is everyone?" Tammo whispered in Carlo's ear. "Asleep?"

"Perhaps they're all praying in the chapel," Carlo said, instantly wishing he hadn't. They couldn't be standing vigil already, could they? What if another cherub child was standing by the altar? A girl this time, shivering in her robe and wings? No. That was just his fear getting the better of him. Celestina was alive.

Tammo suddenly held up a hand. Carlo stiffened. There were voices coming from the room beyond. Carlo could make out male voices saying things like, "I'll raise you three soldi," and "That's twelve fish to me." A solitary violin began picking out a mournful tune.

"Back this way!"

Tammo grabbed Carlo by the sleeve. They doubled back and came out in a gallery of porcelain and astonishing gilt ware. In the middle was a staircase.

"But it only leads down," said Tammo. "How do we get to the other staircase? Do you know this part, Carlo?"

Carlo shook his head.

"My visits have been solely downstairs." He pulled at his lip. "Try that door."

A draught of cold air blew in their faces as Tammo turned the handle.

"It leads outside again," he said with a groan.

He held up the lantern and they both looked. Coronis strutted through the gap as if she knew the place well, and cocked her head knowingly.

"It's a loggia," said Carlo. "See the columns. Someone probably comes here to read or play music in summer."

"And what's on the other side?" said Tammo, indicating a set of doors beyond the furthest columns.

Carlo shrugged.

They tried the door. Behind it was a library, adorned with a great many flowers. Some were arranged in vases and glass jars. Others were pressed between the leaves of open books or in the process of being sketched and affixed to other books. Beyond that was another room, decorated entirely in the style of Mingguo, with delicately painted screens. An image of the Virgin Mother stood in an alcove, arms open in blessing.

"I think these are the Countess's rooms," Carlo said. If he had been anxious before, he was doubly so now. The Countess was the last person he wished to find on the other side of a door. Never mind the fact that he had come to save her daughter. Carlo doubted her ladyship would give him the chance to even begin explaining before she ejected him from the mansion in even more disgrace than he was in already.

"Never mind that," hissed Tammo. "Where in hell is that staircase? We're losing time."

Carlo walked across the painted room and gingerly opened a door that looked like part of the wallpaper.

"There's something through here. But I'm not sure what. Bring the lantern, Tamino."

They both looked. A sliding screen, painted with willow trees, stood half open to reveal a very small room, just about large enough to accommodate nine men standing closely together in square formation. On one wall of the small room was a brass wheel with a handle.

"What in Michael's bootstraps...?" said Tammo.

Carlo gasped.

"But of course," he said. "It's an ascending platform. Like at the Teatro."

"A what?" said Tammo.

"An ascending platform. For Celestina, when she's in

her house carriage. I'll wager it works the same way as the carriage too." He put his hand on the brass wheel. "We just have to turn this to go up."

"I'll do that."

Tammo strode in, Coronis on his shoulder, and pulled the screen shut. He put down the lantern, pulled the handle and began to turn the wheel with both hands. The floor of the room began to sink.

"Wrong way!" said Carlo.

Tammo's face went red as he strained to turn the wheel back again. Veins stood out on his neck. Carlo couldn't help but marvel as the floor rose and Tammo kept on turning the wheel. Through his fustian suit, Carlo could see the movement of muscles around Tammo's shoulders and upper arms. When had his twin become so terrifically strong? It was miraculous that such force could be contained in so lithe a body. With a sigh, Carlo reflected that manly strength was something he would never possess.

Tammo's face was sweating when the mechanism gave a jerk and refused to take them higher. Carlo put his hands over those of his twin, and together they pulled the handle back into position. The jolt of it made Carlo's bones shake.

"Are we there?" Tammo gasped.

The chamber they had come to was stale, as if from lack of airing. Tammo's lantern showed glimpses of a sitting-room and bedchamber in shrine-like hush. A row of toy soldiers stood dusty on a shelf. A riding crop hung, ownerless, from a door. A small but expensive suit of clothes was laid out on the bed, a diminutive sword and belt by its side.

"Orlando." Carlo's throat went tight. He crossed himself. "It's the dead boy's room, Tamino. What if Celestina's is dead too, like the chairmen said? What if we are too late after all?"

His voice trembled. What were they doing here, walking through these silent rooms, whose owners had all flown away? It had been easy to feel conviction in the chapel before the portrait of St. Michael, and even in the sedan chair, pretending to be a virtuoso. But all they had done since they got here was wander from room to room, getting nowhere. What if he had been wrong about the Archangel's intentions? What if their music could not save the noblesse? They were trespassing in a great man's house—in the rooms of his deceased son—with a crow, a storm lantern, and a makeshift flute. They could hang for this.

Tammo gripped him by the shoulder and turned him so they stood face-to-face. Carlo could smell cream cheese on his friend's breath.

"Stop it, Carlo."

His tone was harsh, but not angry. For once, Tamino had managed to control his choler.

"No more talk of death and failure; do you hear? You said we had to do this together as one. That the Archangel would hear us because of our friendship and drive out the evil." He scowled, bit his lip, took a breath. "You've always been the one with faith, Carlo. I didn't believe I mattered a fig to the Archangel until I met you. But I believe now. I believe in the Archangel. And I believe in you."

He screwed up his face, as though he was steeling his mind to drink a foul medicine. Then—so quickly that Carlo didn't feel it until afterward—he leaned forward and kissed Carlo on the cheek.

"Come on," he said gruffly. "Celestina's chamber has to be next."

20. Archangel's Wings

The next door led into the fantastic schoolroom. Tammo shivered, making the lantern beams flicker. Scenes of leopard-clad African princes, golden pagodas, and mathematical instruments appeared and vanished. In this very room, he had once spoken with Celestina. How different it seemed now, how dark and lifeless! No. *Lifeless* was a word he would not speak. At the end of the room was a door, with a light coming from under the threshold. Coronis fidgeted on his shoulder. Tammo reached up and stroked her back to calm her, feeling soft feathers. Carlo crept up to his side.

"What do we do now? There could be any number of people in Celestina's chamber. Physicians, nurses, the Count and Countess..."

Tammo squared his shoulders.

"I'll go first. If I get caught, it will matter less. You have your career to think of."

The fervour with which Carlo clutched at his coat sleeve almost made him drop the lantern.

"No, Tamino! We must do everything together. I'll think of something. Give me a moment."

"You don't—"

The door to Celestina's rooms swung open. A footman

stepped out. One of the innumerable, maroon-coated army Tammo remembered from Twelfth Night. Frantically, Tammo tried to cover the lantern, but it was too late. The footman turned and looked their way, his expression unreadable. Tammo swallowed.

Carlo swept past him with a grand gesture, and made a bow that must have looked extravagant, even at the Teatro.

"Musicians from the opera, if it please you. Come to soothe the poor patient's suffering with the sacred art." He gave a smile that would have melted hearts of adamant.

"Very good. Step this way."

The footman made a bow and held open the door for them. Tammo suppressed a snort. Was the man lackwitted or something? Who would fall for a ruse like that? A servant sees nothing until you tell him to, Carlo had told him, but even so... Tammo hoped to Michael there was no one important behind that door. He couldn't see Carlo bluffing his way past Countess Pageno with a bow and a smile.

Incredibly, there was no one there. A tight passageway led past what must have been the governess's room, and then on into the bedchamber itself. Tammo froze on the threshold. Carlo bumped into him from behind. Celestina's bedchamber! The shrine of the saint herself. Tammo felt his cheeks growing hot, his innards squiggling like worms.

It was not dark here. Candles burned in silver candle stands, giving a soft light. A fire glowed in the hearth. The dancing flames showed a low ceiling with hexagonal patterns, half-moon tables, an elaborate prie-dieu, walls and curtains of rosy damask. A lump came to Tammo's throat. There was the house carriage. How empty it looked, standing immobile by the closed shutters! A toilette table close by was proportioned to fit the carriage underneath it. Everywhere he looked, he saw the accoutrements of a noblesse. Hairbrushes, ribbons, male and female dolls with waxen faces, dressed to resemble the latest fashion plates. Illustrated scores from the opera. Something that Tammo recognised instantly as a covered birdcage. That must be the home of the beloved goldfinches Carlo had told him of. Thankfully, there was no sign of the monkey.

Carlo tapped him on the shoulder and pointed. The bed was against one wall, set into an alcove, its rosy curtains held back by gilded angels. At the foot of the bed, in a chair of the same rosy cloth, a woman slept. Her head nodded on the square-cut neckline of her dress. A lock of black hair had escaped its pins and fell across her forehead. Tammo stiffened.

"The governess," Carlo whispered in his ear. "Come. Let's get to work before anyone else comes."

"And if she wakes?" Tammo glanced back at the governess, her bosom heaving and falling against her throat.

In response, Carlo took Tammo's hand and squeezed it firmly. The eunuch's face was death-pale. It could have been a layer of stage make-up he had failed to remove, but Tammo thought not. This was the moment. Everything rested on it. Either they were right about what the Archangel had given them, or desolate tragedy lay ahead.

Still holding hands, they approached the bed. They could see Celestina now. Her face was flushed, her damp hair stuck to her forehead. She tossed and moaned with a sound like a little sparrow. Tammo retched. There was a smell around this bed that he had smelled before. A smell that in the morning brought wailing mothers and linen shrouds wreathed in carnations. He could see the fatal rash now, climbing Celestina's neck like bindweed, threatening to choke out her sweet life. They must not let it! He lifted Coronis to perch on one of the angels' heads and drew out his flute with a flourish.

"Let's make music," he said to Carlo.

The two friends looked at one another. Tammo could see clearly now that Carlo had tears in his eyes. As he watched, one tear overflowed and ran down Carlo's cheek, making thick paint of the remaining traces of white powder. Tammo ran his thumb over the flute, wishing in vain for the linnets, finches and orioles of the superior instrument. He would not cry. Tears were for girls and babies and eunuchs. He put the flute to his mouth and blew warm air into it, catching a scent of Angel's Wood and the charcoal smoke of Grimaldi's forge. Honest. Truehearted.

"Right, then. What do we play?" he said.

Carlo gave a delicate sniff and dabbed his eyes with a handkerchief. A wistful look came into his eyes.

"I have been working on a composition based upon the song of Orpheus. Our Orpheus, that is." He gave a watery smile. "It has no words as yet, but...it may be appropriate." He plucked his lips.

"Orpheus's song. Yes." Tammo felt a glow kindled in his belly. He clapped Carlo on the shoulder. "The very thing." Companionship. Nightingalising. The woodlands.

Freedom. Everything that bound him and Carlo as friends. As twins. And it included Orpheus himself. The first gift of the Archangel. The winged messenger who had brought them together.

"So, how does it go, Carlo? How does it begin? You start and I'll follow."

He could see Carlo working his face, his shoulders, endeavouring to master his emotions. Tammo made his heart a pine, strong and true. He would not be swayed by Carlo's tears. He would not look at the darling figure in the bed. For this one night he was musician to the aristocracy, and he would not fail.

"Key of A major," Carlo said at last. "Aria form, modulating to the subdominant. Allegretto."

Tammo nodded.

Carlo planted his feet in a wider stance, straightened his back, lifted his chin. He stretched his mouth in a variety of odd-looking yawns, made a few mewing sounds, sliding his voice from high to low. Then he began to sing.

Tammo had heard Carlo sing many times and always thought it sounded angelic, but this time there was something in his song that Tammo had never heard before. From the very first note, his voice filled the chamber, echoing from the damask walls, vibrating along the marble washstand, chasing in and out of the curtains.

The song was light and delicate, the unfurling of springtime blossoms and the dancing steps of dryads. Carlo's voice leapt and trilled in imitation of the thrush's song. Each phrase was repeated twice over, just as Orpheus himself would do, before being balanced by a second phrase that recalled the first and yet subtly differed. Tammo put the flute to his lips and began to accompany Carlo's voice. He echoed Carlo's phrases at intervals, harmonised with them, wove counterpoint around them. Celestina made a soft moan. The governess snorted and fidgeted in the chair. Tammo closed his eyes and gave himself completely over to the music.

A rush of power surged through him. It was not like the power of the dark flute. With that, he would be aware of Carlo as part of his song, part of the gift that enabled him to play. But now, as voice and flute sang together, fluttering about one another like swallows in June, it was as if he was Carlo and Carlo was him. It was impossible to tell where one ended and the other began.

And holding their music together, was a far greater presence. Tammo felt it grow and swell in his lungs, inside his head, in the chamber around him. Not merely a build-up of energy, like a coming storm. But a true presence of heart, mind and soul. An overwhelming sense of power and authority, of compassion, of protection. And most of all, love. That awesome fire of love that burned within heavenly bodies, wheeling in the furthest reaches of the firmament. The same fiery love that knew him intimately, knew how hard he had pounded on that searing door in the craftsmen's quarter, and wept tears of mercury for his pain.

The presence was huge now, pounding in his temples. Tammo could barely hear his music and Carlo's any more. There was another song inside his head: a cold, clear song of awakened light and celestial order. It swelled and swelled, a crescendo of beauty so painful Tammo could hardly stand to hear it, yet he never wanted it to end. Voice after crystal voice joined in the polyphony. Every part was distinct and unique, yet every voice harmonised with the next. There had never been such music on earth. Were he to die now, Tammo believed he would die happy.

Carlo's aria ended. Tammo slowly lowered the flute and opened his eyes. The room looked just as it had before. The silver candlesticks, the empty house carriage. And yet something hung in the air, intangible but so real you could almost taste it. Tammo took one look at Carlo and knew he felt it too.

"Has it worked?" Carlo breathed. "Has anything happened?"

They leaned over the bed. Incredibly, the governess was still snoring in the chair, her head nodding toward her bosom. Celestina was lying peacefully, supported by her pillows. Scarcely a sound escaped her lips. Tammo scowled. Did she look any different? Had the rash begun to fade or was that just his hopes running ahead of him? She looked so tranquil, so completely at rest. Tammo's heart began to pound. What if that heavenly music had been a sign? What if she were, even now, being taken to join the angels? He bit his lip. Heaven must not have her! Not yet. Not now.

A draught made the candles flicker. Both boys glanced round. Tammo's grip tightened on his flute. But it was merely the maroon-coated footman who had let them in. He crossed the room at a slow pace. A glide, Tammo might have said, since the man made no sound of footfalls. A feeling of *déjà vu* came over Tammo. A feeling that some mystery was about to unveil itself. The footman went over to the governess's chair and placed a hand on her forehead.

"She sleeps well. Poor woman! Her cares have been many this last week."

The man looked Tammo in the eye. But the moment of recognition had already come. That voice. That build. That face of devastating beauty, too fair for an ordinary man and yet too stern for any eunuch Tammo knew. How could he not have recognised that face? Had he been so distracted by the footman's coat and powdered wig? He didn't need to see the eyes as well. Those terrible eyes.

"Archangel."

He bowed. Carlo—ahead of him as usual—was already making something between a bow and a genuflection. Coronis cawed and lifted up her head.

"Carlo Bianci and Tammo Capell. "The Archangel shook his head. "I warned you against the pain and sorrow. But you would beg me for gifts."

"We're sorry, Signor," said Carlo, "if we used them ill."

"We confessed in the chapel, Signor. We pledged ourselves to your service," said Tammo.

The Archangel made no reply. He walked over to the golden angel where Coronis perched and reached up to stroke her back. Then he drew back the curtain and placed a hand on Celestina's damp forehead. His face softened to a look of tender compassion. He caressed her tangled hair and placed a kiss on his fingertip, touching it to her cheek.

"How confident you were back then. How certain that you could take care of each other." He stroked Celestina's pale brown hair.

"Yet here you are, four years later. Living separate lives. Losing your gifts yet bearing the cost. Carlo, have you not already suffered the weakness of your body?"

Carlo coughed in the back of his throat.

"Yes, Archangel."

"And you, Tammo. Have you discovered the sacrifice you must make? The fruitless longing for what can never be?"

Tammo scowled. "I don't know, Archangel."

Don't make me say it in front of Carlo. The sight of Celestina, even ravaged by illness, made his very bones ache with love. And yet she would never see him as more than Carlo's messenger. All this talk of sacrifice was making him jittery. A horrible thought came into his mind.

"Is Celestina dying as a punishment to us?"

He blurted the words out, forgetting his fear of Michael's burning eyes. The Archangel wouldn't do that to them. Would he? It wasn't fair. Celestina was innocent.

Michael stood up straight and looked Tammo in the eyes. Had he been asked to guess Michael's thoughts, Tammo would have said the Archangel was sorry he had asked the question.

"Celestina suffers," the Archangel said, "because pestilence preys on the young. It lingers in the air, in clothes and possessions. It infects her as it infected her brother before her." He gave a half-smile. "It has nothing to do with punishment."

He spread his arms wide. The candles flickered as if fanned by a draught. And just for a moment, Tammo thought he could see white wings spread out against the damask wall-covering. Mighty wings, like those of a hawk or a hunting eagle. There seemed to be a light around Michael that didn't come from candlelight, but from those celestial bodies wheeling eternally in the heavens. Tammo clung to his flute like a comforter, knowing a mere musical instrument would be useless to save him had that fire been turned against him. Yet what he felt in his heart was not fear, but warmth. Joy. It made him want to laugh and leap into the air.

"Celestina is not dying," the Archangel said. "You have healed her with the sacred art musical. The music of harmony and love that the seraphim knew on the first day of creation, when the morning stars sang together for joy." He held out his hands towards them. "Together, my sons of Angelio, great deeds can be done."

Out of the corner of his eye, Tammo saw Carlo pull at his lip.

"But if you were here all along, Signor, could you not have done it without us? Our music is but a feeble thing compared to the songs of heaven." He flickered and lowered his eyelashes. "Why wait for our part in it at all?"

St. Michael raised an eyebrow.

"You wish to unravel the mysteries of heaven? Alas, that is something even the Prince of Seraphim cannot do. But know this."

He leaned close. Tammo felt the warmth of barely visible wings envelop them all. Him, Carlo, Celestina. Even Coronis was wrapped in angelic grace.

"You are all a part of each other. As your song has bound you together tonight, so you will be bound by the course of your lives from now on until your deaths. When temptations and separations come—and they must come in this life—remember my words and remember this night." He lifted up his wings once more, so the topmost tips brushed against the ceiling. "And do not forget I am always close by you."

For a moment, there was a blaze of light so bright that it made Tammo's eyes water and he was forced to screw them up. He scrubbed away the tears with the sleeve of his new suit. By the time he was able to look again, the chamber was back to the way it had been. No light but candlelight. Rosy walls and curtains. Wax-faced dolls. Coronis on the statue's head. The governess yawned and blinked, in an uncertain state between sleep and wakefulness. Celestina gave a sigh and opened her eyes. Tammo and Carlo were at her side in moments. Her face was pale, her eyes shadowed, but the rash on her neck was gone. There was no fever in her eyes. Carlo took her hand and pressed it to his lips. Desperate, Tammo tried to think of something he could do to show Celestina that he had fought for her too. That he adored her more than anything on earth. Instead, he felt himself become a statue by Celestina's bedside. A noble pine, just as he had imagined, incapable of speech or movement.

Celestina opened her eyes wide. Those beautiful eyes, dancing with light and life. Tammo felt his stomach flip. The noblesse's face broke into a wide smile.

"Angel-boy! I was dreaming of you."

21. Seraphini

Carlo gave his best smile. Tears were longing to flow from him like fountains, but he wouldn't let Celestina see that. Now was the time to be brave.

"A dream of me, noblesse? But there is no need for dreams. See, I am here, and Tamino too."

Celestina gave the shadow of a laugh.

"Only look! You are wearing your halo." She reached her fingers up toward Carlo's head. "Where are your wings, Angel-boy? Then you would be perfect, just like when we first met."

Carlo's smile slipped. Halo? Was Celestina still seeing fever-dreams? Was she not recovered after all? He turned to Tammo, a question in his eyes.

Tammo made a vague gesture.

"Your head-dress from the opera. You never took it off. Didn't you know?"

Carlo put his hands on his head. His fingertips touched papier-mâché and flaky paint. Gently, he removed a head-dress made to look like a glorious sunburst, a little bent and sodden from its travels, but still the halo of a singing Muse. A giggle bubbled up in Carlo's throat. All his tears turned to giggles that he didn't know how to stop. Celestina was alive and he was a singing Muse! He placed the halo tenderly over Celestina's damp locks, giggling all the while.

"Now you are an angel too."

Celestina touched his face. Her fingers on his cheek made Carlo's heart swell to bursting inside his chest.

"Dear Carlo. I am so glad to see you."

He heard Tammo sigh close by him. Dearest Tamino! He should not be neglected in this hour of wonder. Still smiling, he made a little bow to the beatified noblesse.

"You recall my sworn twin, Tammo Capell? Without the music of his flute, you would not have awoken."

"Tammo Capell..." Celestina turned sleepily towards the blushing Tammo. "Yes, I remember." Her eyes suddenly lit on Coronis. "Oh, is that your crow? How unusual!"

Tammo cleared his throat loudly.

"Noblesse..."

His feeble croak was interrupted by a commotion at the door. The governess immediately leapt from her stupor to the bedside with a suddenness that made Carlo want to giggle again, although he knew he shouldn't. He had recognised one of the voices at the door already. There would be no ghosting away into the night for him and his twin now. They must face the next moment like seraph warriors.

He stood up.

"Bow the minute that door opens," he said to Tammo.

Tammo gave a stiff nod and glanced at the door.

The governess had now noticed there were two intruders by her charge's bedside. With maternal vigour, she elbowed them out of the way, throwing herself upon the pillows. She grasped Celestina's hand in both of her own.

"You're alive, my angel, you're alive." She wept, repeating the words over and over again, in a mixture of Angelian and a country dialect Carlo had not heard since he kissed his mother goodbye.

"Oh, stop that, Teresa. I'm quite well," Celestina said.

The door opened.

Carlo and Tammo stooped double, one knee bent, the opposite arm outstretched behind them. Carlo had just had time to see that one of the men at the door was dressed in a suit of black. As he came into the room, he was saying, "I will bleed her again, your lordship, but I fear the fever is too far gone now—"

But his words were cut short by Celestina's joyous cry of, "Papa!"

"Sweet Michael! A miracle! Oh, my darling!" The Count ran to embrace his daughter.

The governess moved hastily aside. Tammo and Carlo stayed in position. Carlo felt the blood going to his head.

The physician shifted anxiously from foot to foot.

"Let me examine her, your lordship, I beg you."

"Very well." The Count's voice was tight. He pressed a handkerchief to his mouth.

The physician immediately began to take Celestina's pulse and examine her skin. She squirmed at his touch, her eyes darting with impatience.

"Incredible," he kept saying. "The pestilence has receded utterly. *Deo gratias!*"

"Of course, it has." Celestina drew herself up on the

pillows. "Carlo and Tammo made me well with their music. And the Archangel was there, too."

Count Pageno gave his daughter a sharp glance.

"Send a message to her mother," he said to Vittori, who was waiting by the door. "Say that she and the infant can return safely now. Your young mistress is out of danger."

His voice cracked twice, but Vittori gave no sign of having heard. He made a bow and silently left the room. The governess was now kneeling at the prie-dieu, pouring forth a continuous stream of psalms and devotions. Carlo's head began to swim from staying bowed so long. His dread of meeting the Count was beginning to war with a desire to be noticed before he disgraced himself by fainting.

"Call the musicians to the chapel immediately," the Count said to Pompey, who was standing in the doorway, holding a candelabra. "Tell the chaplain to stop offering petitions and to sing *Te Deum* and *Alleluia*. And Vittori," he called after his manservant, who was still in the passageway. "Give a purse to the first revellers you see and invite them in for a cup of spiced wine. We shall have *Carnevale* tonight, and God silence any man who says otherwise!"

"Amen," said the physician, as Pompey and Vittori left.

Count Pageno gave a deep breath. He looked slowly about the room, one hand on his waistcoat. His eye caught Carlo and Tammo. His lips tightened.

"Carlo Bianci and the bird boy. Stand up. What is this my daughter says about your music and the Archangel?"

Carlo straightened his back. The hexagonal ceiling and tiled floor wobbled to kiss each other, then settled back to their normal proportions.

"Your lordship, please accept our apologies for the intrusion," he said. Count Pageno's steady grey eyes were watching him, waiting to see what answer he would make. There was no point resorting to excessive flattery with his former patron. Count Pageno valued the truth. That was what Carlo would have to give him, however fantastical it sounded.

"We would not have come here except on the most urgent of missions. To save the noblesse's life."

"And they did, Papa." Celestina raised herself higher in the bed. "I could hear them in my dreams. First Carlo singing. Then the sound of a flute. It sounded just like birdsong, so magical!"

"Hush, my sweet. Do not tire yourself." The Count held up a hand.

Celestina ignored it.

"And then it changed into—oh, such a beautiful sound! Like stars singing. And the Archangel was there. His face was all glowing and he had such pretty eyes. He held my hand and said, 'Don't be afraid, Celestina.' I thought he was going to take me to Orlando. But he said, 'Your friends are waiting for you to wake up.' So, I did, and here were dear Carlo and Tammo with a crow and a halo and everything. You're not going to punish them are you, dear Papa?"

The Count pressed the handkerchief to his mouth again and lowered his eyes. Carlo wondered if he was going to speak at all. Across the bed, Tammo bit furiously at his lip. The physician made a nervous bow.

"The Song of the Morning Stars, my lord. Music from

the creation of the world. It is said to accompany apparitions of St. Michael of Healing."

The Count made an impatient gesture. The physician bowed again and left the room.

"Papa?" said Celestina again.

"You need to rest, my darling. I must speak to Master Bianci." He pulled a heavy brocade cord, then turned to the governess. "Make sure she has everything she needs." His piercing gaze crossed the room. "Carlo. Come."

When the screen opened, the ascending platform had come to rest on the ground floor, opposite the grand entrance hall. Count Pageno strode through its draughty expanse of marble, past the imposing staircase Carlo had climbed with Rector Bartolomeo the day the Count had become his patron. The footman with the candelabra had to walk briskly to keep up; flames streamed out behind him.

"You may leave us now, Roberto," the Count said.

They had entered a well-lit library where a fire burned in the hearth. A half-empty decanter of brandy and several glasses occupied the hunt table that encircled the fireplace.

The Count eased himself into a stiff-backed chair with a sigh and indicated an empty seat where Carlo should sit. In the improved light, Carlo could now see the Count's unfastened lace cravat, his unshaven chin, the shadows beneath his eyes. He poured himself another brandy and looked around for something suitable to offer Carlo. Finding nothing but even stronger drinks, he swallowed the brandy with a grimace and slammed down the glass.

Then—to Carlo's horror—he took off his wig and rubbed his hands over a bristled head much the colour of Celestina's.

"Merciful St. Michael. My girl, my darling girl," Carlo heard him mutter.

He rubbed his hands over his forehead and eyes, bejewelled rings glinting in the firelight. Then he lifted up his head and replaced his wig.

"Forgive me," he said. "When you are a father... No, I forget. You will never know that pleasurable pain."

He took another sip of brandy and seemed to return to his normal self.

"Forgive me," he said again. "This has been a rare and miraculous night. A night of magnificence indeed."

"Yes, my lord." Carlo thought it wise to keep his voice neutral.

"And now it seems I may owe you a debt of gratitude."

Carlo leaned forward. "Not I alone, my lord. Tamino— that is to say, Citizen Capell..."

The Count held up his hand.

"All in due course, Carlo. It is of you that I wish to speak."

Carlo nodded.

"I fear I may have treated you harshly. Mourning may do that to a man. The loss of a son and heir..." His voice dimmed; he rubbed a hand over his bristled mouth. "The fact is, I placed too many expectations upon you. Attempted to assuage my own grief in welcoming you to my home. Cozened myself into thinking that introducing a young boy to society could somehow fill the empty space left by..."

The Count concealed his emotions in the brandy glass.

"My lord, no expectation you place on me could be too high." Was the Count about to dismiss him for good? Had Celestina been saved only for Carlo to be parted from her once more? "I assure you, I have only myself to blame..." The rising anxiety made him start to cough.

"Have a little brandy." Count Pageno slid a glass toward him. "You misunderstand me, Carlo. I have lost— and almost lost—too many children to wish to lose another." His gaze became distant. "There was another boy like you once. The same clear voice and easy manner. I had only to hear him sing once to know he would be fêted throughout the Empire. But his passions were as intemperate as his performances were brilliant. He contracted that sickness which every lover fears. His talent was cut short far too soon." The Count sighed heavily. "I only wished to keep you from his path, Carlo."

Carlo clung to the glass of untouched brandy. To grow up only to live a satyr's life and dally with Venus to the point of... It was all he could do to suppress a shudder. In ways he couldn't explain, he knew he would not share his fellow-castrato's fate.

"It angered me to see you truanting in the street, I do confess. But not enough to justify cutting you off for two whole years."

Count Pageno took a sip of brandy and straightened the lace at his cuff.

"I have said I mean not to lose any more children. You will recommence your weekly engagement in my chapel and at any private concert I command. And, when I judge the time is right, I will present you to the Duke."

Carlo's cheeks flushed. This was beyond generosity. It was everything he had dreamed of since Signor Bernardi had first begun training him for the conservatorio. The future of a primo castrato. He stood up and made a bow.

"My lord Pageno, how can I ever—"

"Sit down, Carlo." The Count waved a hand. "In view of this, I think the time is right for you to take a name. Naturally, you will wish to name yourself after your patron. What do you say to Papageno?"

Carlo hesitated. It would be a dreadful thing to anger the Count just now. But Papageno was not the right name. Not with the future Carlo had foreseen tonight.

"My lord, I am truly grateful for the restoration of your patronage. More than I can ever say. But I must tell you that I have already decided upon my artistic name. Will...will my lord forgive me that I choose to name myself in honour of an even greater patron? In view of tonight's events, I believe there is only one name I can take. I dedicate my music to St. Michael and choose the name Seraphini."

The Count looked into his brandy glass and nodded slowly. "Seraphini? A bold choice. And yet... And yet..."

He gave a deep sigh and swirled the brandy.

"Yes. Yes, I think you are right, Carlo. Seraphini. Let us begin with the Archangel's blessing and go on from there. His grace will approve, I'm sure. Seraphini it is. I shall have your portrait commissioned on the morrow. Now sit down, Carlo. There is no call to stand upon ceremony tonight."

Carlo planted his breeches in the chair.

"You do me great honour, my lord." He gave a nervous smile.

"Do you think I could withhold anything from my daughter's saviour? I almost lost her once before, to the fever that left her crippled. And tonight..." He put the handkerchief to his lips.

"One of your daughter's saviours, your lordship," Carlo dared to say.

The Count took another sip of brandy and dabbed at the corner of his mouth several times before speaking again.

"Ah. The bird boy. You seem very keen to take his part."

"There is...an understanding between us, my lord. A kinship." Carlo tried his best to relax his hands, to maintain an open profile. Sweet Michael! Let the Count not dismiss Tamino as a mere intruder! Let him recognise Tammo's worth.

Count Pageno fingered his cravat.

"I have no opening for a flautist in my household at present. That post is filled. The Cavalier Marchesi may be able to do something for him...."

The Cavalier Marchesi. Security. Future prospects. Count Pageno was generous indeed tonight. But this wasn't the reward Tammo wanted. Confinement in lace and embroidered waistcoats. Subject to a great man's beck and call. That was Carlo's dream; his twin wanted the woodland and the song of the nightingale. He wanted to be free in a way Carlo found hard to understand, yet he knew it touched the very essence of Tamino's soul.

"My lord..." Carlo gave a slight cough, swallowed, and tried again. The steady grey eyes were watching him, intrigued. "I humbly beg your lordship's pardon, but Citizen Capell is not a flautist as the common man would understand the term. He is a bird-charmer, skilled beyond his years. Live avian capture is his speciality. Any bird my lord could wish for, he can provide, tamed and trained, in tricks or in song. If my lord Pageno would secure him noble patronage within this trade, his gratitude would be limitless. I give you my word."

Carlo's cheeks were glowing by the time he finished this speech. He tried to take a sip of brandy, choked, and erupted into a fit of coughing that made his eyes water. Count Pageno patted him firmly on the back.

"Easy, my fine fellow. In time a eunuch may learn to drink like a man, but not tonight, I think."

Carlo nodded, coughed again, and dabbed at his eyes and nose with a handkerchief. Count Pageno smiled.

"I see I must give your companion's reward some thought. Live avian capture? I take it this explains the crow in my daughter's bedchamber?" He raised an eyebrow. "Most men would take that for an ill omen, but in this case, it seems the usual laws of nature are turned on their heads."

"Only in the case of Citizen Capell." Carlo tried to smile through his watering eyes. "My lord Pageno will find he is one of a kind." The brandy made him cough again. Count Pageno gave him another pat on the back.

"Ah, dear! I forget what delicate creatures you eunuchs are. I shan't have you going out in the night air again. You will sleep here tonight. I will send word to the conservatorio and have my carriage take you home in the morning."

Carlo tried his best to look grateful rather than astonished. A bed in the Pageno mansion? A carriage home? His lordship was the very soul of generosity. A flicker of doubt crossed Carlo's face. What about Tammo? Where was he to be sent? The count caught Carlo's eye and gave a fatherly smile.

"I can see you are itching to ask me about my plans for young Citizen...what is his name again? Camille?"

"Capell." Carlo lowered his gaze.

"Yes. Your fortunes are set to be entwined, I think. Pray, don't distress yourself. I will have the apricot room made up; it has an alcove for a manservant. Is there anyone who should be informed of his whereabouts?

Carlo thought hard, trying to remember the name that escaped him.

"I believe there is, my lord, but someone will need to ask for the details."

The Count made another minute adjustment to his cuff. Carlo took a deep breath.

"My lord, if you are to send to the conservatorio, there is one more favour I would ask."

22. Promises and Friendships

Celestina gave a genteel yawn as the governess disappeared into the schoolroom. She stretched her arms and smiled at Tammo. His stomach flipped.

"Why are you standing there silent, Tammo Capell? Won't you come here and play your flute for me? Since it did me such good when I was asleep, it should benefit me even more now I'm awake, do you not think?"

Being in the same room as Celestina made Tammo hot in the forehead and fidgety. He wanted to retrieve Grimaldi's storm lantern, which had now burned itself out, but he didn't want the governess to suddenly remember he was there and send him from the room. Celestina looked lovelier than ever against those pillows, framed by the damask curtains. She had scowled a little as the governess and physician continued to fuss, but Tammo thought her a model of patience. In her place, he was quite sure he would have thrown something at that hysterical woman if she had kissed and prayed over him one more time.

This was his first chance to prove to Celestina that he was more than Carlo's friend and messenger. And he had become a silent cypress.

"I know what you're thinking," he muttered, as Coronis

gave him one of her best corvid stares. "And I'm not afraid. Not of anything."

"I beg your pardon?" Celestina raised her perfect eyebrows.

"Noblesse." Tammo scratched his neck. Coronis cawed and flew to land on a console table. Her wings narrowly avoided displacing a vase of oleanders.

"Are you blushing?" Celestina covered another pretty yawn. "Will you play the tune you played for the birds the night Carlo sang for Papa's guests? I heard it through the curtains, but only a little."

Tammo tugged at his brush-like forelock as he made his way back to the bedside.

"I fear I don't have the instrument I had that night." He held up the makeshift flute. I should make a poor shift on this old thing. It's only good for enticing pigeons into traps."

Celestina arched her brows. "Play, Tammo Capell. I command you!"

"As your young ladyship wishes." Tammo made a bow that he knew was not as good as Carlo's.

He began to play a ballad, something suitable to the rustic instrument. There was no point attempting a gavotte or sarabande. The Archangel had departed, and with him the celestial song. Nevertheless, he tapped his toes and dipped his head in time to the beat. The song would bring a little of the street carnival into the chamber, if nothing else.

Celestina clapped her hands and smiled all the way through. When the ballad ended, she gave a happy sigh.

"That was beautiful, Bird-boy. I should reward you but, alas, I have no largesse to give."

A lock of your beautiful hair would be gift enough, Tammo wanted to say. Carlo wouldn't have hesitated, he knew. But the thought of saying such words made Tammo's skin itch, and his feet want to run out the door and home to Grimaldi. He scratched his neck.

"At your service," he managed to mumble.

Damn. Why was he wasting opportunities like this? The governess, or even the Count could be back through that door at any moment. This was his one chance, alone in the chamber with Celestina, to make her aware of his worth. She had just praised his flute playing, hadn't she? Couldn't he follow that up somehow; leave some token of remembrance?

Token of remembrance. Gift of worth. Of course. He reached inside his chemise and drew out the leather thong he'd used to fasten the carnival ring about his neck. The cheeky little face seemed to wink at him in the candlelight. He didn't have the right to keep a treasure like this, whatever Carlo said. But as a gift for a young noblewoman... Ah! Celestina would not forget him now. He knelt at the bedside and held out the ring toward her.

"Noblesse, would you accept this token?" His voice was so hoarse, he could scarcely get the words out. "In remembrance of tonight's miracle?"

The silence that fell after his words seemed endless. Celestina turned the ring over in her hands, held it up to the candlelight, touched the little face.

"A carnival ring!" she said. "Oh, it's perfect! I shall

treasure it always." She slipped it onto a delicate finger and admired it, smiling.

Tammo managed an awkward smile too. Then he frowned again. Carlo might not understand his need to give the ring to Celestina. If he saw it on her hand, he might say things. Impulsive, emotional things. He might tell Celestina where the ring really came from.

"Ah. Noblesse..." He held up his hand. "It might be...er...better if this were kept secret." He tried to assume a playful expression, which probably looked ghastly. "Not a word to anyone, eh? No wearing it openly. Your ladyship," he added.

Celestina's eyes sparkled in her wan face.

"A secret token? Oh, how delicious! I love secrets. It's just like the opera!" She removed the ring and slipped it inside a pillowcase. "Never fear, Tammo Capell. I shan't breathe a word to a living soul, not ever. I swear on the Archangel's sword."

Tammo wanted to make a pledge of his own in return, something about defending her for the rest of his life and never betraying her trust. But by the time he'd done blushing and biting his lip and changing his mind back and forth, the door had opened, and the governess had come back.

"I don't have lice," Tammo protested when the under-servant came to tell him he must take a herbal bath. "And nor does Coronis," he added, in case the man might take it into his head to start bathing her too.

"Lordship's orders," was all the man said, before giving a wide yawn. His poorly-fastened neck-bands and bleary eyes suggested he had been awoken from sleep to perform this task, and resented it.

With a lumbering gait, he led Tammo down a servants' staircase that seemed to go on and on. Tammo stumbled on behind as best he could. Shadows loomed, tall and thin, on the cream-painted walls. He wondered if Carlo would be taking a bath too. He didn't like being alone in the mansion without him. When that footman had come to say he must stay the night, Tammo had nearly choked with shock. Him? Sleeping in a nobleman's bedchamber? It was like something from a crazy dream, the sort where furniture turned into cheese and biscotti.

Only Celestina had not been surprised.

"Of course, you and Carlo must stay the night." The monkey was climbing up her neck. She stroked its back and tickled it. It chittered, and looped its tail around her.

"And maybe Papa will let you spend the week. I have so much to show you. Teresa and I made a new figure for the toy theatre. A winged Victory, with a golden wig. Carlo simply must see it."

"Hush, my dear." The governess fussed with Celestina's coverlets. "You've been very poorly."

"It's just for tonight, your father says." The footman kept a respectful tone. "The young citizens must go home in the morning." He turned to Tammo. "I have been I instructed by his lordship to take from you the name and abode of your master. To let him know you are safe."

"Grimaldi the blacksmith. Angel's Wood," Tammo

said, without thinking. He forgot to argue that Grimaldi was not his master. The old man would be fretting about him. "You won't get there tonight, though. The gates will be closed and it's dark."

"The Count's messengers go wherever he tells them to go," the footman replied. "And the Count will see you in the morning. He wants to hear about your skill in live avian capture."

Tammo coughed violently.

"He wants…?"

"Oh dear, Tammo Capell!" Celestina laughed. "How red you have gone! Why should Papa not want to hear all about you? I daresay he can make you as famous a bird-catcher as he can make Carlo a singer." She scratched the monkey's back. "There now, Giacomo. Have you missed me, my darling?"

Tammo took hold of the console table to steady himself. This was becoming more unreal by the moment. He needed Carlo. He needed his friend by his side, to make sense of everything.

But all he got was a bleary-eyed man who wanted him to take a bath.

"Where's Carlo?" he said to the under-servant's back.

"I don't know Carlo," the man grumbled. "I know I was having a dream about a fabulous eel risotto…"

"The young castrato." Tammo tried again. "The singer."

"Singers are all in the chapel now. They woke me up, with all those alleluias. Right when I was tucking into the juiciest eels you ever tasted."

Tammo began to recognise where he was. The dining hall. The pantry. The long servants' passageway. Next came the courtyard he had visited that first night with his cages of nightingales. He remembered it all. The well, the stables, the kitchen buildings.

"Should have woken my brother from his bed instead of me." The under-servant grunted with a nod towards the gatehouse. "Sent him trotting round in the dead of night to give baths to lice-ridden boys. That would give him something to whinge about. Heh, heh, heh!"

The man gave a wheezy laugh and walked off, leaving Tammo standing in shadow.

If all this patronage business isn't a dream, Tammo thought, *I'm going to make damn certain I get some respect in future. I'll have some trade cards printed:* Bird-tamer to the aristocracy. *And I'll refuse to speak to anyone lower than a first footman. That'll show them.*

Tammo trotted after the tallow light to a scullery at the back of the kitchen. Clouds of steam flew out as the under-servant opened the door. For a moment, Tammo could make out nothing beyond a hazy impression of wooden tubs and linen towels. As the steam subsided, he could see kettles, irons, slatted wooden mats on a terracotta floor and—steeping dried herbs in a kettle—a staunch and familiar figure.

"Tammo Capell!" Fenice flicked a lock of damp hair back into place and put her hands on her hips. "I should have known it would be you getting me out of bed on

Lenten Eve to fill great bathtubs in the middle of the night. Wherever there's trouble..."

She hip-walked over and reached up to pinch his cheek. Coronis gave an outraged caw. Tammo looked over his shoulder to see whether the gatekeeper's brother was watching his humiliation, but he had gone to dream up more eel risotto.

"What became of you, young blackguard? Running off and leaving me in the marketplace, and me in tears and all. The young eunuch wants to teach you some manners."

"I'm...er...sorry, Fenice." Why did she have this gift for making him squirm so? Every time they met, he was torn between pleasure to see her and toe-curling embarrassment. And what did she have to go touching him for?

"An improvement," she conceded. "An improvement in your dress too, I see." She tugged at his fustian coat. "Too bad you'll have to take it all off now." She nodded to where a manservant in shirt sleeves was pouring hot water from a copper into the bathtub, neck veins straining.

Tammo felt certain his very elbows were blushing.

"You're not going to...? I mean, you won't still be here when...?"

Fenice snorted with laughter.

"A young starveling like you? Now, maybe if you had the proportions of Pompey..."

Sweat trickled down Tammo's forehead.

"Aren't you going to congratulate me anyway, Tammo Capell? Signora Rosamunda has agreed I can join the seamstresses. I start after Lent. So, this is the last bath you'll enjoy with me."

She pouted and thrust her bosom somewhere near Tammo's belt.

The shirt-sleeved manservant put down the copper and straightened his back. "Leave the poor lad in peace." He clapped Tammo on the shoulder. "She doesn't mean any harm by it."

"He knows that." Fenice gave a vixen's grin.

As the manservant turned his back, her face softened. "Was it really you who saved the noblesse's life tonight?"

"Me and Carlo." Tammo shrugged. "But mostly the Archangel."

He scratched his neck. Discussing these things with Fenice didn't seem right somehow. And yet it didn't seem completely wrong either.

"Oh, I see you're talking like a priest now. Keep your little secrets, then. I like a man with an air of mystery. Very gallant, don't you think?" She shook her head. "You're a rare one, Tammo Capell. When first I heard the good news, what's the first thing I said to Maria? Tammo Capell will have a hand in this. I can feel it in my waters."

"I thought you were asleep in bed until they woke you to run a bath." Tammo scowled.

Fenice slapped his arm. "Do you think any of us could sleep with the little noblesse in danger? Lackwit! We've been sitting round the kitchen hearth these five hours, praying to St. Michael." She blew out air. "Asleep in bed!"

Tammo wondered if it was time to have the bath soon. Talking with Fenice made his head spin.

"Dark horse, aren't you?" She grinned. "Come on and

kiss me then, Tammo Capell. I have to be up again at sunrise."

"I..." Tammo felt terror mix with an awkward stirring that made him want to jump in the bath there and then to cover it. Fenice cackled like a fishwife.

"One day." She wagged her finger. "One day you'll be begging me, Tammo Capell."

"And it's all true?"

Carlo smiled his cupid's smile.

"Of course it's all true, Tamino. I am to be Seraphini the castrato, and you are to be bird-charmer to the nobility. We will need time to hone our skills, of course, but in years to come, I doubt there will be two such famous men in Angelio."

Tammo scratched his neck. "I don't want to be famous..."

Carlo threw up his hands in mock horror. "Tamino, I declare you try the patience of a seraph. I believe you must be taught a lesson this instant."

He slipped his hands under Tammo's armpits and began tickling. Tammo wriggled and snorted, and tickled Carlo back. The eunuch squealed with laughter. Together, they tumbled onto a patterned rug, giggling and sighing.

"Is this not the most splendid room?" Carlo stretched out, his arms over his head. When I become primo castrato at the opera, I shall have one just like it."

Tammo looked about him. There was no need to guess how the room had acquired its name. The wallpaper, the furnishings, the curtains, and the ceiling were all decorated in the same shade of apricot. He found it overwhelming.

"Close your eyes."

Tammo scowled. Was this really necessary? He felt awkward as it was, his nightshirt smelling of lavender, his wet hair stuck up like a hog's back. A drip of water ran down his back.

"I said, close your eyes, Tamino."

Carlo was feeling around under a pile of pillows, deep enough to support any number of princesses from antique tales. A spark of mischief was in his eye. Oh Lord, let it not be itching powder! He shut his eyes.

"Hold out your hands."

Something long and smooth was laid across the palms of his hands. Something wooden, with the texture of carvings upon it.

He opened his eyes. The dark flute. He was holding the dark flute in his hands. The instrument of his dreams, come back to him once more!

"Where did this come from?"

"The conservatorio, of course. With Maestro Aquila's compliments. You know, no one else has played it since you left. It's like it was waiting for you."

Tammo nodded slowly.

"Like the Archangel willed it."

Carlo yawned.

"I suppose we should consider retiring to bed."

Tammo sat up and stared at the bed. It looked as if an apricot creamed ice had taken on the form of a night couch. Lace curtains frothed over bolsters, cushions, sheet and coverlets, all of the same apricot hue. A golden crucifix shone on the back canopy. Inlaid steps led up to the toweringly high mattress. No wonder Count Pageno had wanted him to bathe before bed. He should have peeled Tammo's skin into the bargain.

"I am not sleeping in that!" he declared.

"No, you certainly are not, dear twin. I am to sleep in the apricot bed. Your humble couch lies behind these curtains. Perchance Coronis will line it with her breast feathers for you."

Carlo got up and walked over to the alcove. He drew aside an embroidered curtain to reveal a simpler mattress surrounded by cushioned walls also the colour of apricot.

"For my loyal manservant." Carlo fluttered his eyelashes. "To reward his diligence in the hailing of sedan chairs."

"Manservant, my foot!"

Tammo grabbed Carlo by the waist and tickled him again until the eunuch kicked and shrieked with laughter. They both collapsed onto the alcove mattress, sniggering under their breath. Carlo sighed and put his head on Tammo's shoulder. Tammo gave him a sly push.

"You're not going to start singing into mirrors in the middle of the night, are you?"

Carlo narrowed his eyes. "Only if you decide to treat us to some graceful tumbling."

Tammo made his hand a tarantula. "I'll tickle you again," he said.

Carlo batted his hand away and sighed. Silence stretched out. Tammo took a deep breath.

"I always knew the Count would take you back. You will be primo castrato one day." He felt his face redden.

Carlo rolled over and smiled. "And I always knew you would get the dark flute back. You will be the greatest bird-charmer who ever lived. My Tamino."

Carlo stretched and sighed again. Tammo opened his mouth in a cavernous yawn. Coronis had already fallen asleep, her head tucked under her wing.

"Prayers and candles out?" Carlo suggested.

They knelt together on the tiled floor and recited the familiar words. It was strange how the same prayer could bring back such bad memories of the intermediate's dormitory and such good memories of the Archangel's constant presence. They both said *amen* together. Carlo climbed the stairs to the apricot fantasy of a bed. Tammo stretched out on the alcove mattress. It was so soft, it felt like lying on a cloud. Across the room, Carlo lay back on the frothy pillows. Neither boy had drawn draw the curtains around his bed. Tammo made the resolute decision that he would watch over Carlo the whole night, even in sleep. He would never fail to protect him again. He looked up to find Carlo was watching him by the light of the still-burning candle. The steadiness of his gaze made Tammo blush.

"What are you looking at?" he said.

Carlo gave a mysterious smile. "You're a wonder, Tammo Capell. I knew it from the moment you tumbled through my window."

Tammo snorted. "You look tired to death. Go to sleep, Carlo."

Carlo raised an eyebrow. "Yes, maestro."

The next moment, his expression softened again. All Tammo could see in the candlelight were those limpid eyes and cupid's lips. As much girl as boy. Tammo wondered if he would ever truly understand his friend. Carlo smiled.

"Goodnight, Tamino."

Tammo smiled back.

"Goodnight, Carlo."

His twin blew out the light.

End

About the Author

Elizabeth Hopkinson is the author of the *Asexual Fairy Tales* series and podcast. Her short stories have appeared in many anthologies and magazines, and won several prizes.

She lives in Bradford, West Yorkshire—home of the Brontë sisters and the Cottingley Fairies—with her husband and cat.

Elizabeth is a romantic asexual and is committed to asexual representation in fiction.

http://www.elizabethhopkinson.uk/

Instagram: @angeliocitystate

Also from Deep Hearts YA

L.I.F.E.
Felyx Lawson

Rider Williams is your typical high school student. He has classes, hangs with friends, plays video games, writes for the school paper, plays guitar, collects comics, and is gay. Okay, so he's not your typical high school student.

Rider is trying to finish his senior year of high school while struggling to accept himself and hide his secret. It's difficult and he might have succeeded if not for two challenges in his way. The first, an assignment about the one thing he doesn't understand and hasn't experienced: love. The other, Cameron Walker, a transfer student who looks like a stereotypical jock, but seems to be so much more.

Can Rider survive the weight of his secret?

It's only the start of the school year but Rider already knows L.I.F.E. isn't as easy as it seems.

Available now in ebook and paperback

Also from Deep Hearts YA

Gerald Ribbon and the Bird in His Brain
Maxwell Bauman

Gerald Ribbon has a habit of ruining his love life.

The bird in his brain gives him terrible advice, and he is stuck dealing with the consequences.

He screwed up his relationship with Jessica, who has now moved on and is seeing someone new. But the fear of damaging another friendship prevents Gerald from openly expressing his feelings for his best friend, Allen. When Allen begins to date Diana, Gerald feels himself getting left behind and tries to form a wedge between the two. Ultimately, Allen and Diana's relationship reaches a breaking point, and Gerald needs to be louder than the noisy bird in his brain and do what is right for his friend and himself.

Available now in ebook and paperback